Terrible Secrets

Steve Higgs

TERRIBLE SECRETS

'Terrible Secrets' is a work of fiction.
Names, characters, businesses, organisations, places, events and incidents

either are the product of the author's imagination or are used fictitiously. Any resemblance to actual persons, living, dead or undead, events or locations is entirely coincidental.

Contents

Chapter 1

The windows exploded outward into the street, a spectacular shower of glass particles falling to the asphalt like a cascade of diamonds beneath the streetlights. An alarm was already wailing, triggered more than a minute earlier when the intruder chose to enter the shop. The damage to the windows was unnecessary – he could have left by the same door he used to enter the shop, but where was the fun in that?

Stepping through the wreckage of the shop's front façade, his satchel stuffed full of cash and slung over one shoulder, he adjusted the hood of his coat to make sure his face was obscured. He held no concern for the police he could hear approaching at speed – he knew they would come.

Provided he kept his face hidden from any CCTV cameras, there was no danger of being caught. It wasn't as if the police could do anything to stop him.

As if on cue, a black and white power-slid into sight at the end of the road. Its rooflights were spinning, the strobes bouncing off the windows to its left and right as it accelerated toward him.

Taking his time, he took out his phone, posed for a selfie, and changed the track playing through his earbuds. He was about to go toe to toe with the cops and that demanded something with a sick beat. Sliding his phone away again, he unwrapped a Baby Ruth candy bar and bit off the first inch. The cops in Chippewa Falls were on edge, he knew that, and it was for good reason. They lost one of their own two nights ago, exploded from inside to create a surprising mess.

A chuckle escaped his lips as he remembered the horrified look on the officer's face when she realised she wasn't in control. She had been so full of herself, barking orders and expecting them to be obeyed.

Her attitude sure changed when the first lightning bolt hit her.

The cop car was coming right for him. It had to be doing at least eighty and was going to have to brake hard soon. There was no chance they hadn't seen him, but to make his intentions clear, he stepped into the road.

The candy wrapper drifted down to the asphalt, his jaw working to break down the last bite of chocolate and peanuts.

Officer Chris Burton, holding tight to the steering wheel, squinted at the lone figure framed in the car's headlights. 'What's he doing?'

In the passenger seat, Burton's partner, Officer Sarah Kirke gripped the butt of her issue weapon. Her pulse was banging in her head, adrenalin coursing through her body to make her feel jangly and weak.

Her response came out as quiet as a breath.

'Magic.'

In the street, the hooded figure drew in energy from the city's main ley line. It ran beneath the river heading north, branching out like legs on a spider or a metro rail system. It fuelled the spell he was forming, water molecules coalescing when he pushed his will through them.

Officer Burton hit the brake pedal, expecting the car to instantly slow. He planned to get close enough that the figure in the street – almost certainly a man, he believed – would dive out of the way. If he drew a weapon, or did anything ... magic, Chris was just going to hit him with the car.

It came as a shock when the car kept on going.

'Chris!' Sarah blurted in panic.

The car's tires were braking. They had stopped completely, in fact, but that made little difference to the car's velocity as it shot across the sheet of ice coating the road.

Officer Burton pumped his brake pedal in a fruitless attempt to regain control and both officers stared open-mouthed at the hooded figure who refused to move out of the way.

They were heading right for him. He was filling the windshield and there was no time for the man to avoid being struck now.

Sarah wanted to scream at the madness of their situation, but an invisible force slammed into her side of the car, bowling it sideways across the street like a wrecking ball.

The hooded figure felt a shudder of excitement spread through his body as he watched the police car flip side over side twice before it slammed into a parking meter, tearing it from the ground.

Everything was so easy now. The magic had come to him more than two years ago. He had no idea what triggered it, but it gave him the ability to fulfill dreams other men couldn't even imagine. It was ultimate power.

Dropping the air spell employed to flip the car, he swivelled his body to face the wreckage. The car had come to rest on its side, the passenger side caved in where the B post sat between the front and rear doors. With the damaged portion uppermost, it almost looked like a shark had taken a bite out of it.

Renewing his charge of line energy, the hooded figure manipulated the elements to create a fresh spell. Holding his right hand aloft, he produced flame.

There was no good reason to kill the cops, but then again, he couldn't think of a reason not to.

The flame flickered, minimal power keeping it alight as it hovered just above the skin of his right palm. Did he torch the car with the cops still in it? Taking a second to weigh up the pros and cons, he let the flame go with a disgruntled grimace.

He doubted it was within anyone's power to stop him, anyone not imbued with greater power than his, that is. He knew there were others out there like him; everyone did. The news channels were filled with reports of supernatural events and the appearance of terrifying creatures.

A worldwide attack just a few weeks ago, when people who looked human but were clearly something else, shattered the illusion that humans were the only players in the game. Filmed by eyewitnesses all around the globe, the existence of magic could no longer be denied.

Police and armies in the affected countries had been swept aside like ants before a lawnmower, the supernaturals – that's what the TV people were calling them – had abilities beyond our comprehension. Where had they come from? Where did they go when they suddenly vanished? Will they return? What do they want? All these questions and many more were fodder for dozens of TV debate panels filled with so-called experts.

The hooded figure had no answers, but he knew people were afraid and the authorities were looking for anyone they could finger as a supernatural just so they could show they were doing something.

They had no clue, and no chance of stopping him even if they knew who he was, which they didn't. Nevertheless, he acknowledged that drawing attention to Chippewa Falls would do him no favours.

There were noises coming from inside the car, grunting, cussing, and cries of pain as the occupants struggled to get free.

He pulled his hood just a little tighter to his head and turned away, strolling from the scene of devastation without the slightest trace of haste.

Chapter 2

I n the kitchen, Cassie patted bacon strips dry using a kitchen towel and laid them on a platter ready for her father. He was in his study, going over his notes for the sermon he would give in church this morning.

Having a pastor for a father and a detective for a mother ensured Cassie and her sisters grew up in a house filled with love and rules in equal measure. They knew no different – this had always been their life, but it meant their new-found abilities had to remain the utmost secret. Both the church and the police department had strong views on the use or even existence of magic – their parents would find it hard to accept their daughters were all witches.

'Breakfast,' Cassie called, raising her voice so that everyone would hear. Everyone except her sister, Jennifer, that is. Cassie knew her twin would be listening to music, her ear buds drowning out all other sound.

Mercifully, the elder sister, Naomi, would grab Jennifer as she passed their room.

The sound of the front door opening drew Cassie's eyes in that direction, so she saw her mother coming into the house. Though still beautiful, her mother was looking tired recently - work stress as much as anything was to blame. Grey was beginning to appear in her wonderful hair, changing her appearance and adding to the fine lines around her eyes as her fiftieth birthday approached.

'Hi, Mom,' Cassie wafted a hand across the counter to demonstrate that breakfast was ready. The timing was serendipitous, not planned - she had no idea when her mother would return, such was the nature of her job.

Detective Michelle Stevens offered her daughter a thin smile.

'Hi, Cassie. Thank you for doing breakfast.'

Picking up a piece of bacon and biting off the end, Cassie mumbled, 'No problem.'

The sound of footsteps on the floor above heralded the arrival of her sisters just a few moments later. They gathered at the breakfast bar, taking plates, and giving thanks to God before they all started eating.

Naomi asked. 'What's the subject for today's sermon, Dad?'

Across the table, Cassie and Jennifer exchanged a glance. The question was not a casual one, it was a veiled warning from the elder sister to the twins. Cassie had been looking for a way to introduce the subject of magic for several weeks. She believed that they could make their parents understand. They were not dangerous, and they would never use their magical abilities to cause any harm. Quite the opposite, in fact. They wanted to do good.

Naomi argued that they could never allow anyone to know their terrible secret. Both mom and dad had given their opinions on the subject, commenting on the news coverage the family had watched together. Their father believed it was an abomination against God. Their mother believed anyone attempting to wield magic must by default be a criminal, their intention only to use it for criminal purposes.

Before he answered, Pastor Stevens reached across the table to place a hand upon his wife's.

'I think perhaps that may depend on what your mother has to tell us,' he remarked. It was clear from what he said that he knew more about what had driven mom from bed and kept her out of it all night.

Jennifer and Naomi both stopped eating, waiting to hear what their detective mother might have to report. Only Cassie continued chowing her food, unwilling to remain hungry and excusing herself because she'd been breathing in the delicious scents for the last twenty minutes.

'There was another attack last night,' Michelle revealed. 'Sarah and Chris were both hurt. They're in the hospital now. They're fairly banged up, but not in any danger,' she clarified. The girls knew most of their mother's colleagues, and rather liked Sarah. She had been a senior when they started at high school, and well known because she was captain of the volleyball team. 'They expect to be released later today,' Michelle concluded, 'but will not be back in work for a while.'

With a horrified tone, Naomi asked, 'What happened?'

Michelle flipped her eyebrows, grasping the pot of coffee to refill her mug as she said, 'Someone broke into Collins' Pharmacy on Bay Street. I say they broke in, but it looks like they exploded the bricks in one wall to gain entry. Of course, I say exploded, but CSI needed about eight seconds to confirm nothing explosive had been used. It was magic,' she confirmed what her family were waiting to hear. 'Then whoever it was flipped Chris and Sarah's cruiser, slamming them across the street. You should see the state of it. It looks like it was hit by a train.'

Pastor Stevens reached out with both hands, grasping his wife's and eldest daughter, Naomi's. In turn, Cassie and Jennifer lifted their arms and soon the family were linking hands around the table.

'Let us pray,' the pastor closed his eyes and bowed his head.

As their breakfasts cooled, and Cassie questioned whether she could duck her head to snag a piece of bacon from her plate without being noticed, the man of the house turned his words to God. He asked the Almighty to look after Chris and Sarah, and to give them all the strength they needed to lead the community through this troubling time.

He finished with, 'Amen,' which his wife and daughters echoed before releasing hands once more.

Cassie fell upon her breakfast, eager to quell the rumbling emptiness that plagued her core.

Ignoring his own plate of food, the pastor asked his wife, 'Is there any indication who is behind this attack? Is it likely to be the same person?' He didn't say, nor did he need to, that he was referring to the most recent magical attack before this one.

Officer Tammy-Jo Spencer had been killed in a most terrible manner three days ago. Her body was found in the woods bordering the northern edge of the town in the early hours of Friday morning. Her injuries were catastrophic, her internal organs all ruptured, and her skin burned.

The medical examiner listed the cause of death as organ failure, but everyone knew she had been killed with magic. Tammy-Jo had been responding to a resident who reported strange lights coming from the woodland behind their house, but her last transmission said only that it was all quiet when she arrived. She told dispatch she was going to have a quick look around before returning to her police cruiser.

She never made it back to her car.

The hunt was on, but there were no clues to lead them in one direction or another and Michelle had gotten far too little sleep in the times since the terrible scene was discovered.

Yet more tired from getting almost no sleep last night, Michelle gripped a coffee cup with both hands. It was a little hot to the touch, though she barely noticed it. Her head was filled with terrifying thoughts of perpetrators she would not be able to stop even if she could identify them. The images they had all seen on television were like something from a science fiction movie. That what they were seeing was not only real, but was in their city, gave Michelle cause to question whether God had abandoned them.

She would never voice such a thought, certainly not in the presence of her husband who believed strength in their faith had never been more necessary. But the subject of God was being discussed by everyone. On TV, at work, by the people in the streets – it was everywhere.

Many acted as if the appearance of these magical beings was proof that God did not exist. Michelle wasn't ready to join that side of the debate, but her faith had been rocked.

There was no official response from the White House, and it was the same story all around the globe. Governments were forming committees to address the new threat, but they were as in the dark as everyone else.

To answer her husband's question, she said, 'No, not yet. I will have to get back to work after church.'

Her statement was startling enough that even Cassie stopped chewing. Crime didn't stop just because it was Sunday, but mom hadn't worked on the sabbath in years. She was a senior detective and the wife of a pastor. Her shifts were arranged around Sunday service and family lunch. Every other Sunday for years had seen a gathering of family members as dad's sister, Alicia, arrived with her husband and their four children, plus grandmas Ruth and Christine, mom and dad's mothers.

It was a gathering that had not been interrupted for anything for so long the sisters could not remember the last time.

It was the in-between Sunday this week, the one where no one came to the house and they Stevens family was able to enjoy some quiet family time. Nevertheless, not having mom around would be weird.

Pastor Stevens nodded, quelling his natural urge to comment. If his wife felt she needed to work, it would be with good reason.

Breakfast ended, conversation turning to school and college when mom forced it away from the worrying subject of magic and the sense of unease everyone felt.

The sisters responded dutifully, telling their parents what they wanted to hear. Not that they needed to lie about their schoolwork ever – they were all straight-A students, but the pressure of their own terrible secret had been building for weeks and threatened to erupt like a volcano if left unchecked.

The crux of it was the difference of opinion they held. When Jennifer found online footage of a young woman throwing glowing orbs of energy from her right hand in the midst of a magical battle, they had all been excited to know they were not alone. They each had magical power – raw, untrained, and untested, but utterly undeniable.

Cassie and Jennifer wanted to explore it, their excitement such that their more cautious elder sister, Naomi, would not have been able to stop them if she tried. They all understood the danger in what they were proposing, and how their newfound abilities might be perceived not just by their parents, but by everyone in their community. However, it was only Naomi who argued for patience and caution.

Jennifer was always the one who walked a line between her sisters, doing her best to keep the peace as the middle-born – even though she was only a handful of minutes older than Cassie. She wanted to explore her magical abilities, but was holding back so it wasn't two against one.

Research allowed them to discover the woman they saw online was a British girl called Anastasia Aaronson. However, it strengthened Naomi's argument when she was declared a fugitive from the British police and then spotted in New York less than two weeks ago where an enormous battle had taken place. Several police officers died in that battle and though it was not clear by whose hand, the sisters could not deny that Anastasia Aaronson had been there.

Since admitting to each other they all possessed the same magical ability just a few weeks ago, the world had changed. Initially they practised in secret, finding time and space to go somewhere secluded. Then the existence of magical beings became common knowledge and Naomi insisted they all stop.

Public condemnation for supernaturals was instant and harsh. Anyone identified as possessing magical powers would be swiftly ostracised, possibly arrested, and most certainly hounded out of town by decent folks who were all secretly questioning where to buy a pitchfork.

Naomi was scared, quite rightly so, and she believed they could avoid detection by simply never practising magic again.

Cassie's opinion was that they would need to develop and refine their skills so that they could use them when they had to. If there were magical beings who might hurt and kill, and were able to defy the laws of physics in such a way the police and armed forces could do little to stop them, then surely it fell to the sisters and others like them to stand against the new enemy.

Cassie argued that they had no idea if they were alone in possessing these powers, or if there were lots more like them. The supernaturals had appeared and then disappeared again as swiftly and completely as they came – their attack around the globe captured on cell phones for all to see. Now though, there were magical events happening in singular, unconnected occurrences.

Did that mean that some supernaturals stayed behind when the others retreated, or was it people like the sisters with powers they could not explain or even fully understand?

Jennifer dithered between her sisters' polar opposite opinions, unable or unwilling to decide whose side she was on.

There would be another heated discussion later today, all three girls knew it already. Their glances across the breakfast table as they argued with their eyes, made it clear Cassie intended to defy Naomi, and Naomi would do all she could to stop her impetuous younger sister from exposing all three of them.

In truth, it was a miracle neither parent picked up on the expressions passing between their daughters.

After breakfast, Cassie and Naomi retreated to different portions of the house. Having made breakfast, Cassie was exempt from any kitchen cleaning up duties. Naomi and Jennifer took care of it, but neither was willing to talk about the biggest subject on their mind while their parents were still in the house.

Their father left half an hour before the rest of them needed to go, heading to church to prepare for morning service. When their mother went for a shower, cleaning herself up before changing into appropriate church-going clothes, Naomi sought out her errant sister.

'You heard mom this morning, Cassie,' Naomi pointed out as she came into the twins' bedroom. 'If she finds out ...'

Cassie was bent over slightly at the waist, leaning towards the mirror as she applied a swipe of mascara. She finished the task, controlling her rising ire before she turned to face her sister.

'What is it that you're proposing then, Naomi?' Cassie cocked a hip to one side, letting her body language match the sass on her face. 'Try and keep this a secret until we are old enough to move out? Or do we just wait until mom and dad are buried in the cemetery? Do you really think this is something we're going to be able to keep a secret forever?'

Jennifer came into the room, edging around Naomi to do so, and putting her hands up in a gesture that indicated she wanted no part of their argument.

'I don't need to get involved,' she remarked, 'I just need to get my phone.' The electronic device was never far from her hands, though she'd fallen asleep without plugging it in to charge the previous evening. It almost dead when she awoke. Half an hour of charging while she got breakfast had been sufficient to ensure it lasted while they were out.

'You are involved,' Cassie insisted, a hint of venom in her voice. 'Whether you like it or not, Jen, you have to decide whether you are going to use your gift or not.'

'We're calling it a gift now, are we?' Naomi challenged. 'It's hardly the term I would use.'

In absolute defiance of her sister's concerns, Cassie pulled line energy into herself. Like her sisters, she didn't fully understand where it came from, but had the ability to feel the ley lines running underneath the city and to pull on them whenever she needed to fuel her magic.

Her hair began to float, lifting away from her skull slightly as magical, elemental energy filled her body. Lifting her arms, she drew moisture from the air, forcing the tiny molecules to join together.

Behind her, Jennifer gasped when she saw what her sister was doing.

Naomi narrowed her eyes, her expression conveying a threat that Cassie took to be a challenge.

'In the house?' Naomi growled.

The tiny water droplets were beginning to form a mist in the air between Cassie and Naomi. Like a small cloud hovering in the air, it carried water which Cassie intended to throw at her older sister.

Her own anger rising, Naomi drew in line power of her own. If her sister wanted her to back down, she was in for a nasty shock. Creating an air spell with nothing more than a murmur of will, Naomi planned to throw the gathering cloud of water back at Cassie before she got the chance to use it.

The sound of the shower shutting off and the shower door opening preceded their mother calling through to check on them.

'Are you ready, girls? We need to go in ten minutes. That's you I'm talking to, Cassie. You are always last.'

Their mother's voice broke the spell, literally and figuratively, both girls panicking that she might come to check on them. How could they possibly explain if she saw them conjuring magic inside the house?

With no magic to support it, the water inside the small cloud fell to the floor like rain, a sudden downpour on an area of carpet less than twelve inches across.

Jennifer snorted. 'I ain't cleaning that up,' and flounced from the room to leave her sisters still glaring at each other.

Backing from the room, Naomi agreed whole heartedly with her younger sister.

'Neither am I. It's your mess. Don't think this is over though.'

Tension between the three girls was a new thing. There had been scraps in the past, of course, what siblings don't have an occasional battle at some point? However, they had been born into a loving family and were about as tight knit as three sisters could be. They helped and supported each other in all things.

For years Naomi had been their defender in the school yard. Eighteen months older than the twins, she had never questioned whether it was the right thing to do when she made sure the kids in her sisters' year group knew the consequences for messing with them.

Only now that the challenge of negotiating their newfound abilities created a rift in opinion were they at each other's throats.

Ten minutes later, the three girls were leaving the house with their mother. It was a short walk to church and the weather outside was pleasant and warm despite the leaves falling from the trees. They hadn't spoken since the standoff in the twins' bedroom, but their thoughts on the subject of their most recent fight were soon distracted by the appearance of a figure they had seen too many times before.

Chapter 3

I t was perhaps the tenth or twelfth time they had spotted her. The twins had seen her outside their high school, and agreed that that was the first place they saw her. They thought nothing of it for a time, until they saw her watching them at the mall last weekend. They had been with Naomi at the time, and it was Naomi who spotted the old woman.

The fact that their elder sister had seen her too removed any chance that it was a coincidence. They had chosen to approach her that day, but in the bustle of people at the mall, they lost her almost as soon as they set off in her direction.

Now she was on the opposite side of their street. A couple of doors down but clearly watching their house, the old lady was standing in the shade of a sycamore tree. There were leaves around her feet where they fell overnight, and a small blanket of them covered the sidewalk where a line of trees edged the road.

Naomi had her phone in her hand, hastily snapping a picture while Jennifer asked, 'Mom, do you know who that lady is?'

Michelle was checking her phone, making sure there had been no messages from the station. Consequently, she had to look up and about to see who it was her daughter was referring to.

'What lady?' she asked.

All three girls had taken their eyes off the old woman to see what their mother would say and when they looked back, their stalker had vanished. Had she stepped behind the tree, disappearing from sight behind its trunk?

Confused, all three sisters moved as one, stepping into the road and crossing it, their footsteps hurried.

'Where are you going, girls?' their mother wanted to know. 'We don't have time for shenanigans.'

The fact that Michelle's feet had come to a stop meant that she was no longer on her way to church. They had been a few minutes late leaving anyway, her need for a shower to fight off her fatigue delaying the process of departing the house. The girls were not to blame for that, but they really needed to get moving now. Instead, they were now scurrying across the street.

When Michelle got no response, her eyes flared a little. Her daughters were grown women now, but she wasn't about to change the nature of their relationship. If mumma said something, that was how it went.

Ten yards away, Cassie, Jennifer, and Naomi all reached the far side of the street. They had fanned out slightly, approaching with Cassie in the middle, so she reached the tree they thought the old lady might have gone behind first. Her sisters to her left and right made sure to box the woman in.

They wanted to know who she was, and why she was following them - a natural enough question to ask.

When they discovered there to be no one there, and no direction in which the old lady could have escaped, the three girls looked at each other with wide eyes and worried expressions.

Jennifer stared up into the tree, not that she thought that was where the old lady might have gone.

From across the street, they heard the impatient tone of their mother and knew they really needed to go.

Hurrying back, lest they incur their mother's ire, Jennifer whispered, 'What do you think she wants?'

'The old lady?' Naomi sought to confirm, thinking for a moment Jennifer was referring to their mother. Seeing Jen's expression, she said, 'I don't know. But I don't like it, and I think we need to find out.'

Cassie couldn't believe her sisters. 'What about the fact that she just vanished?' she hissed at the pair of them. 'She's using magic.' It was a flat statement that trucked no argument.

None came, but that was because they were nearing their mother, whose face matched her impatient tone.

The three girls fell silent, quickening their pace to make sure they got to church in plenty of time. Their mother liked to be there early enough to greet people when they arrived. As a law enforcement agent, she was a central figure in the community in her own right. Being married to the pastor simply added to that and she would often remind her daughters of their responsibilities.

Feeling nervous, Jennifer slipped her hand into Cassie's, the two girls staying like that the rest of the way to the church.

Their father railed against the voices who were calling God into question. His sermon was all about the need for faith in troubling times, and how through God's grace the worrying threat would be overcome. The congregation agreed, the whispering voices condemning magic users though there were many who still simply refused to believe what they were seeing on TV was real.

Before and after the service, there was really only one conversation to be had – everyone was talking about the robbery at Collins' Pharmacy and what happened to the two police officers. Details were sketchy, but there were pictures of the police cruiser doing the rounds already. There were pictures of the ruined wall and front façade of the pharmacy too.

Cassie got one from Sheridan Cookson, a girl her mother didn't approve of because she wore too little clothing and showed far too much skin. They had been friends since kindergarten though and Sheridan had made sure to drive by the scene this morning.

One side of Collins' Pharmacy had a hole in it that a person could walk through. The bricks were lying on the ground outside as if blown out from within.

Showing Jennifer, she asked, 'How did they do that?'

Jennifer shook her head. 'I have no idea. How much power must it take to do that?' Her question highlighted what concerned them both about what they were seeing – their powers were insignificant. They could freeze water and turn it into steam which was great for making drinks. If it wouldn't terrify everyone, it would be a neat party trick.

They could also make the air move and conjure water from the air. Last year, Naomi created fire, sending a stream of it from her right hand to scare off a mountain lion but she had always claimed to not know how she did it and hadn't been able to pull it off again since. None of them knew they had any power at all until fear acted as a catalyst to release the magic within the eldest sister. That in turn made all three girls question what they could do, and in secret all three began to experiment.

But how could they test themselves and really learn? If you want to learn to play the piano, you get lessons. For most things there is an App or online classes. Not so for learning to control elemental magic. Not that they knew to call it that.

Keeping it hidden from their parents, they had searched the internet, finding hundreds of online videos that claimed to be able to show a person how to do magic. They were all nonsense, and the footage they found of people wielding magic, filmed in secret by people caught in close proximity to events they would rather avoid, told the girls nothing about how to perform the spells they could see.

Cassie wanted to practice, Naomi refused to let her, to which Cassie had, of course, scoffed. Jennifer attempted to mediate, but neither her younger or elder sister would back down, and the air had grown frosty.

It was nearing noon when they left the churchyard, the congregation drifting away after the usual round of cakes, coffee, and chatter. The Stevens ladies followed, but the pastor remained behind – there were always tasks to which he needed to attend.

Mom wanted to get to the hospital. She wasn't due to be working, but fellow officers had been hurt in the line of duty and the girls understood that the police department, their mother included, were all pulling together. There was a new threat in town, one who would happily attack and kill police officers, and the police department would focus on little else until they were able to identify and stop the person behind the crimes.

By half past twelve, their mother was going out the door and without her to act as a pressure cap, the fight that had been brewing for days was bubbling to the surface.

Chapter 4

The SIA

C olt Ironbolt, Head of the Global Supernatural Investigations Alliance, called SIA for short by everyone who knew about it, stifled a yawn and berated himself for daydreaming. He was not a man given to idle fantasy, yet he had struggled to find sleep last night because his brain was sounding a bugle alarm calling him to arms.

He had always aspired to greatness. He wanted recognition for achieving great things. He wanted museums and airports named after him. He wanted to be the President. And what might have been a laughable proposition a few months ago was looking ever more tenable.

Humanity was heading for a war against a race of supernatural beings which they knew almost nothing about. Thanks to his organisation – not that he founded it, but he ran it now and that was what counted – humanity knew only of the threat, not how potentially cataclysmic the threat might be.

He knew though.

He knew because it was his job to know. Thanks to Ayla Pendragon, his new special advisor, he knew all about the history of the demons and why the planet now found itself plagued by them. The death curse of their supreme being was failing and soon they would flood the Earth. They meant to reclaim it, and with the source magic they possessed they expected it to be easy. Ironbolt didn't fully understand how there could be more than one kind of magic, yet he accepted what he was told. He also accepted Ayla's word when she assured him the demons' source magic was vastly more powerful than the elemental magic she could wield.

The demons would sweep humanity's best weapons aside like kindling before a hurricane.

There was another faction, those who called themselves Angels. Essentially the same, yet following a different set of principles, they were also planning to rule over humanity. They might be nicer about it if Ayla was to be believed, but humanity would still be under their rule.

Neither outcome was acceptable, but that gave Ironbolt the opportunity he needed. Like General Grant after he won, if Ironbolt could pull off a victory – he was going to make the world know he was at the helm of the force fighting to win – his ascension to the ultimate seat of power would be all but guaranteed.

'President Ironbolt,' he said it aloud just so he could hear it.

How could a nation say no to the man who saved them all from enslavement? It wouldn't be just America though, would it? He would have saved the whole world. He would have joined the human race together to fight against a new enemy ...

He realised he was daydreaming again, pinched the bridge of his nose with his eyes closed and attempted to clear his head.

There were a million things he needed to do and none of them were getting done. Domestic and foreign issues all fell on his desk, and all had to be prioritised and dealt with expediently.

His number one task remained the formation of a supernatural army. Ayla Pendragon was helping him with that, helping to recruit people who demonstrated any magical ability. The problem was finding them.

Otto Schneider, the annoying German wizard, was doing the same thing. Sort of. He refused to cooperate with the SIA, dictating terms to them rather than fall in line and work directly for Ironbolt. Schneider claimed to have rescued hundreds of familiars from the demon realm – a claim backed up by Ayla as she was one of them. Something had gone wrong though, and the returned familiars got scattered across the planet. A few had been found, or more accurately, had been identified because they arrived back where they were originally taken from years, decades, and in some cases centuries after being kidnapped.

Ironbolt could only imagine what it must be like for a person from the 17th century to arrive in modern-day anywhere. Cars, planes, heck - how about electricity? Those people stuck out, but according to Ayla they had found less than fifteen percent so there were hundreds of powerfully magical former familiars at large across the planet. Trained by their demon masters to serve them, there could be no better recruits for Ironbolt's army.

To add to that, every single day, the SIA was uncovering more and more people who were developing magical abilities of their own. They woke up one morning and could freeze water or transform into a werewolf or other creature or ... well, who could guess what might be next.

The SIA needed to find and recruit these people as swiftly as possible, creating an army that would stand against the demons and angels when they next appeared. Ironbolt wanted to run a public campaign to encourage such individuals to identify themselves, but the federal government squashed his suggestion like a bug the moment he raised it. They were worried about backlash, about the danger to regular folk if they were to raise their hands. The populace was scared, and the papers were filled with reports of mobs forming. All it took was a rumour and the odd little man at the end of the street would find angry neighbours on his stoop. No one had been killed yet, but there had been hospitalisations.

To that end, three floors beneath Ironbolt's feet, a team of agents, mostly supernaturals but joined by a few humans from various special forces and elite law enforcement agencies, were analysing the latest reports coming in from across the US and prioritising which to investigate. There was no point sending agents to a place just because something supernatural happened. Their resources were too spartan for that. If they could identify an individual, then they would go.

Agent Frank 'Ferris' Bueller, a wizard, asked, 'What about this in Chippewa Falls?'

The report was fresh in, no more than a few hours old and the second incident recorded in the town in a few days.

Agent Debs Wallace, another wizard, though one with limited powers, said, 'I spoke with the local police two days ago when their officer was killed. They have no leads. Sending someone would be a waste of time.'

Bueller acknowledged her comment with a nod, and they moved onto the next report. The incident in Chippewa Falls was noted and filed. Further incidents would result in a flag on the system, but would only warrant greater scrutiny if there was a high likelihood of finding the supernaturals involved.

Chapter 5

'We need to practice!' screamed Cassie. 'All of us,' she made daggers with her eyes. Naomi was refusing to listen, too concerned for the consequences of being discovered. Cassie and elder sister Naomi had been going at it for fifteen minutes already and neither was going to change their stance anytime soon.

'What will mom say when she finds out the evil magic users the police are hunting live in her house?' Naomi shot back. 'Do you care what impact it will have on our father when the town discovers all three of his daughters are witches?' It was the same point she'd been making for days, just voiced a different way.

Cassie hated that her big sister always went for guilt first. Of course she cared, but Cassie knew she could scream that until she was blue in the face because Naomi wouldn't accept her words unless they were backed by action.

Choosing to hit back with this same weapon her sister chose to employ, Cassie narrowed her eyes.

'What will you say to dad when mom comes up against whoever it is who killed Officer Spencer? What will you say when the next person is killed or hurt and people later find out that we could have stopped them? We have a responsibility to this community, isn't that what mom is always saying? What if no one else can stop them?'

Forcing her voice to be calm, Naomi replied, 'The people in this community are not ready to see us as anything other than monsters. If they find out what we are, it will be like the Salem Witch Trials all over again. We won't be able to stay here, and neither will our parents. If you do this, Cassie, if you refuse to listen to reason and expose us all, I will never forgive you.'

Jennifer set out to keep the peace, but had given up more than five minutes ago, retreating across the room where she waited to see if the argument would escalate. It looked to be petering out but not in a good way. Her sisters were not going to agree.

'Surely we can find a happy medium?' Jennifer suggested hopefully. 'I think Naomi is right that there is a danger in being discovered. The people in this town will not understand, Cassie. You know that, right?' Jennifer then shut Naomi off before she could remark, 'Cassie is right too though. The people on TV were saying that conventional weapons are no use. We all saw the October 12th event,' Jennifer employed the term by which everyone was referring to the day of the supernatural invasion, 'Police and soldiers around the world were swept aside as if they were nothing. So if it is only magic that can fight this, doesn't it fall to us to be ready?'

Cassie nodded her head with an exaggerated show of satisfaction.

'Exactly. Thank you.'

Jennifer wagged a finger at her twin.

'Not so fast, Cassie. If we do this ... if we do anything, we need to be one hundred percent safe. Don't you agree, Naomi?'

Both twins looked at their elder sister expectantly.

Naomi felt her teeth grate against each other as she clenched her jaw to stop the first words in her mouth from escaping.

When she had her anger under control, she said, 'The only way to be one hundred percent safe is to do nothing at all. I am done talking about it. I'm going to get some lunch.' Her announcement was followed by her departure from the twins' bedroom. Jennifer and Cassie got to hear their elder sister stomping down the stairs.

'Lunch?' Jennifer asked, the question aimed at Cassie in a hopeful tone that they might all make up over a meal.

'You go,' Cassie replied. 'I'll be down in a minute. I need to clear my head first.'

Jennifer accepted her twin sister's answer without comment, collecting her phone from the end of her bed before leaving the room.

Cassie waited until she could hear her sisters talking downstairs in the kitchen. Then she picked up her jacket, slipped her arms into it and silently slid her bedroom window open. She hadn't gone out the window and down the Maple tree outside in a long time. It was something she and Jennifer had started doing as kids. She could not remember which one of them had dared the other the first time, but it proved to be easier than expected.

They used it as a way to escape whenever one of them was banished to the bedroom, not that such a thing happened very often, but their mother was strict, and the tree provided them with a method of disobeying her without getting caught.

Until they did.

Of course it had been Cassie, who grew overconfident and fell that day. Had she not broken her arm, the two of them might have continued to get away with using the tree. Instead, by the time Cassie returned from hospital with a pink cast around her broken limb, the tree limbs nearest their window had been removed by dad's saw.

That was three years ago, and the tree had sprouted new growth as one might expect. Nevertheless, as Cassie balanced on the window ledge and looked where to put her foot, she felt nervousness rising that she might repeat her fall but from a greater height this time.

Five minutes later, when she had failed to appear for lunch and Jennifer had grown curious, Cassie's absence was discovered. By then, Jennifer's twin was two streets over and heading for the woodland where she knew she would be able to practise with minimal risk of being caught.

That her sisters knew she had snuck out was not in question – Jennifer had phoned her and then sent a text message. They would seek her out too, she knew, which was why she chose to return to the place where they had practised many times before. Let them come - Cassie would prove her point by knocking Naomi on her ass. Then her stupid, bossy, older sister would have to use magic to fight back – they would be practicing whether Naomi wanted to or not.

Feeling agitated and a little angry still, Cassie had to force herself to wait and listen for several minutes to ensure she was alone in the woods before she began to draw on ley line energy.

She wanted to produce a ball of energy in her hand the same way she had seen Anastasia Aaronson do. As a weapon it looked far more powerful and more practical than moving air or conjuring water. She was getting better at manipulating water as an element to produce steam or ice and could do it at speed now, but how much help would that be in a fight?

However, until Anastasia turned up to show her how to do the sizzling ball of magic thing, Cassie had to accept that she could only practice what she knew how to do. She blew out a hard breath in a bid to expel all other thoughts from her mind and focused on the spell she wanted to produce. Cassie could feel the water molecules in the air. They were all around her - in the trees and the plants, and in the soil beneath her feet. She pushed out with her senses, closing her eyes to better focus her mind by removing the input of other senses.

With a snap, Cassie raised her right hand, feeling magical energy flowing through her body. Holding the spell in her mind, she drew in water vapour from all around, forming a ball of it above her open palm.

When she opened her eyes, a smile teased at the corners of her mouth. It had taken her no more than a couple of seconds to perform a spell that would have taken almost a minute a few weeks ago. Not only that, but the ball of floating, shimmering water was twice the size of any she had conjured before.

The smile faltered, ultimately failing when she reminded herself that this was just another party trick. The police cruiser had been slammed with a force of magical enemy so strong that it had destroyed the car. She could create a ball of water. Big deal. She would go down a treat at kids' parties.

Changing the spell, with the ball of water still floating above her hand, she manipulated the water molecules, reducing the temperature until ice crystals began to form. Yet again she was able to produce the effect she wanted far faster now than she could have a few weeks ago so that within a few seconds she held a ball of ice above her hand.

The size of a softball, when she abruptly shifted the spell once more to create an air manipulation that flung the ice at the trunk of a tree, the effect was impressive enough. Had her ball of ice hit a person, it would have done them some damage.

She needed more though. Not that Cassie wanted to get into magical battles, that was just a tactic she used in a bid to win her argument with Naomi. Nevertheless, she made a valid point. If nobody else could stop Officer Spencer's killer, perhaps it would come down to someone with magical abilities.

Indeed, if she needed to expose herself as a witch in order to prevent a further death, or worse yet her own mother becoming entangled with such a dangerous person, then she would do so without hesitation. At least that was what she told herself.

Dropping her arms to her side, Cassie shrugged and rotated her shoulders and then her neck, kind of giving herself a massage as she psyched herself up for the next spell. The sight of Collins' Pharmacy and the exploded wall in one side of it had been plaguing her thoughts since she saw it. Whoever had done it, they used a spell Cassie had never considered before. But how had they manipulated the elements to create that effect? Could it be done with air? Could it be done with water? How do you make a wall explode? Better yet, how does a person practice such a feat without a wall to practice on?

She needed something to practise on. Looking around, nothing presented itself. Perhaps she could do something with a plant?

With a shrug, she decided the only way to find out was to try and see what happened. Selecting a young birch sapling, reaching for the sky in a bid to escape the forest floor, she conjured a new water spell.

She was able to sense the water inside the young tree but, had to focus hard to narrow her aim to just that one plant. Feeling it with her mind and augmenting her thoughts by moving her hands, Cassie isolated the moisture in the central part of the young tree's main stem.

'Now what?' she challenged herself. She wanted to produce something spectacular just like the bricks blowing outwards from the wall of the pharmacy. Could she burst the stem of the tree? How would she do that?

Only one answer presented itself, so with an absentminded lick of her lips, she frowned slightly and leaned towards her target as she applied as much heat as she could create with her mind as swiftly as possible.

The birch sapling made a small hissing noise followed by a pop. Then at exactly the point where she had been aiming her efforts the top half of the plant folded over and sagged to the floor.

Cassie let her arms fall and her shoulders slump with a groan of displeasure.

'You're doing it wrong.'

The voice came from behind her and was so sudden and unexpected that Cassie shrieked with alarm as she spun around to face the direction of danger.

Chapter 6

Two miles away at the Sacred Heart Hospital, Michelle Stevens was talking to Officer Sarah Kirke. Sarah and Chris had been brought in together, but last saw each other in the emergency room triage unit. Sarah knew that Chris was okay - the hospital staff was good enough to keep her informed, but they were in separate rooms and neither felt ready to get up and move about to find the other.

The terrible trauma to the cop car damaged their internal organs, the sudden shift from forward momentum to sidewards could have killed them both. Sarah had terrible bruising to her face where she had broken her nose on Chris's skull, sustained breaks to her right forearm and collar bone and there was blood in her urine from the damage to her kidneys. The doctors assured her she would make a full recovery and there would be no lasting damage.

There were cards and flowers and a fruit basket already in Sarah's room before Michelle arrived. She had stopped off in the hospital reception area to buy magazines and candy - two things she believed no one else would have thought of.

'Thank you, Michelle,' Sarah managed to groan. She was groggy from painkillers, but lucid enough to answer questions. The chief had been in already, so too almost every member of her family, and her ex-boyfriend who somehow seemed to think that her being injured might make her want to get back together with him. He'd been politely sent on his way, but it had been nice to see everyone else.

'I won't ask you how you're feeling,' Michelle remarked with a smile, 'but you look like you lost a fight with a wizard.'

A surprised laugh escaped Sarah's lips at the unexpected comment from her colleague, quickly followed by a sharp intake of breath and a groan.

'Oh, God, please don't make me laugh,' she complained good naturedly. 'You're going to ask me what I saw and I'm afraid I'm going to have to give you the same answer I gave you when you first asked.'

Michelle raised her eyebrows. 'I wasn't sure you even remembered that,' she remarked. 'You seemed so out of it.' Michelle had been one of the first officers on the scene following the attack the previous evening. Others had dealt with the scene and organised removing the cruiser while Michelle liaised and coordinated with CSI, not that they found any evidence of anything. It seemed criminals using magic didn't leave fingerprints. There was a slim hope that hair or fibre might be found, but otherwise they had nothing to go on.

Naturally, she had wanted to visit both officers in the hospital anyway because they were her colleagues, and she was concerned for them. But in her role as a detective investigating the case, it was necessary to interview them. She did that as best as possible the moment she was cleared by the doctors to do so, however just as she said, Sarah and Chris were not really with it at the time.

Sarah groaned again, shuffling awkwardly on the bed to change position.

'I remember it,' she claimed. 'I even remember what I said. Unfortunately, I'm going to say the same thing now. The suspect was probably Caucasian, approximately six feet two inches tall and athletically built. However, wearing a nondescript black hoodie and grey sweatpants with white sneakers, it was difficult to gauge body shape accurately. My assessment that the suspect was athletically built is based on shoulder to waist ratio. I cannot be certain that it was a man, but I believe that to be the case, again judging by nothing but body shape inside baggy clothes. He kept his hood up the entire time, so neither Chris nor I got to see his face. Nor did I see him move at any point.'

That Sarah – a seasoned police officer – was unable to even determine the suspect's race did not bode well. Sighing internally, Michelle referred to her earlier notes. Sarah hadn't changed her record of the suspect one bit.

'Yes, you said he was in the street as you approached. Officer Burton was driving and when he attempted to stop, the vehicle continued moving.'

'That's right,' Sarah agreed. 'It was as if the suspect had control of our vehicle. Chris pumped the brakes and attempted to steer, but nothing happened. Then an invisible force struck the right side of the vehicle just behind my seat. Honestly, if it had hit the car a few inches farther forward, I don't think I would be here now.'

Michelle drew in a slow breath, held it for a second, and let it go again. She had absolutely nothing to go on. It was just like when they found Tammy-Jo. That crime scene had been so devoid of physical evidence that it was almost sterile. There wasn't so much as a footprint that didn't belong to the fallen officer.

She needed help. She needed somebody with magical abilities of their own to work alongside her. The very thought was abhorrent. Would she be able to trust such a person? Were they even trustworthy?

Pushing Sarah to remember something that might help, Michelle asked, 'Is there anything else? Anything at all that might help us to identify him?'

Dutifully, Sarah racked her brain, replaying the scene in her head as forensically as she could manage. There was simply nothing for her to add. It had all been over in a flash, and truthfully, she felt lucky to be alive.

Knowing that Sarah was due to be discharged later today and both cops would be off work for some time, Michelle wished Sarah a swift recovery and then left her to visit Chris instead. But her conversation with Officer Chris Burton was no different from that which she had with Sarah. The result was the same too.

Leaving the hospital less than an hour after she arrived with the sum total of nothing achieved other than to wish her colleagues 'get well soon', Detective Michelle Stevens headed to the station.

43

Chapter 7

'I wasn't doing anything,' Cassie protested. Her conscience kicked in the moment the lie left her lips, but her heart was thudding in her chest, and Naomi's voice was echoing in her head - the warning she had failed to heed catching her out far sooner than she could ever have imagined.

Feeling almost sick from the rush of adrenalin flooding her body, Cassie suddenly realised who she was looking at. It was the old lady, the one who had been watching them, and her expression changed, shifting from guilty and afraid to accusatory and righteous.

'Hey, I know you. Why have you been watching us? Me and my sisters have all spotted you.' She was challenging the old woman, and in some ways attempting to deflect from the worry that her acts of magic had just been witnessed. The old lady did not appear to be carrying a phone, so she could not have recorded what she'd seen.

Cassie was getting her first proper look at the mysterious stalker. African American, with dark skin that carried a sun-worn appearance, the old lady had to be close to eighty if not somewhere on the other side. Her hair was completely turned to white, and cut fairly short so it clung around her skull. She was short – maybe five feet and two or three inches, but stooped so her real height might have been an inch or more than that in her twenties and thirties.

She wore a long skirt that might have been a dress – a shawl over the top in muted greens and reds fell to below her knees so the only other item of clothing Cassie could see was the lady's boots. They were sturdy and hewn from a thick brown leather with a thick sole.

The unwelcome intruder was yet to speak, but watching her Cassie was feeling more confident by the second.

Until the old lady raised her arms that is.

With a flourish of her right hand, and without even looking in its direction, the same birch sapling Cassie had been torturing exploded into pieces. Wood pulp like confetti showered the small clearing they were standing in.

'That's how you do it,' said the old lady, refusing to take her eyes from Cassie's.

Cassie's lower jaw was hanging wide open. From being caught performing magic and having her heart race one moment, to believing she could get away with it by simply lying and denying all knowledge of what the old lady might think she had seen the next. Now her heart was almost refusing to beat such was the terror gripping her.

'I'm not going to hurt you,' the old lady said as if sensing what Cassie was feeling or perhaps reading her expression correctly. 'My name is Bethany Cromwell,' the lady introduced herself as she closed the distance between them and reached out with her right hand.

Cassie's feet took an involuntary step backwards, fear making her want to run, curiosity demanding she stay. Staring down at the hand coming toward her and back up at the engaging smile spread across the old lady's face, Cassie let her upbringing take over.

'I'm Cassie Stevens,' she mumbled, gripping the offered hand to shake it, but barely noticing she had done so until Bethany let it go again and it fell back to her side. 'You're a witch,' she managed, the words coming out indistinct because there was so little moisture left in her mouth.

The old lady studied the teenager, looking her up and down like she was a piece of meat in a butcher's window, and she was trying to decide if a purchase were warranted.

'I prefer the term wizard,' she replied.

Cassie blinked twice slowly. 'I thought wizards were men?' she questioned. Just like Bethany, she was drinking in the features of the person opposite. Yes, she was old, but there was an intense energy to the woman that belied her years. Was that to do with the magic?

Bethany smiled generously. 'Unfortunately, Cassie, very little of what you think to be true will prove to be so. The world ... the supernaturals as people are calling them, are not what people think.'

'What are they?' Cassie blurted her question, keen to learn something from the old woman.

Bethany smiled at the girl. 'We'll get to that later. Why don't you tell me what you think you are?'

'Um,' Cassie stuttered. What kind of a question was that? How was she supposed to answer? 'I'm a wizard?' she asked hesitantly.

Bethany let a small chuckle escape her lips.

'Perhaps,' she replied, somewhat cryptically in Cassie's opinion. 'You are human, dear child, with just a little extra something in your bloodstream. If you want to know what that little extra something is, or why you can now do what everyone will call magic, I'm afraid I'm going to come up a little short on answers. That is not why I approached you, and it's not why I've been watching you.'

Seeing an opportunity to ask a question she wanted an answer to, Cassie grabbed it.

'So why have you been watching us? Some people would call that stalking, you know?'

Bethany's smile stayed in place. 'I could see what you were, but I am new here,' The old lady paused her sentence, her eyes flitting left as if confirming her claim against an old memory, 'sort of old, but new now, I guess. Anyway, I was unsure how to approach you. I guess I was worried I might come off as creepy or scary.'

Cassie flared her eyes a little, pulling a face. 'Well, you did.' Feeling nervous, Cassie forced herself to ask a question she felt she had to know the answer to. 'Did you kill that police officer?'

Bethany nodded her head as if she had expected the question or was pleased that Cassie had asked it.

'I did not,' she replied. 'If your next question is going to be whether I know who did, then the answer is *no*. There is someone else in the town, someone with power. I don't know who it is. Not yet, but … well, that is one of the reasons I have come to you.'

Cassie shook her head slightly. She got the impression Bethany almost told her something but decided at the last second to hold it back. Regardless of that, she wasn't following what the old lady was trying to tell her.

Cassie asked, 'What do you mean?'

'I fear that the person behind the death of that police officer a few days ago might not be human at all.' Seeing Cassie's eyes flare in surprise and horror, she quickly pressed on before the teenager could interrupt. 'I'll explain what that means a little later if you'll allow me. Suffice to say that if the guilty party is human, then they are powerful, and I suspect they will attempt to recruit anyone else displaying magical abilities.'

Suddenly, Cassie understood. 'You mean me, don't you? And my sisters.'

'Yes,' Bethany confirmed. 'I do not wish to alarm you, but what you can do, your abilities, while completely untrained and in their infancy, make you an enticing target. He - I'm going to call him a *he* until proven otherwise - will want to train you.'

Warily, Cassie asked, 'What is it that you want to do?'

Bethany showed Cassie a serious face. 'Well, that's a really good question, young lady. I want to train you, but not because I want to use you. I am motivated because I can sense the good in you and want to empower you to protect yourself and others. Your fledgling skills are going to get you into trouble. Since there is no way to rid yourself of the magical ability you possess, the only thing you can do is increase your ability so that you can defend yourself.'

Cassie recognised a natural inclination to want to walk away. She had no idea who this woman was. Getting her name and shaking her hand didn't mean they knew each other or give her any reason to trust. However, her entire argument against Naomi was for the need to be able to increase their power and ability for such a time when they might need to use magic. Now she was in the presence of a woman who appeared to have honourable intentions, who was vastly more capable when it came to wielding magic, and who was offering tuition.

Really, how could she say no?

Imagining returning to her sisters an hour from now imbued with five times the range of spells that either one of them held, Cassie allowed herself to feel optimistic.

'Show me,' she encouraged, in that bored teenager's tone that suggests they do not expect to be impressed.

Bethany considered the young woman for a few moments, questioning how to approach the subject of training. She had been a familiar in the demon realm, and her own ability to wield elemental magic was well developed. However, she had never been required to teach anyone, only to learn. She elected to go right back to the very basics and see how much Cassie understood.

'What do you know about the source of your magical energy?' she asked.

That was an easy question for Cassie to field. 'Absolutely nothing,' she admitted without hesitation.

Bethany spluttered a laugh. She really was going to have to go back to basics.

Chapter 8

'Where have you been?' Jennifer gasped. Cassie had just walked back through the door, and was still in the process of taking her coat off. 'Naomi has been going nuts, Cass. Why didn't you answer your phone or at least send a message?'

Cassie fixed her twin with a disinterested look.

'When isn't Naomi going nuts? She's always got something to get excited about. That's why I didn't answer the phone. Is mom home yet?'

'No, Cass. It's a good thing too, don't you think? Anyway, where have you been?'

Cassie bit her lip, thinking about what she wanted to do and holding back for just a second while she thought about it. Abruptly, and with an almost imperceptible nod to herself, she threw caution to the wind and tapped into the ley line just as Bethany had taught her.

When flames danced in the air an inch above her right hand, she was watching Jennifer's face for the shock she knew she would see there.

Jennifer let out a squeak of surprise as she jumped back, but caught herself before she'd retreated more than a foot. Her fascination for what Cassie was doing was greater than her fear.

'How are you doing that?' she asked, her voice a gossamer thin whisper. She moved in closer, stopping when she began to feel the heat emanating from the flames. 'Doesn't it burn?' she asked.

'Not at all,' Cassie assured her. 'The spell insulates me from the heat. This isn't all, Jen. I have so much to show you.'

Jennifer asked, 'How?'

Both girls squealed in shock as the front door opened less than two yards from their position. In an instant, Cassie doused the flame in her hand, stilling the magic that powered it and dropping her connection to the nearest ley line.

'Girls,' mom said as she came through the door, already unzipping her winter coat. Noticing their startled expressions, she asked, 'What are you two up to?'

'Nothing,' blurted Cassie, lying to her mother guiltily. 'You just scared us is all. We were not expecting you.'

Michelle could tell when her daughters were not being truthful. It was a mixture of mom intuition and experience as a cop, but she was far too tired to have it out with them now. She hung her coat on the peg in the closet by the door and slipped off her boots, placing them inside the closet before closing it.

'I'm going for a nap, girls. I would appreciate it if you would keep the noise in the house down, thank you. It's been quite a long day already. Is your father not home yet?'

Not knowing the answer to that particular question, Cassie shot her eyes at Jennifer.

'Um, no, mum. He hasn't been back yet.'

Feeling like she was running on empty, Michelle accepted the information as her daughters presented it and pointed her feet towards her bedroom. She could do with more than a short nap, but a couple of hours would go a long way to reviving her - she was due to be back on shift later tonight.

Once their mother was out of sight, and the two girls heard her bedroom door close, they both breathed a sigh of relief.

Cassie sagged against the sideboard, her heart still racing at how close she had come to getting caught.

Jennifer took a moment to recover, but then turned her attention back to her sister. She wasn't letting Cassie off the hook.

'You better start spilling, sister. How is it that you can suddenly create fire? And what else is it that you can do? You've only been gone a couple of hours.'

Cassie enjoyed the additional power her new secret gave her, but she knew she needed to share it. She hoped that by meeting Bethany, Naomi could be convinced of the need to learn the craft of weaving magic. With Bethany's tuition they could advance at speed. They could keep their secret, they just had to be careful.

'Where's Naomi anyway?' Cassie asked. She just realised that her elder sister wasn't in the house, she couldn't be, for if she was, by now she would be in Cassie's face.

'She went looking for you, Cassie,' Jennifer remarked, a little harshly in Cassie's opinion. Jennifer was already putting her phone to her ear having dialled Naomi's number.

It rang and continued ringing, switching over to answer phone which invited Jennifer to leave a message. She chose instead to send a text message in which she let her big sister know Cassie was home. Then she sent another, adding that mom was taking a nap and to be quiet coming in when she returned.

'So come on, Cassie. In two hours, you've taught yourself to conjure fire? I don't believe you. So what's going on, little witch?' She had an eyebrow hitched and a smile crossing her face to let her twin know that she was only being semi-serious. There was altogether too much drama right now to be getting into another fight.

Cassie leaned inwards, getting closer to Jennifer so that she could talk quietly as if they were conspirators and all around them might be people who could hear their discussion.

'I met someone,' she revealed. She said it with a smile, because she was thrilled by what had happened today and by what she had learned in such a short space of time. She was excited to share that with Jennifer. And with Naomi, she reminded herself. She loved her older sister dearly, but wished she didn't have to play the role of mom whenever mom wasn't around.

However, in contrast to Cassie's expectations, Jennifer's forehead creased with confusion.

'You met someone?' she echoed her twin's words. 'What does that mean?' In the next second, her expression changed, two neurons colliding in her brain like a switch flicking and her eyes widened with sudden realisation. 'You mean someone like us.'

Cassie nodded, unable to keep the excitement from her face.

'It's that old lady who's been watching us. She is amazing, Jennifer, you wouldn't believe the things she could do. She taught me, she explained things, and she wants to help us.'

Jennifer wasn't sure how she wanted to react or even what her reaction ought to be. She was part terrified by the news, but also undeniably enthralled by the suggestion that there were more people like them in the city. The old lady had been appearing for more than a week, or rather, it had been more than a week since they first spotted her. It occurred to Jennifer that possibly they'd been getting stalked for far longer than that. Was that safe behaviour?

'Where did you meet her, Cassie?' Jennifer wanted to know.

Cassie shrugged. She'd expected her twin to be more excited than this. In contrast, Jennifer seemed … apprehensive. Cassie would be able to understand it if Bethany was still a complete stranger and they knew nothing about her, but Cassie had just explained that she'd met her and talked to her and learned from her. No ill had befallen her from the encounter, so surely there was little to fear.

'She found me in the woods,' Cassie replied, seeing no need to be lenient with the truth. 'I guess she must have followed me. She caught me practising, and honestly I thought I was busted for a moment. But let me tell you, she is so much more powerful that I could even imagine.'

Jennifer gave a small, disbelieving shake of her head.

'Powerful enough to knock a police cruiser across the street?'

Cassie couldn't believe what she was hearing. 'If she was behind the recent attacks, why was she so friendly to me?' Cassie was about to say something else when a terrifying thought suddenly occurred to her. Bethany, if that were even her real name, claimed that the crimes were committed by another person, a powerful person. Maybe that was true and maybe it wasn't, but the old lady had talked about the desire to recruit other persons with magical ability. She talked about it in an abstract way, as if it was what the cop-killer would want, but she was the one attempting to train Cassie. Was it out of the good will of her heart, or because she was trying to recruit her?

Glancing down at Jennifer's phone, she asked, 'Has she replied to that text yet?'

Jennifer tilted her hand upwards so she could see the screen on her phone and touched it with her thumb. The screen came to life, but showed no messages. It had only been a couple of minutes, but that was more than enough time for Naomi to have responded.

With the creeping sensation of worry making her skin feel clammy, Cassie asked another question.

'You said she went to look for me. Where did she think I would be?'

Jennifer lifted her face away from her phone to lock eyes with her twin.

'She went to the place in the woods.'

Chapter 9

The girls were running by the time they hit the sidewalk, all caution thrown to the wind as they hightailed it to the woods where they hoped they would find Naomi. It frustrated them that they had to rely on their feet while Naomi, eighteen months older than them had a full driving licence and her own car.

Most of the time they just put up with it, but right now it was a serious headache.

'She's still not answering,' Cassie grumbled, speaking as though Naomi was doing it on purpose as she gave up trying to ring her number.

Though she knew it would do no good, Jennifer couldn't help but feed her desire to say something in response.

'You always have to push her buttons, don't you, Cassie? Why would you just ... why couldn't you have answered the phone? Naomi went out looking for you because she was worried.'

'I know, okay,' Cassie tried not to snap though she really didn't need to be reminded of her shortcomings. She knew she could be irritating, but perhaps if Naomi listened to her once in a while, there wouldn't be so much friction.

The sun was already setting, the cool air of late autumn turning cold as the warmth of the day escaped into the sky. It was more than a mile back to the woods no matter which route they took. They used every shortcut possible, but stopped on every street to look for their sister's car.

Fit and athletic, from hours of track and volleyball, the sisters fell into an easy yet swift pace as they covered the ground. There were few people around to see them, just a couple out walking their dog and an old lady on her front porch calling for her cat. There were a few cars around, coming back from dinner with their relatives, or wherever else they had been, but traffic was sparse at this time on a Sunday in the suburbs.

They reached the final row of houses at the edge of the town and skirted around them to reach the woods. It was twilight now, long shadows cast by the trees as Jennifer and Cassie left civilization behind and ran into the woods.

'I didn't see her car anywhere, did you?' asked Jennifer.

Cassie slowed to a stop, her sister going another few paces before she realised. Then she too applied the brakes.

The girls were looking at each other, enough light left in the day for them to see each other's faces despite the water vapour forming from their breath.

'She's not going to be in the woods,' Cassie stated. 'Naomi will be in her car. Either driving around looking for me, or back at home.'

'So why isn't she answering the phone?' Jennifer challenged her sister's claim.

All Cassie could do was shrug her shoulders, an exaggerated gesture to ensure Jennifer would see it in the dark.

She guessed, 'She's punishing me?'

Jennifer huffed out an annoyed snort of breath through her nose and balled her hands on her hips as she looked about and tried to think of what to do next. It wasn't like Naomi to fail to respond to multiple texts and calls.

'Did you at least get a number for this Bethany woman?' she demanded to know. 'I want to know where she is.'

Starting to feel that she acted foolishly silly now that she was massively on the backfoot, Cassie hated that she had to admit that she didn't.

'She said she didn't have a phone.'

Jennifer made a scoffing noise. 'Oh, come on, Cassie. Everyone's got a phone. Did you get her address?' she asked in a tone that suggested she thought Cassie had acted even more ridiculously than usual.

Starting to get defensive, Cassie snarled, 'I didn't bother to ask her, Jen. If the two of you hadn't been so obstinate … no, check that. Naomi was obstinate, you were cowardly. If you'd picked a side,' she pressed on when she heard her sister draw in a sharp breath of outrage, 'then maybe we could have resolved something. Especially if you'd picked the right side. You know that I've been right all along. We need to learn how to use these skills. If the two of you had been with me, I wouldn't have been racing to get home, and none of this would have occurred.'

'You've got some nerve,' Jennifer could feel her fists bunching. She hadn't hit her sister since they measured their age in single digits, but she was giving some serious consideration to it now.

Sensing the tone of her sister's voice, and reading her body language, Cassie reacted by tapping into the nearest ley line. Jennifer could do the same if she wanted, but she'd missed out on this afternoon's lesson, and Cassie was itching to prove her point about the need to be able to wield their magical power.

She wasn't going to hurt her sister, but she was prepared to prove a point. In a display of superiority and confidence, she widened her stance just a little and splayed her arms one at a time first right and then left to her sides with the palms facing upwards like she was holding two softballs.

She could feel magical energy fizzing inside her body. It was like having an energy drink flowing through her veins instead of blood and it made her feel powerful.

Jennifer didn't realise what Cassie was doing until she saw her sister's hair begin to float. Adrenaline flooded her body, the instant reaction of fight or flight causing her to draw on ley line energy herself. In contrast to Cassie, who understood things better from the brief instruction she received from Bethany, Jennifer was doing it on instinct, and thus getting a far weaker charge.

Cassie hadn't intended to actually create a spell to fling, but there were other things that Bethany had taught her. Due to those teachings, she knew how to engage her second sight and saw when her sister drew on the nearby ley line, a thick branch coming off the mainline that ran under the river.

They were facing off against each other, the situation escalating so fast that neither one of them had the opportunity to really consider what it was that they were doing. So it was to their great fortune when they both heard a twig snap.

The sharp noise pierced the night, bursting the bubble the girls had found themselves caught in as they both spun around to face the direction it came from.

From the darkness stepped a shadow in the shape of a man. Wearing a dark hood to hide his face, he said nothing as he moved into the late afternoon moonlight.

Cassie knew Jennifer couldn't see it, she wouldn't have been able to herself if she hadn't met Bethany, but with her second sight, the trail of ley line energy filtering through the earth and into the hooded figure was impossible to miss.

There was only one conclusion to draw: they were facing the killer.

Chapter 10

'Jen get behind me!' Cassie screamed the panic she felt. Her brain demanded she conjure a spell, any spell, anything that would convince the hooded figure to back away or leave them alone. Wasn't that the trick to beating bullies? Show strength and they will look for a weaker target.

Jen hadn't moved though. She was frozen to the spot. Filled with line energy, she could produce a spell of her own. Jen was good with air spells and surely two against one would give them an advantage of some kind.

The unseen face inside the hood said, 'Interesting,' and raised his hands. Instantly, the volume of ley line energy flowing into him trebled and the air began to shift as he moved his hands to manipulate it.

Jennifer cried out in fear, 'Cassie?'

Was she asking what they should do, or begging her sister to save her? Cassie couldn't be sure which, but with her twin yet to react in a way that might help them, she took it upon herself to do what she could.

The thought of using flame on another human being made Cassie feel physically sick, but she manipulated the element to produce it anyway. Flame burst into her right hand, illuminating the dark trees instantly. What now though? She couldn't throw it. Largely this was because she didn't know how – Bethany hadn't taken her that far, but also it was because she knew she could never set fire to another human being.

The opportunity to use it was never hers it turned out, the world going sideways when a blast of air so strong that it felt solid hit them from the right.

Cassie and Jennifer were lifted from the ground and thrown a yard across the clearing. They managed to land on their feet, but momentum ruined any hope of staying there. The power of the hooded figure's air spell startled Cassie, but what the hooded figure said next terrified her.

'You are more capable than I was led to believe. Now surrender, or the next blow will be more than a gentle tap.' He was speaking more loudly than the situation required and employing a gravelly edge to his voice so that the girls would not recognise it. The thrash metal blasting into his ears made it hard to hear his own voice, hence the raised volume, but the effect on the girls was as if he were shouting and they cowered away.

In a terrified squeak, and flailing to grab Cassie's arm, Jennifer managed to stutter, 'Cassie who is that?'

Cassie didn't answer. She wasn't even listening, she was thinking. Conjuring flame, and bringing up her second sight were not the only things Bethany had shown her this afternoon. She had no idea if she could pull it off; she had only tried it once before she realised the time and hurried back to the house. Now though she was reaching out with her senses, pushing elemental magic into the ground beneath her fingertips and telling herself that it would be the last thing the hooded figure expected.

'Last warning, ladies. I can easily take you by force,' the hooded figure growled at them. 'I see you trying to cast a spell there. What do you hope to do?' he sniggered.

'Cassie, what do we do?' Jennifer squeaked. She still held tightly to Cassie's right forearm. They were both in a crouch, low to the ground with the hooded figure just a few yards away where he towered over them.

Cassie focused on her spell. Refusing to let doubt enter her mind, she pushed more energy into the ground. She was going to get one shot to make this work, or they were in serious trouble. Whoever was inside the hood was stronger or simply more experienced. They were outmatched and the man in the hood knew it.

Yet his superiority gave Cassie an edge - one she hoped to exploit. His assured self-confidence, staring down at two women huddled on the ground, robbed him of his caution.

With a shout that was nothing to do with the spell and all about making herself feel brave, Cassie released the energy in her spell. It ripped at the soil, burrowing into it where the man stood. Her skill with such a spell was entirely untested, but she knew it was possible and if nothing else she felt motivated.

When Bethany explained to her a little about what was possible through mastery of elemental magic, the old lady performed some demonstrations. In one of them, she forced soil up out of the earth as if a mole on turbo-mode was about to breach the surface.

She got to have one go at it, but had done nothing more than disturb the loose dust on the surface.

There was significantly more energy and will behind this spell. Coupled with fear-driven adrenaline, the effect, while not quite the explosive force she hoped for, was sufficient.

The hooded figure stumbled as the earth shifted beneath his feet and he dropped the spell he was holding when he threw his arms out for balance. His left foot sank where the soil beneath it loosened, and he almost fell.

Cassie wasted no time. The moment she released her spell she was thrusting off with both legs and dragging Jennifer off the ground to follow her.

'Run!' she screamed, twisting her body around to face back towards the street some forty yards behind them.

That was all the encouragement Jennifer needed. Just as fit and as fast as her twin sister, the pair of them burst into action, exploding off the ground and into a full sprint like runners at the Olympic Games.

They could not see it, but behind them the man in the hood was readying another spell. Annoyed that he demonstrated weakness and inexperience in allowing the two girls to catch him off guard, his latest conjuring was fuelled by anger. Moisture gathered in the air above his head, the atoms within it agitated as he pressed them to create lightning.

His teeth were gritted, the process of creating the most devastating spell in his personal arsenal taking longer than he wanted. The girls only needed another couple of seconds. After that they would be in the street and able to escape from his sight.

They were too fast for him and had a head start. But if he got this right, they would be stopped dead in their tracks. The hardest part of using lightning, so far as he was concerned, was in directing it accurately. However, he felt confident that over such a short distance he only needed to throw it in the general direction.

Cassie and Jennifer felt the ground change beneath their feet as their boots left the dirt and hit the sidewalk. They had covered forty yards in a few seconds and were leaving the terrifying hooded figure behind. They were not, however, going to slow down until they got home.

Leaning into the turn as they attempted to go right and place a house between them and their attacker, Cassie risked a quick glance back the way they had come. That was when the blast of lightning hit them.

The hooded figure allowed himself a moment of jubilation, fist raised he punched the air, then dropped his connection to the ley line to focus on extracting his foot from the ground. The lightning strike was less powerful than he had wanted, but he'd had no more time to push energy into it. It had done the trick, and perhaps it was for the best that it was a weaker charge - he did not want to hurt them for they were considered too valuable.

The twins landed in the road, thrown almost from one sidewalk to the other, they struck the unforgiving surface, scratching their skin and raising bruises that would remind them of the experience for many days to come. In many ways it was a good thing it was cool out, because they were fully clad from head to toe. Had it been summer, the asphalt might have shredded their exposed skin.

Their attacker stalked after them, moving fast but not running. Ahead of him the girls were moving. It told him they were still conscious, but he did not think they were about to get up. Reaching around to his back right pocket, he withdrew his phone to make a call.

It wasn't as if he could carry both girls by himself.

He had nothing about his person that he could use to bind them, so help would need to be swift to arrive. Music blasting, too focused on his phone and the opportunity to brag, he didn't see the car coming when he stepped into the street.

Naomi was giving the area by the woods one final drive by. Her concern for her sister, and the fact that she couldn't find her, was entirely secondary to the anger she felt over having to look for her. She had been muttering uncharitably to herself in her car when a blinding flash of light occurred almost simultaneously with both her sisters suddenly appearing.

They ran from the woods and onto the sidewalk a hundred yards ahead of her. But just as Naomi questioned what Jennifer was doing here when she was supposed to be at home waiting in case Cassie showed up there, an arc of lightning illuminated the woods. Moving sideways as if it were chasing the girls, it lifted both Cassie and Jennifer from their feet. Big sister, Naomi, got to watch as her younger siblings were thrown across the road like pins before a bowling ball.

Automatically, her right foot mashed down on the accelerator pedal, her nifty Toyota hybrid responding like a scared cat as it leapt forward. Her eyes were glued to the two girls lying in the street, her heart refusing to beat as she waited for either one of them to get up, or even start moving.

There was no way for her to see the dark character step out of the shadows and into the road, and it would have been hard to spot even if she'd been looking in the right direction.

The front right quarter of the car caught the hooded figure with a glancing blow. He bounced off the passenger's side of the car, his body folding the door mirror inward as he rebounded off and into the undergrowth at the side of the road.

Naomi screamed in shock, a familiar sound that broke through the confused fog filling Cassie's head. By the time Naomi's brakes had stopped the car and she managed to get the door open, her sisters were getting to their feet.

'Naomi?' Cassie questioned, groggily trying to get her feet moving in the right direction. As she took her first step, Jennifer latched a hand onto her shoulder for support.

'I just ran someone over!' Naomi blurted, twisting her torso to look back at where she had seen the person fall. 'I hit them!' she added unnecessarily, words tumbling from her mouth as shock forced its way to the front of her brain, snatching the driving seat away from her senses.

Cassie nodded. 'Yes, thank God. Now let's get out of here.'

Cassie and Jennifer staggered the yard and a half to get to their sister's car. Naomi was still rooted to the spot unable to work out which direction she needed to look in. She'd seen her sisters thrown across the road, a bolt of lightning doing the damage, but she'd hit someone with her car. They might be injured, they probably were, she decided. She had to go and check.

When she attempted to move away, Cassie hooked a hand into her elbow, arresting her motion.

'Where are you going?' Cassie gripped Naomi's arm tightly. 'We need to go.'

Jennifer's head was pounding, and there was a ringing in her ears. She had bright coronas in her eyes which made it difficult to see, but she could think. Placing a hand against the roof of Naomi's car to keep herself upright, she lifted her head to lock eyes with her sister's.

'That's the killer,' she managed to gasp. There was no moisture in the voice and talking made her head hurt worse. 'We have to call mom,' she wheezed.

Her eyes wide and her mouth open, Naomi twisted to look back at the spot where she saw the hooded figure land.

'The killer?' she echoed.

'Yes,' Jennifer managed to say, wincing and closing her eyes against the pain in her head. 'He attacked us.'

Cassie took a deep breath, drawing in fresh ley line energy to fuel another spell. Jennifer didn't need her help to stay upright any longer, she was holding onto the car. Naomi appeared close to catatonic, but at any rate, Cassie believed that she was the only one of the three with enough juice to do anything to the killer if he attempted to resist.

Seeing her younger sister attempt to head in the direction of the man they were claiming had attacked them, was enough to break Naomi from her reverie. It was her turn to grab Cassie's arm, stopping her from going any farther.

'Cassie, what are you doing?' she demanded to know.

Cassie flexed her arm, attempting to break free, but her elder sister's vicelike grip wasn't going to be removed so easily.

'Let me go, Naomi. I can handle him.'

Naomi's jaw dropped open again. 'Handle him? Handle him? What on earth are you talking about, Cassie? I just watched you get thrown across the street. Did he create that lightning?'

Jennifer groaned, 'Is that what it was? That would explain why I'm struggling to see anything. I'm going to be sick,' she remarked, swivelling to her left and bending at the waist to get her head lower.

Now unable to decide which sister she needed to deal with, Naomi let go of Cassie's arm to check on Jennifer.

'Don't go anywhere,' Naomi ordered.

Cassie stayed in place for almost two seconds, just long enough to make sure that Naomi's attention was diverted. Then commanding her legs to work, even though they felt oddly disconnected from her body, she walked away from the car and back towards the spot where Naomi had been looking.

'Hey!' Naomi shouted.

Cassie stopped, not because her sister had called her, but because there was no one there. There was enough moonlight shining down on the road for her to clearly see the short skid mark behind Naomi's car and a patch of flattened undergrowth where the hooded figure must have landed.

While they were arguing, he had escaped.

Chapter 11

Parked on the driveway outside their house, the three sisters continued to argue. The focus of their heated, yet quiet discussion was what they did now. The one thing they agreed upon, was that they weren't going to tell their parents anything.

Naomi's phone had died while she was out looking for Cassie. It was an older model and overdue for an upgrade. Her parents were holding off, probably planning to replace it at Christmas, and to be fair, it worked just fine, but the battery lasted less than half as long as it used to. If she forgot to charge it twice a day, it became as useful as a paperweight.

As elder sister, Naomi did what she could to make sure her younger sisters understood everything that had happened was their fault. Her phone dying wouldn't have happened if she had been at home. She wouldn't have left home if it wasn't for Cassie's need to constantly rebel. When Cassie returned home the pair of them should then have stayed there until Naomi returned.

'We couldn't,' insisted Cassie. 'You didn't answer your phone and we were worried about you.'

Jennifer felt sure Cassie was about to tell Naomi about the old lady, but her head was pounding, and she wanted to get inside. If she let Cassie say another word, a fresh round of questions would ensue, so to head her off she changed the topic.

'We were attacked by the killer, Naomi. You get that, right?' Jennifer drew the attention of both sisters. 'It was the killer and he escaped, but you must have hurt him.'

'We have to investigate this ourselves,' Cassie insisted. 'Maybe he went to hospital for treatment. He might have a broken bone, but even if he doesn't, he will be badly bruised. We can check that out and if we can find him, then we can find a way to let mom know who he is.'

They had already gone over and over whether they recognised his voice or had seen his face, Cassie getting irritated by Naomi's need to repeat her questions when she'd already been given answers.

They had no idea who he was. In fact, the only thing they had to go on, was the twins agreeing that the voice they heard was young and had been exaggerated to sound deeper than it otherwise might. Looking for a young man with bruising in the city of Chippewa Falls was a task akin to finding a needle in a haystack. He could be young, but what did that really mean? He might be a high school senior or thirty years old. They weren't even sure what colour his skin might be.

'Then we have nothing to go on,' Naomi concluded.

'So what are you suggesting?' Cassie wanted to know. 'Do we just let this go? Is that your big idea?' she challenged Naomi.

Fed up with them arguing, and wanting to get inside, Jennifer introduced another new topic – this time going for the big one so she could distract them both.

'Why don't you tell her about Bethany?' she suggested.

Naomi shifted her gaze, hardening her eyes as she looked from Cassie to Jennifer.

'Who's Bethany?'

'Good question,' remarked Jennifer. She had her eyes closed still and one hand against her head. She no longer felt sick, but her head continued to pound, and she wanted to take some painkillers. With that in mind, she gripped the door handle to let herself out. 'We can continue this inside. I need to lie down.'

She was out of the car and walking towards the front door before either of her sisters could stop her.

Faced with a fresh threat - that of their mother questioning where they had been and what had happened to their clothes - Naomi tore after Jennifer.

'Okay, look. I'll go in first and distract mum. She's probably fixing dinner. I'll offer to help and make sure that I'm blocking her view. You two,' she growled out the word with a jab of her right index finger, 'need to get yourselves cleaned up. We'll talk about this more when there's less danger of being discovered by our parents. And you,' she jabbed her finger firmly in Cassie's direction, 'are going to tell me who Bethany is.'

The smell of rib roast filled the air inside the house, welcoming them into what felt like a safe environment before they even crossed the threshold. As expected, their mother was in the kitchen.

Michelle looked up at the sound of her daughters returning home, so too their father who was also in the kitchen. Not that he ever took part in the preparation of family meals – Michelle learned very early in their marriage that it was safer to just do it herself if she wanted to produce something edible.

What was missing from the equation in her opinion was a deeply satisfying and oaky malbec. Michelle always allowed herself a glass of wine while making Sunday dinner, but she was working tonight, so alcohol was off the menu.

'Where have you three been?' their mother asked, a slight frown creasing her forehead. The frown increased as all three daughters froze. 'You look guilty,' she pointed out in her cop voice.

As planned, Naomi was using her body to shield her sisters. If their mother took a good look at their clothes, she would know they had been up to something.

Why hadn't they concocted a believable story? They had sat in the car on the driveway for almost ten minutes, arguing back and forth about what they were going to do. Why had it not occurred to any one of them that they might need to explain where they had been?

Like criminals caught in a searchlight, the three girls were rooted to the spot. Naomi was closest to her parents, but ensuring her sisters would be less visible behind her meant that her mother's eyes were boring into her own.

At the breakfast bar sitting opposite his wife, where he typed notes on his laptop, Pastor Stevens chuckled.

'Ever the detective, Michelle. You have three perfect daughters. Allow them a little slack, why don't you? When was the last time any of them ever got into any bother?'

Michelle's eyes narrowed slightly, squinting at her three girls before she turned her attention back to the stove.

'Dinner will be ready in ten minutes. It's a good thing you ladies didn't arrive late.'

Naomi breathed a sigh of relief, putting on her best innocent face as she hung up her jacket and strolled as nonchalantly as she could across to the kitchen area. She refused to look back, confident that her sisters would know to walk casually across to the stairs and only then hurry up to their room.

'What can I help with?' Naomi asked her mother, pausing to place a kiss on her father's cheek.

Dinner came and went, the meal itself was delicious as the girls had learned to expect from their mother, and the conversation mercifully, stuck to neutral topics, rather than returning to the city's morbid curiosity for all things magical as a reaction to the recent murder and last night's attack.

The girls, nevertheless, sat in fear that their mother might endeavour to pin them down on where they had been this afternoon. She had awoken to find all three of them absent from the house. The squirming sensation of nervousness in her belly made Naomi not want to eat. It had robbed her appetite, but failing to eat her mother's delicious beef rib would cause her to question why, so Naomi forced the morsels down.

Less than an hour after dinner, just before seven o'clock, Detective Michelle Stevens announced that she had to get going. She was back in her suit, and though tired she felt charged with a responsibility to bring the mysterious killer to justice.

With his wife out of the house, Pastor Stevens announced his intention to take a long bath - something he rarely had the opportunity for in a house filled with women. The girls watched as their father collected a book from the sideboard and retreated from the living area.

Cassie counted to see how long it would take after their father departing before her elder sister started to berate her.

She got to two.

'Start spilling, Cassie. Who is Bethany?' Naomi demanded, her fists balled and placed on her hips. 'Where were you this afternoon? I came out to the woods looking for you and you were not there. Why weren't you answering your phone, for that matter?'

Jennifer was sitting in the corner of the long couch that faced the family's television. She felt a little bruised from being thrown across the road and had endured dinner with the sensation of her head splitting into two pieces. Just before mom served dessert, the painkillers she'd taken finally caught up and forced her headache to subside. It wasn't gone, but she felt a lot better.

Always the peacekeeper, Jennifer knew already that Naomi's comment was going to instantly rile Cassie. She often wondered why Naomi couldn't be more tactful when dealing with the feistiest person in the house. She and Naomi got her father's character, whereas Cassie was a younger double of their mother - full of righteousness and easy to annoy.

'Let's just calm it down a little, shall we?' Jennifer suggested. 'Instead of starting a fresh argument, how about the three of us look at this calmly and objectively? I'm quite certain Cassie will explain all about Bethany. Won't you, Cassie?' Jennifer remarked pointedly, essentially giving her twin an order. 'I for one will feel better if the three of us approach this together. Can we do that, please?'

Jennifer fell silent, looking from Naomi to Cassie and back to Naomi, daring either one of them to argue with her.

Cassie had her right hip cocked to one side and her arms folded across her chest. It was a classic defensive posture, ready to repel all who stood against her. Mercifully, Naomi was mature enough to cave first.

'Fine,' she said, heading for the couch adjacent to the one on which Jennifer sat. 'I'm listening.' Settling into the centre seat she fixed Cassie, the one sister still standing, with an open and engaging expression. It was tantamount to a fresh challenge.

Jennifer held her breath, wondering how Cassie was going to react.

'Nice to see that you can be reasonable for once, Naomi.' Cassie smiled at the barb in her comment as she formed a third side of the square by relaxing into their father's lay-z-boy.

Heading off the argument which still rumbled in the distance like a storm threatening to arrive with a deluge, Jennifer got in quick.

'Bethany, Cassie. Let's start there.'

With a sigh of annoyance, Cassie began retelling the tale of meeting the old lady in the woods. She had to backtrack slightly to explain that when she went out of the window to escape the house in defiance of her elder sister, she chose to practise at one of the spots they had used before. She defended her actions, speaking quickly so that Naomi couldn't when she explained how much she'd learned in such a short period of time.

'It's true,' Jennifer commented. 'If nothing else, the old lady, whether her name really is Bethany or not, showed Cassie things we would never have figured out for ourselves.'

Feeling that her twin had done a good job of cueing her in, Cassie produced a flame in her right hand, and then another one in her left. Between the two flickering lights, a smile spread across her face to challenge Naomi.

'That's not all,' Jennifer added, turning her face to look at Cassie. 'What was that thing you did with the ground?'

Naomi was yet to say anything about the mysterious old lady who had been following them and had now revealed her own magical abilities. She had comment upon comment lined up in her skull, but was fighting hard to bite her tongue until her impetuous younger sister had finished showing off.

Cassie was wise enough to know that Naomi was going to pick her apart the moment she gave her an opportunity. Also, she had to admit that she knew almost nothing about Bethany, and what she did know could easily be lies or half-truths.

Since running from the house with Jennifer in search of Naomi, she had been going over the time she spent with the old lady in her head. Nothing Bethany said gave Cassie any reason to believe she harboured any ill intent towards her or her sisters. Nevertheless, she was prepared to admit there was something distinctly fishy about her.

The old lady had been stalking them for more than a week that they knew of. She claimed she didn't have a phone and when Cassie asked how she would contact her, Bethany had said she would come to her. What kind of an answer was that? Cassie was rushing to get home at the time, so hadn't challenged the old lady.

With that in mind, she did her best to disarm Naomi's argument before she was given a chance to raise it.

'I have no idea who this old lady is,' Cassie admitted much to Naomi's surprise. 'I don't think she's the killer or connected to the killer. If she were, or if she wanted to do anything to me, she had more than enough opportunity this afternoon. What I'm saying,' she attempted to explain, 'is that I want to trust her,' she got to see Naomi roll her eyes a little, 'but I think we need to find out who she is.'

Satisfied they had covered the topic of the old lady adequately, and could move on to finding out a little more about her shortly, Jennifer was desperate to hear what the old lady had told Cassie about their abilities.

Prompted by Jennifer's request, Cassie switched topics.

'Bethany said that we have the ability to control nature's elements. She did not explain where that power comes from, and perhaps she doesn't know. Whatever the case, we can control air, water, fire, and earth. By manipulating these elements in different ways, we can generate heat, or cold, so that we can blow a chill wind or a blast of heat so hot it is like a furnace. We can generate fire, which I have to say was surprisingly easy to learn. We already know we can control the movement of water and create ice, and we just witnessed lightning being generated. Earth spells are hard – I tried to create a hole beneath him – whoever that was in the hood,' she added for clarity. 'But all I managed to do was shift a little dirt around. It made me sweat just to do that.'

'It worked,' Jennifer pointed out. 'What else?' she prompted Cassie to keep going.

'Second sight.' Both Cassie's sisters stared at her – they had no idea what that meant. Cassie tried to remember how Bethany had explained it. 'It's your inner magical ability to see.' Her sisters' expressions didn't change, but they did exchange a glance to confirm they were in the same confused boat.

Naomi spoke first. 'What are you talking about?'

Jennifer looked it up on the internet. 'It says here that second sight usually refers to a person who claims to be able to see into the future.' She finished reading and looked up. 'That's not it, is it?'

Cassie shook her head. 'No, when I bring up my second sight, I can see the magical energy in the ground. It's coming into my body almost as if it's entering through my feet. Yours too,' she added. I can also see magical energy in other people. Like when we cast a spell. When the killer appeared, I could see the ley line energy drifting up through the ground to touch his body, and when he began conjuring, his hands were controlling the magical energy. It was like a dance of light. Bethany said that our second sight would enable us to see through enchantments that might hide a creature's true nature.'

'Creature?' Jennifer repeated her twin's word. 'You mean like ... vampires and stuff?'

All Cassie could do was shrug. 'I didn't get that far with her. She showed me how to do it. I can try to show you, if you like.'

'No magic in the house,' Naomi snapped as if giving a command. 'We have to draw the line somewhere.'

'It's not like doing spells,' Cassie replied calmly but firmly. 'In fact, all I need to do now that I've got it figured out, is blink.' She made a big show of closing both of her eyes and opening them again. 'Right now I can see an aura around each of you. It's quite beautiful, actually.'

Too excited at the chance to try it to care about Naomi's opinion, Jennifer was blinking her eyes.

'How do you do it? I can't get it to work. What should it feel like?' she fired out rapid questions as she continued blinking like a mad person having a fit.

Cassie disengaged her second sight by blinking once more.

'The blinking isn't really part of it,' she said, failing to really explain anything. 'I just do it because it helps me to focus. The first time Bethany got me to do it, she had me close my eyes and then visualise everything around me. She wanted me to form the most complete image that I could, and then feel out with my senses so that I could touch the magical energy. Try that,' she instructed.

Cassie had her eyes closed too, but snuck a peek to see what her sisters were doing. In truth, she wondered if Naomi might just be staring at her with an angry glare, so was pleased to see that her older sister's eyes were also closed.

She closed her eyes once more and asked a question, 'Can you feel it? Can you feel the magical energy in the air and in the ground and in each other?'

'Yes,' Naomi's answer came out as barely more than a murmured breath.

Jennifer echoed Naomi's answer.

'Now I want you to imagine that you can see that magical energy. What would it look like? To me it looks like fine golden dust. As each of you pulls on the energy flowing through the earth, there is a thread of it wending through the ground to enter your bodies.'

When Jennifer squeaked excitedly, Cassie's eyes snapped open.

'I can see it!' she reported. 'Now what?'

Before Cassie could answer, Naomi announced that she too could see the energy all around and flowing between them.

Cassie sucked in a breath through her nose, filling her lungs before she said with an air of hope, 'Now you open your eyes, and you should be able to see it still.'

She watched as both of her sisters slowly opened their eyes. Jennifer was gripping the seat cushion of the couch as if it were anchoring her to the planet. A broad smile spread across her face.

'This is amazing,' she gasped. 'This is absolutely next level.'

Naomi did not disagree, but she asked, 'What use does it have? Did Bethany tell you what you could do with it?'

Cassie had not enjoyed a moment of unity like this with her sisters for some time. It was rare when the three of them agreed on anything. Not that they were always fighting, but the three girls were of a similar age but vastly dissimilar temperaments. It led to friction, which combined with the pressures of adolescence, school, boys, and a strict mother, caused them to aggravate one another far more often than was necessary.

To answer Naomi's question, Cassie said, 'I believe it has a number of uses, such as seeing through enchantments like I said, but Bethany did not have the time to reveal them to me before I chose to leave.' Trying to repair some of the damage of this afternoon's arguing, and offering the olive branch, Cassie added, 'I was rushing to get back home. I didn't want the two of you to worry.' she saw Naomi begin to react, and held up a hand to stop her. 'I know, Naomi, you're going to tell me that I shouldn't have gone out in the first place. We're going to continue to disagree about that, and about our need to improve our magical abilities. Rather than continue that argument now, can we instead discuss what we should do about Bethany, and how we can find the person who attacked me and Jennifer earlier?'

'She's right, Naomi,' Jennifer got in quickly, reaffirming her position as peacekeeper. 'We won't gain anything by arguing. He made it sound like he knew about us, didn't he, Cassie?'

Cassie nodded. 'He said that we were stronger than he expected, or something like that.'

Naomi held up a hand with her index finger extended to beg a moment's grace. Then with an exaggerated blink, she cleared her second sight.

'That is going to take some getting used to,' she commented, using both hands to rub at her eyes. 'Okay, girls, in the spirit of collaboration, let's ignore the problems Cassie caused this afternoon and focus on the problems we have to come. How did your attacker know you would be in woods? Do you think it was blind luck or coincidence?'

Jennifer and Cassie looked at each other, both encouraging the other to provide some kind of answer.

Naomi provided one before they could. 'Bethany sent him.' Naomi was already rising from her seat, twisting off her right foot to make her way across the room as she said, 'I'm not saying that is the case, but it is one that I feel we should consider to be a distinct possibility. It worries me, but we know so little about her, and she seems to know quite a lot about us. Cassie, you said that she was nothing but friendly, and seemed keen to meet Jennifer and me. Could it be that she was friendly to you because she needs all three of us together if she intends to ensnare us?'

Rather than answer her sister, and largely because she knew Naomi was making some good points and didn't want to admit it, Cassie asked, 'Where are you going?'

Over her shoulder, Naomi's voice drifted back as she disappeared through a door towards mom's office, 'I'm going to see what I can find out about this Bethany lady.'

Jennifer and Cassie exchanged a confused look. Naomi was going to look Bethany up? How was she going to do that? And what was she doing in mom's office?

Before they could voice their questions, Naomi reappeared. Hanging through the door frame so her fingertips and her head were visible, she made a conspiratorial, 'Pssst!' noise. 'Are you coming or what?' she asked with the eyebrows high on her forehead. 'Oh, you don't know that I know where mom keeps the password to get into the police database,' she commented before varnishing back through the doorway.

Jennifer and Cassie looked at each other again only this time in stark shock. Their straightlaced, obey-all-the-rules sister was about to do something completely illegal, and had clearly done it before.

The sound of their footsteps as they raced across the living room echoed throughout the house. Mercifully, the only person to hear it was their father, and he was far too absorbed in his book to even notice.

Chapter 12

Detective Michelle Stevens was on her way to the house of Ethan Clarke. The forensic team had worked nonstop since they began gathering evidence at Collins' Pharmacy last night. There had been almost nothing to find, and of course any evidence such as fingerprints, hair, or fiber, would be thrown out of any courtroom because it was a place of business and had hundreds if not thousands of the city's residents trailing through it every single day.

However, in the street near to the ruined police cruiser, a candy bar wrapper with a smear of saliva on it to mark it as fresh proved interesting enough for one of the diligent team to lift a set of fingerprints. Those fingerprints belonged to Ethan Clarke. That the saliva also belonged to him, seemed likely, which was why Michelle was on her way to his house.

In the passenger seat of her car, her partner, Lakota Blackrock, one of only three Native Americans in the Chippewa Falls PD, questioned why a high school student with a bright future would rob a local pharmacy.

'Because he could,' Michelle commented. 'If he is one of these new supernaturals, then he is capable of blasting out a wall without touching it, and able to throw a moving police cruiser across the street. Does a person imbued with such power care about rules? When we come face to face with a supernatural, will they surrender? Will our guns even provide a tangible threat? There are no protocols for how we're supposed to approach this, Lakota.'

Lakota could hear the nervousness in his partner's voice, and it unnerved him more than any thoughts he had about what they might be walking into. Michelle Stevens had never shown the slightest trace of fear in the years that he had known her. Now she sounded rattled.

'Do you think we should call in a couple of uniformed units?' He knew what she was going to say, but wanted to hear her say it anyway.

Michelle shot him a surprised look. 'We can't. Besides, we don't know that he is a supernatural. In which case we're on our way to the house of a kid in high school. How would it look if we turned up with three units and six officers?'

'Which is all very well, until we have to arrest someone who is a supernatural.' Lakota didn't need to say anything further, the dangers inherent in the new reality were obvious to everyone.

The rest of the journey was conducted in silence. So much so that when the radio squawked, a unit reporting in from a domestic violence case across town, it made both Michelle and Lakota jump. They laughed to hide their nerves, neither willing to fully acknowledge how on edge they felt.

The house on Mansfield Street was attractively lit from inside, with additional lighting outside to illuminate the garden. Michelle gave it a single drive by, both detectives looking out the left-hand side of the car for any sign of ... anything.

'Looks like a nice place,' Lakota remarked.

Michelle agreed though she did not bother to voice her thoughts. It was the home of the football coach from her twins' high school. Had her daughters been sons, she would have known Coach Clarke very well, but as it was, she knew him well enough. They would speak if she bumped into him in the street and she could pick Ethan out of a line up easily enough. Not that he was a bad kid, but his prints were on record for a reason.

She wrapped her knuckles sharply on the front door and rang the bell for good measure. The muted sounds of television filtering out from the house competed with thrash metal coming from an upstairs bed-room, and a change in volume as someone opened a door let Michelle and Lakota know that someone was coming.

It was Coach Clarke who opened the door, a curious expression in-stantly changing to one of concern when he saw who was on his doorstep.

'Michelle? What is it?' he wanted to know.

Keeping things calm, Michelle said, 'Can we come in, Bruce?'

As if remembering his manners, Bruce Clarke backed up a pace, clear-ing the way for the two detectives to enter his home. Initially startled by the presence of the police at his home late on a Sunday afternoon, his brain was working overtime in a bid to work out what might have driven them to his door. There had been a brief moment of panic, when he worried that a member of his family might have been hurt, but his wife was in the kitchen, and his son was upstairs.

'What is this about?' he tried again to extract some information.

Amelia Clarke appeared in the hallway. She'd heard her husband talking to someone and was curious to see who it was.

'What's going on, Bruce?' she asked as she approached, drying her hands on a small towel. 'Oh, hi, Michelle.' She gave a friendly wave and a smile that didn't make it to her eyes. Then her smile froze completely when Michelle's partner spoke.

Lakota met Bruce's eyes. 'Is Ethan home?'

Chapter 13

Naomi was doing her utmost best to hide how terrified she felt. It wasn't the first time she had ever done this, but it was the second. She could only imagine what would happen if her mother were to ever catch her, and in a way it felt good to have accomplices.

All three of them held their breath as she punched in the ten-digit alphanumeric code to access the police department's database.

'How many times have you done this, Naomi?' Cassie asked. She felt as if the world had just tilted a little on its axis. Naomi never did anything wrong, or against the rules.

Skirting around the truth, Naomi replied, 'More than once.' She pressed *return* and felt her heartrate spike when the screen changed. She was in. Had the system spat her out, she would have been able to make herself look super cool, but avoid actually going through with that which she knew she ought not to.

'What now?' whispered Jennifer.

Naomi was desperately trying to remember where she had to navigate to next in order to perform a personal search. There were so many options, but telling herself that it was too late now to undo the crime she was already committing, she clicked on a tab to see what it was.

She got it right first time and found herself on a page that invited her to enter a name.

Trying to make it sound like she knew what she was doing, she said, 'I believe this performs a basic search. If Bethany has a criminal record or things like parking violations, then it will find her. I also think it finds basic information such as home address and phone number and suchlike, but we might need more information than we have to get that stuff.'

'Such as?' ask Cassie.

Naomi turned her head away from the screen slightly.

'Social Security number might be helpful,' she replied in a mocking tone. Then becoming more serious, she asked, 'What's her last name again?'

She got her answer and typed in Bethany Cromwell. A little clock face appeared to show that the computer was working, and no one spoke as they all waited to see what results it might yield.

Without the fanfare of a beep or any other noise, the page changed to reveal the results of their search. There was only one Bethany Cromwell in the system, and she did have a criminal record. With a tiny adjustment of the mouse, Naomi clicked on the file to open it.

Naomi was expecting to discover that the old lady in question was some kind of con artist. She had a criminal record, but when the page opened, the photograph they saw was not the woman they knew. The Bethany Cromwell shown was a white woman in her late thirties and her list of crimes included prostitution, petty theft, aggravated assault, and possession of a controlled substance.

Cassie allowed herself a small smile though she kept it to herself.

'Maybe I didn't spell it right,' Naomi remarked, going back to the search page so she could try again with a few permutations. Just a few minutes later, she accepted that the Bethany Cromwell they were looking for, assuming that was indeed her real name, simply wasn't in the police system.

It didn't really tell them anything, other than the lady had no criminal record, again assuming that she was using her real name.

'So what now?' asked Jennifer.

Naomi had pushed back slightly from the desk and turned her chair around so she was facing her sisters. She wasn't sure what she was going to say, though she knew she wanted to advise caution when it came to the old lady. She felt there was no reason to trust her. Why was she so willing to give them free lessons? However, she didn't get to say any of that because Cassie's phone rang.

The sudden noise in the quiet of mum's office made all three girls jump, Jennifer squeaking in fright as it startled her.

Cassie had the phone in her hands, where she was twiddling it nervously until it went off. She almost dropped it, losing her grip, and then catching it in mid-air before it could reach the carpet. Hurriedly turning it over to see who might be phoning her, her eyes went wide in shock when she saw the name 'Robert Cameron' displayed.

Robbie, the captain of the high school football team and its quarterback, was tall, handsome, and lean. More than that, he was expecting to get a scholarship to Yale at the end of the school year. He was the sort of boy her parents might actually approve of her dating, though he had never shown her much interest.

They had kissed once, at a party in Arnold Kissinger's house. Though since it was Arnold's eighth birthday at the time, Cassie didn't think it counted.

Robbie didn't date much. He'd been going out with Pandora Simmonds for most of the summer, but it was well known that he chose to end it, and he hadn't been seen with anyone since.

'Are you going to answer that?' Jennifer asked. She could see the name on the phone from where she stood and was arguing with herself that she wasn't jealous of her twin.

The question acted as a catalyst to snap Cassie out of her reverie, otherwise she might have stared at the phone until it switched to voicemail.

Stabbing the green button with a nervous forefinger, she twisted away from her sisters to head out of the room. Far too curious to miss out, Jennifer and Naomi exchanged a quick glance before following her.

Naomi got two steps, before she went back and closed down her mother's computer, erasing, she hoped, all trace that they had ever been in the room.

Telling herself to be cool, Cassie answered the phone.

'Hey, Robbie, what's up?' she asked, making it sound like she was busy doing something interesting and only answered the phone because she was curious about what he might want.

'Hey, Cassie,' Robbie's deep voice purred in her ear. 'I was wondering if you might want to catch the new Marvel movie together?'

Cassie's eyes dilated with the shock of his sudden invitation. Robbie hadn't mumbled his words and didn't come across as nervous. He never did though. He was self-assured and confident in all things – at least that was how it always seemed to Cassie. So it wasn't so much that he knew she would say yes – he wasn't that arrogant. His confident manner was just the way he was. It was a big attractor.

Hearing a snigger, Cassie felt her face flush and turned around to make a face at her sisters. They were both watching her and grinning.

Replying to Robbie, Cassie said, 'Sure. When were you thinking?'

'Friday night?' he suggested. 'There's a whole gang of us going.'

Cassie did her best to not sound disappointed that it wasn't going to be just the two of them, but hey, it was still her he was inviting and not someone else. He could have his pick if he wanted.

Forcing her voice to sound pleased but casual, she said, 'Sure. See you in school tomorrow?'

'How about if I pick you up on my way to school?' he suggested.

Cassie's heart skipped a beat. He lived a block away and had his own car. Thoughts of jealous whispers, most notably from Pandora when she saw them arriving at school together, filled her head. There was a certain delicious satisfaction to be had from it.

Unable to fight her smile, but managing to keep her cool, she said, 'Sure. I'll see you then.'

He made a comment about needing to get back to their history assignment because he'd been putting it off and had run out of time, then said he really had to go, but was excited for Friday.

With the call ended, Cassie found her mind adrift on a sea of confusing emotions. Robbie Cameron had asked her out and then claimed he was excited for Friday to come. The captain of the football team wanted to date her, and her head was already filling with dreams of arriving at the prom with him and of the homecoming parade. They looked set to win the state championship this year – the first time in the history of the school and it was making Robbie Cameron into something of a local superstar.

'Hello! Earth to Cassie,' Jennifer's voice broke through Cassie's daydream. 'What was that? Did Robbie Cameron just ask you out on a date?'

Cassie offered her twin a hard frown.

'So what if he did?' she demanded, instantly adopting a defensive posture. 'Are you saying I'm not good enough for him? Think I need to lose a few pounds?'

Naomi got in quick while Jennifer's face was still reeling with surprise at her sister's unwarranted attack.

'She didn't say anything of the sort, Cassie. Don't you think it's just a little bit suspicious though?'

Cassie's frown deepened further. 'Suspicious. A boy asks a fine sister out on a date, and you think it's suspicious.'

'Come on, Cassie. Open your eyes,' Naomi implored. 'Two hours ago, you got attacked by a hooded figure at the edge of town and the only thing you and Jen could agree on was that he had a young voice.'

Cassie's eyes bulged from her head.

'You think the killer is Robbie Cameron?' she blurted.

Naomi shrugged. 'I'm saying I don't know, but don't you think the timing is a little odd?'

'She's right, Cassie,' Jen added her weight to the argument. 'When was the last time Robbie even spoke to you? Now he's asking you out.'

'It wasn't his voice we heard,' Cassie snapped. 'I know his voice and that wasn't it.'

'People can change their voices,' Naomi pointed out, doing so in a calm and patient voice that only served to annoy Cassie further.

She snapped, her anger bubbling over. 'You bitch!'

'Hey.' The voice of their father ended the conversation abruptly. 'That is not the kind of language I expect to hear in this house, young lady,' he chided.

All three sisters had spun to face their father, guilt and embarrassment ruling their features though none so much as Cassie who had been caught losing her temper. There was no profanity allowed in their house. Not ever. Name calling got banned when they were young enough to learn to speak.

Pastor Stevens wore a deep frown on his face. He had three teenage girls and he loved them with every fibre of his being. They were beautiful and intelligent, brave and resourceful. He could not be more proud, and he knew other parents suffered problems with their children that never found a place in his home. He knew for certain because those parents often came to him for guidance.

Nevertheless, his daughters were no longer children and the twins had reached that tough age when they were not quite adults either. He didn't feel the need to say anything further on the subject – his daughters, even Cassie, the most precocious of the three – deserved some credit and it was just one slip of the tongue so far as he knew.

'I think you should all retire to your rooms,' he suggested, though the girls knew it was the same as an order. 'You have school tomorrow, and I am sure you have assignments to finish or to check over.'

Naomi felt like protesting – was she to be punished for her sister's foolish mouth? Her mouth stayed closed though for she knew her father would question why Cassie felt the need to break a house rule and that Cassie would point the finger of blame her way.

Instead, Naomi led the way across the room to kiss her father's cheek and make her way up to her room. He was right that there was school-work – her college tutors kept her busy.

Chapter 14

While the girls were silently ignoring each other and dealing with their own issues, their mother was feeling frustrated.

Ethan Clarke had a perfect alibi. One provided by his parents who were unanimous in agreeing their son hadn't left their house the previous evening.

'How can you be so sure?' Michelle challenged them as politely as she could.

Coach Clarke did little to hide that he was unhappy about being questioned.

'You think I don't know when my son is in the house?' he snapped his reply without needing to think. 'Ethan is a great kid.'

'No one's saying he isn't,' Lakota interrupted.

Coach Clarke swung his head around to stare at Michelle's partner. He didn't know the man and in a way that made his intrusion easier to take. He knew Michelle was a cop, but he knew her better as the twins' mom – they were in the same year group as Ethan and had known each other for years. It made her presence at this time feel personal.

Looking at her again, he said, 'Where were your kids last night?'

Michelle tilted her head to one side. 'That's not how this is going to work, Bruce. We can place Ethan at the scene of an incident last night. I have to ask you again how it is that you can be so certain your son couldn't have snuck out of the house?'

Ethan's mother looked horrified by the accusation.

'He would never...'

'You seem to forget,' Michelle cut her off, 'Amelia, that Ethan has a juvenile record.'

Coach Clarke was fighting to control his temper. 'That was a decade ago, Michelle. Ethan was seven years old, and I still believe he was falsely accused. Besides, we're talking about a candy bar he allegedly stole from a shop.'

'The same shop where the incident took place last night, Mr. Clarke,' Lakota pointed out.

From above them on the landing, a new voice joined the conversation.

'What's going on?' Ethan asked, appearing on the stairs as he made his way down.

Michelle looked up, recognising the boy she knew in the young man descending toward her. Ethan had grown strong and tall in the last few years and was almost a man. That didn't make him guilty of anything other than growing up, but it did mean his physique fit the description given by Sarah and Chris.

'They think you were out of the house causing trouble last night,' snapped Ethan's father, any pretence at tolerating his guests' presence dismissed. 'I've already told them you didn't leave the house at any point, but they're refusing to listen.'

Michelle had played this game too many times before to get drawn into a discussion. She chose instead to address a question directly to her suspect.

'Ethan, tell me why it is that we found your fingerprints and DNA at the scene of the crime outside Collins' pharmacy last night.'

Both detectives watched the boy's face to see how he would react - it showed nothing but surprise.

Looking at his parents, Ethan screwed up his face in confusion. 'Last night?' he questioned. 'What happened last night?'

Michelle noted that he hadn't answered her question, but before she could prompt him, Coach Clarke was talking again.

'There was a break in and a robbery at Collins' pharmacy, Ethan. Some cops were hurt.' News travels fast in Chippewa Falls, so Michelle was not surprised that Ethan's parents knew the details already. Coach Clarke turned his face to glare at Michelle. 'The cops believe you are behind it.'

'We are following a lead, Mr Clarke,' Lakota corrected Ethan's father. 'As we are duty bound to do.'

'Well, dad's right,' Ethan gave a response to the accusation finally. 'I never went out, but you don't have to take my word for it. I was online gaming with Robbie Cameron and Ramy Vance until almost midnight.'

'You were supposed to be doing your history assignment,' Coach Clarke rounded on his son, more concerned with his academic results than the police investigation.

Ethan shrugged. 'I finished it this morning. I needed a break last night.'

Suddenly seeing that he had the perfect reason to usher the police from his house, Coach Clarke switched his attention back to the two detectives.

'You can check with his friends, yes? He never left the house and now has several alibis to confirm his whereabouts. Are we done?'

Michelle sucked in a deep breath through her nose, giving herself a moment to think. She would follow up to make sure his story checked out, but saw little reason to doubt it would. It wouldn't mean that it was true, of course, only that his friends were prepared to lie for him.

She cut her eyes at Lakota. He was doing the same thing – giving himself a second to think. When they locked eyes, he gave an almost imperceptible shake of his head – they were done here.

Back outside on the street, they got into their car, but Michelle didn't turn the engine on yet.

'What are you thinking?' Lakota asked. He had a lot of respect for his partner. She was tenacious and kept a clear head when it came to examining evidence. He'd worked with several detectives during his eighteen years on the job, but Michelle was his first female partner and by far the best.

Michelle blew out a breath as if she had been holding it and made an exaggerated show of deflating her shoulders.

'Honestly? I'm questioning what we would have done if Ethan had no alibi. What do we do when we catch up to the person behind this, Lakota? What if we try to arrest them and they start doing magic?' She was voicing her fears – not something she could ever recall doing before. Going up against an armed perp would make her heartrate rise, but she was trained for such a situation and had experience.

Now the rules had changed, and she couldn't be sure what they even were now. The cops at the station were waiting for new protocols to come down the line. What were they supposed to do if they came up against a supernatural? Could their current rules of engagement apply? An unarmed perp was no longer to be considered less of a threat. The person who threw the cruiser across the street possessed enormous power. What if they turned that on a person instead of a car?

Then she remembered Tammy-Jo's ruined body. They all read the coroner's report. It was one thing to go after a cop killer, but Tammy-Jo had been fried from the inside. How do you fight that?

Lakota reached out to touch Michelle's arm, invading her space which was something he never did.

'What would your husband say?' He employed a tactic he knew would work.

'Ha!' Michelle laughed though it sounded fake even to her ears. 'He would tell me God will guide us.' Turning to face her partner in the car's dim interior, she spoke quietly when she asked, 'What if God is a lie?'

Chapter 15

Breakfast in the Stevens household was a stilted affair on Monday morning, few words being said, and eye contact largely avoided as the girls fixed their food and retreated to a stool on the breakfast bar. All the while they each pretended to be too engrossed in the news playing on the TV or whatever they were looking at on their phones.

Michelle's ability to notice the drama at play was reduced by fatigue - since she had only just gotten in - and by her own musings on the investigation at hand.

Pastor Stevens had parishioners he needed to see in the coming hours, including two members of his community who were terminally ill. His attention, therefore, was not in the room.

It remained like that, the sisters tiptoeing around each other with their parents blithely oblivious to it, until just before the twins were getting ready to leave. A car pulled up out front, and Michelle saw who was driving it because she was near the door, checking in her purse for her phone.

Frowning deeply to herself, she questioned aloud, 'Why is Robert Cameron here?'

'He's here to collect Cassie,' Jennifer did a good job of getting one back at her twin by throwing their parent's attention her way.

She and Cassie had discussed the subject at some length last night. Jennifer would not commit to taking a side and it was infuriating her twin. Cassie was adamant that the person who attacked them wasn't Robbie and Jennifer could give no reason why she remained suspicious other than to agree with Naomi that the timing of his sudden interest was a hard coincidence to accept.

Cassie accused her twin of jealousy, and the conversation went downhill from there.

Upon hearing the name, Michele cocked an eyebrow. 'Oh, really?' she pinned Cassie in place with a look.

Starting from a position of already angry, Cassie had to bite her tongue fast to avoid snapping at her mother – a move that would instantly annihilate any chance of going on a date on Friday.

'Yes,' she replied. 'He called to ask me out last night. He wants to take me to a movie on Friday. That's okay, isn't it?'

Michelle lifted her chin, looking across the room at her husband who was, as usual, engrossed in something else and not paying attention.

'Martin!'

The tone and volume of his wife's voice penetrated his concentration.

'Yes, dear?' he questioned, aware that he had clearly missed something.

'Cassie has a date with Robbie Cameron this Friday. Opinion?'

Pastor Stevens wanted to let a smile cross his face. As their father, he was supposed to be the one vetting and approving any boys his three daughters wished to date. The truth though was that his wife proved to be a far scarier proposition for any young suitors to overcome and she carried a gun. It was nice that she pretended to include him.

In a serious voice, he asked, 'Isn't he the captain of the football team?'

'He sure is, Dad,' Cassie replied with a broad grin.

'Very well, but I expect you home by ten thirty and he is to pick you up from inside the house so that I get to meet him.' He would rather his daughters found dates from within his own church, but the town was such that the catchment areas of churches and schools was not the same.

'Thanks, Dad,' Cassie felt a wave of relief. Now that her father had said she could, she knew her mother wouldn't argue, but when she turned back toward the door, she found her mother was no longer there.

She was outside and heading directly for Robbie's car. Cassie darted after her, but not fast enough to prevent her mother from starting an interrogation.

'Hi, Robbie,' Michelle said, using a smile to disarm the boy. 'I hear from Cassie that the two of you are going out this Friday.'

'If that is acceptable, Mrs Stevens,' he replied, meeting Cassie's mother's gaze with an endearing smile.

'Mom what are you doing?' Cassie hissed.

Ignoring both her daughter's question and the one posed by Robbie, she asked one of her own. 'Where were you on Saturday evening between ten and midnight, Robbie?'

'Mom!' Cassie blurted, shocked at how embarrassing her mother was acting.

Robbie's cheeks coloured and he squirmed a little under the detective's gaze.

'I was at home, Mrs Stevens. I was gaming online with Ethan and Ramy, two of the boys from our class. Is there a problem?'

'Was Ethan online the whole time?' she pressed.

'Um,' Robbie's jaw worked up and down a couple of times as he tried to figure out how to answer the question. 'Sure, yes ... he must have been. We were playing HALO, it's an immersive teamplay game. We would have noticed if he was away from the controller at any point. I mean, he took a break to go to the bathroom or whatever, but that's all. What's this about?' he asked.

Michelle nodded her head to acknowledge his words, but made no attempt to answer his questions.

'Has Ethan displayed anything ... have you noticed anything different about Ethan recently, Robbie?'

Again, Robbie glanced across at Cassie as if asking for help. His expression made it clear he wanted to know why he was getting the fifth degree.

Cassie was getting angry – not an emotion any of the sisters would willingly display toward their mother unless they wanted to get themselves grounded, but she felt that enough was enough.

'Mom, what is going on? Robbie stopped by to give me a ride to school. That's all, Mom. Can we stop with the questions?'

'Have you?' Michelle pressed, wanting Robbie to answer the question. 'Have you noticed him acting differently recently?' She wanted to ask if Robbie had seen his friend using magic, but doing so would tip her hand a little too far.

Held in place by her eyes, Robbie felt no option but to provide an answer.

'No, Mrs Stevens. Other than being tired from all the football practice his father puts us through and the endless assignments from school, he's just the same Ethan he has always been.'

Not exactly satisfied, but accepting that Ethan's alibi was supporting his story, Michelle ended her interrogation.

'Thank you, Robbie. Sorry about that. There's some strange stuff happening in the town right now and I needed to be sure Cassie's friends aren't mixed up in it.'

Not meaning a word of it, Robbie said, 'That's okay, Mrs Stevens.'

'Are you done, Mom?' Cassie asked, not even trying to keep the cool tone from her voice.

She got a look from her mother that told her not to push her luck, and turned away to smile at Robbie before she could rise to the challenge. With a sigh and an embarrassed expression, she checked over her shoulder to make sure her mom was returning to the house before she spoke.

'Oh, my goodness, I am sooo sorry. I don't know what has gotten into her,' Cassie gushed while holding her hands to her glowing cheeks.

Robbie laughed. 'It's fine. It's just your mom being a mom. Well, and a detective, I guess. She was at Ethan's house last night, grilling him about the thing at Collins' Pharmacy on Saturday.'

'What!' Cassie was shocked. 'She thinks Ethan is behind it? It was a magical attack, wasn't it?'

'That's what I heard,' Robbie replied with a shrug. 'Do you need to get your things? We should probably get going or all the good parking places will be gone.'

Cassie began to back away. 'Sure, I just need a moment.'

Spinning around to head back to the house, she saw Jennifer and Naomi in the windows to her right. They were both staring out at Robbie.

'What?' she demanded once she got back inside. 'It's a boy. I'm sure you have both seen one before.'

Jennifer's bag was next to Cassie's on the sideboard next to the breakfast bar. She timed it so they would arrive there together and when Cassie bade her parents goodbye and started toward the door, she found Jennifer hanging back to wait for her.

They exchanged a look but no words until they got outside.

The moment they were out of the house, Jennifer whispered, 'Look, Cassie, I just wanted to tell you that we watched to see if he would show any signs of tapping a line and he didn't.'

Cassie's mouth dropped open. 'You're still going with ulterior purpose thing? You can't just let it be that he actually wants to date me? Not everyone is evil, you know.' She couldn't believe her sisters could think Robbie might be the one behind the recent murder.

'That's not what I am saying,' Jennifer hissed back, frustrated by her twin's pig-headed refusal to see sense. 'I just wanted to tell you that we checked, and it looks like you were right.'

Cassie was too mad to accept her sister's attempt at an apology, especially since it was such a weak one. She might have spat a reply, but Naomi was coming out of the house behind them, her car keys jangling in her hand. She had to get across town to college, but had no reason to leave yet, which to Cassie meant she was only outside to spy. Robbie interrupted before Cassie could react.

'Hi, Jen.' He waved and smiled. 'Can I give you a lift too?' he offered, wafting both arms toward his car, a new model Nissan Titan utility vehicle.

'No, she's fine to walk,' Cassie answered for her sister.

Jennifer had been about to say the same thing – getting in the car with Cassie and Robbie would be like playing gooseberry, but her twin's attitude changed her mind.

'Sure, Robbie, that would be lovely, thanks.' She glided by Cassie and into the back seat before her twin could reply or argue.

Robbie held the door open for Cassie, and left with no choice, she clambered in next to Jennifer.

Chapter 16

Naomi watched them go, noting the plate number on Robbie's car when he pulled away – just in case she lost sight of it.

Her second sight, something she had practiced engaging for more than an hour last night before bed, had revealed nothing, but all that really told her was that Robbie hadn't been drawing magical energy from the planet when she was looking at him.

She heard her mother's questions and Robbie's answers. So did Jennifer, the two girls urgently whispering to each other while they watched through the window.

Their mom suspected Ethan, another boy in Cassie and Jennifer's school year, that much was clear, and he could be the one who attacked the twins at the edge of the woods yesterday. If so, he would be carrying the bruises today.

Naomi insisted they needed to find out and Jennifer didn't argue. Someone in their town was using magic to commit crimes and to hurt people, that much they knew. What they didn't know, and what troubled them most, was the very real possibility that it would take another person or persons using magic to stop them.

Naomi had a short list of tasks for her day and none of them included attending class. She had never ditched school in her life, but today she would. She intended to find out who Bethany really was, even if that meant confronting her, and she was going to help Jennifer figure out if one of the boys at her high school was the hooded figure who attacked them last night.

Nervously, she turned her ignition key and eased onto the street fifty yards behind Robbie's car.

Chapter 17

The SIA

'What did you find out?'

The question came from Agent Bueller and was aimed at his partner, Debs, who had been up half the night looking into what she claimed might be a promising case. He'd called to check she was in already when he arrived at the coffee shop down the street and was carrying diesel-strength flat whites and bear claws when he arrived at her desk.

'There's definitely something in Chippewa Falls,' she thanked him with a nod as she accepted her beverage and sugary treat, one in each hand. The brew came first, Debs taking a quick chug to clear the funk from her mouth and to scare away the last of the fatigue she felt. 'I already booked out a car. We leave as soon as we are ready.'

Agent Bueller swung his left leg around and over the arm of a chair to slide down and into it next to Debs' desk. With sugar from the bear claw dropping from his upper lip, and flecks hanging from his facial hair, he cleared his mouth before asking a question.

'What?'

'That's what we have to go there to find out. However, they have a dead cop who was fried from the inside by her own blood and then two more got banged up when their cruiser was thrown across the street. I've been reading the police report,' the SIA had all kinds of backdoor access granted to them by the government, 'and they have no clue what they are doing. I think, given the power being wielded, that it might be one of Otto Schneider's missing familiars.'

That snippet of information was enough to get Agent Bueller interested. Finding the familiars – those individuals who escaped the demon realm when Otto Schneider busted out – was one of the SIA's top priorities. Finding one and bringing them in would gain recognition for the agents involved.

'Have you told Pendragon? Frank Bueller asked, holding his breath while he waited for the answer.

'Tell her what, Ferris?' Debs used his nickname – most people did – and snorted a derisive laugh. 'I'll let her know when we are on our way back with a familiar in our custody. Until then, I'm not drawing any attention to Chippewa Falls at all.'

Good. This was good news. Agent Bueller nodded along with his thoughts. Familiars were considered of such worth that any suggestion they might have found one could result in a different team getting assigned to the task of collecting them, or even one of the other teams swooping without permission to get there first.

It wouldn't matter that Bueller and Wallace had their collar snatched from under their noses when they had done all the leg work, everyone would be too excited and interested by the fact that there was another familiar in their camp.

Assuming they could get the familiar on board, that is.

This one was on their radar because he or she had been misbehaving. It was almost expected. According to Ayla Pendragon, some of them had been away for centuries. Now returned, the world they knew was unrecognisable and they were imbued with unthinkable power due to all those years of magical use and practice in the service of a demon.

Either way, they still had the task of identifying who it was when they got to Chippewa Falls.

When Agents Barrow and Furness arrived at the office ten minutes later, there was nothing left to show that Bueller and Wallace had ever been there. Unless one counted the tiny flecks of sugar on the carpet tile next to Debs' desk.

Chapter 18

R obbie did most of the talking at the start of their journey, which was mostly because the girls weren't talking at all and the vibe coming off them was tense to the extreme.

Of course, when Jennifer started to join in, happily chatting with Robbie despite the stink-eye coming from Cassie, she got involved too.

Jennifer asked what movie they were going to watch – a good conversation starter which led to Robbie talking about all the Marvel movies he'd seen and enjoyed.

Approaching the school gates, Cassie's attention was focused outside the car where she surveyed the streets for any sign of Bethany. Ever since getting home last night she had been arguing with herself about what the old lady was. She came across as a friend – someone who wanted to help them and believed that not only was it the right thing to do, but a necessity. Bethany hadn't explained why, but it was clear she believed the girls needed to learn to control their ability if only so they could defend themselves.

What motivated her remained the question at the top of Cassie's list. Was she grooming them? Had she spoken with and then sent the hooded figure who attacked them? He'd heard about them from someone, and Cassie certainly hadn't shared her secret with anyone other than her sisters. Jennifer swore she hadn't either. So too did Naomi for that matter, and if that were true then it only left Bethany to have spilled the beans.

Cassie desperately wanted to ditch school so she could learn more from the old lady, but she needed some reassurances and a good reason to trust her first.

Robbie's car glided through the school gates, a parking lot attendant with his yellow vest directing traffic to turn left for parking and to filter right for drop off.

Around the parking lot, Cassie continued to scan the fence line, looking for any sign of the old lady.

'You okay there, Cassie?' Robbie asked, catching sight of her in his rear-view mirror. 'You looking for someone?'

'Um, no,' she lied guiltily. 'Just seeing who else is about.' A coy smile when she caught his eyes in the mirror suggested she was checking around because she wanted to be sure other people got to see her arrive with him. Her sister being in the car too kind of ruined the effect, but since that wasn't why she was looking around at all, it didn't really matter.

With a jolt, Cassie sat forward in her seat, almost pressing her face against the window as she squinted into the distance through the gaps between the cars. When Robbie turned the steering wheel to pull into a parking space, she had to crane her head right around and look out through the rear window.

She wasn't mistaken though, she had just seen Naomi's car cruising along the road outside their high school. What was her sister doing here? She heard Robbie say something, but did not respond, too transfixed to even consider acknowledging that he'd spoken.

Tracking Naomi's direction of travel, she caught a quarter glimpse of Bethany on the far side of the road and moving away. It was hard to spot her - there were too many obstacles in the way, including the trees bordering the street.

When her car door opened, seemingly of its own volition, Cassie jumped a little, snapping her head around to see who was there as if it might be someone coming to attack her.

'Whoa!' Robbie darted back a pace upon seeing Cassie's startled expression. 'Everything okay?' he asked. 'Is it me, or are you a little on edge this morning, Cassie?'

Cassie twisted around to look back where she had last seen Bethany, but neither the old lady, nor her sister's car were in sight. Forcing herself to smile, she grabbed her bag from the floor of the car and twisted her legs around to get out.

Robbie offered her a hand, which she took gratefully and kept hold of once her feet hit the ground. She had just spotted Pandora Simmons across the car park, and better yet, Pandora had seen her.

She was going to parade across the parking lot, however, the plan forming in Cassie's mind had nothing to do with school or boys or rivals and was entirely to do with ditching school to find Bethany and Naomi. Nevertheless, whatever else she got up to today, she had time to make a statement first.

Jennifer was waiting just a couple of yards away, her phone in her hand and her attention on it. Cassie knew she needed to put their differences aside, but she couldn't talk to her twin about it here.

Robbie locked his car and pocketed his remote, pleasingly accepting Cassie's hand in his as he turned to walk towards the school. There were dozens of other kids around them, all moving in the same direction, though there were other cars still arriving.

Cassie didn't want to, but could not avoid sneaking a glance in Pandora's direction. The skinny girl had a flat chest and was only half as pretty as all the boys seemed to think she was. Her flaming red hair, set against her green eyes gave her a certain something, but with a smile, Cassie reflected that whatever it was she had, couldn't be all that much, or she would be with Robbie still.

There would be trouble, Cassie understood the dynamics of such things, much the same as anyone else. Pandora was popular, and would enlist her bitch friends to cause trouble if she could. Or perhaps her aim would be to split Cassie and Robbie apart.

The instant that thought made its way into her brain, the emotion that came with it caused Cassie's inner magical ability to seek out the energy flowing through the nearest ley line. Catching herself doing it, she quickly quashed the spell beginning to form in her head.

'Robbie!' a boy's voice trumpeted as they neared the edge of the car park.

Cassie's head turned along with Robbie's to see Ethan coming in their direction.

Jennifer saw him too, and Naomi's comment about what they overheard their mother saying earlier echoed in her head. Could Ethan be the one behind the recent spate of magical attacks? Was he the one who came at them as they left the woods yesterday?

'What's this?' Ethan asked, pointing at Robbie and Cassie's intertwined hands. 'I take it you finally got around to asking her out then?' Ethan remarked.

A swell of excitement surged through Cassie's chest. Robbie had been talking about her for some time? His decision to ask her on a date wasn't a sudden thing because he was somehow involved in the attacks and knew about their magical powers. It was nothing to do with that at all. Naomi's concerns had no foundation.

Robbie muttered something in reply, basically telling Ethan to stop talking, and when Cassie glanced, she saw a tinge of red colouring Robbie's tanned cheeks. It made her feel good.

They crossed out of the car park and onto the forecourt of the school. There were kids all around them – a few rushing to get inside. It was much cooler to hang out and chat, and that was precisely what Cassie wanted to do.

At the top of a short flight of the steps, they turned right and onto the grass where several more of Robbie's teammates were already hanging out by a large oak tree. There were girls with them, many from Cassie's year group.

This was to be the first time that she joined them, before today she'd always been considered bookish and largely to be avoided because her mother was a cop. Arriving on the football captain's arm was a whole different story and acceptance was instant.

However, when she looked around, she noticed that Jennifer was no longer with her. Slipping her hand from Robbie's just before they got to his friends, she looked for her sister in the crowd behind them.

'Hold on a second, Robbie, I need to speak with Jen.'

He gave her a nonchalant shrug to accompany his smile.

'Sure thing, Cassie. I'll be right here with the guys.'

Spotting her sister, Cassie hurried over to her without making it look like she was hurrying.

'What are you doing, Jen? Why didn't you come with me?' Cassie wanted to know, the words framed as an accusation.

Jennifer snorted derisively. 'That's your crowd suddenly is it, Cassie? Robbie Cameron asks you out for one date and all of a sudden you're in with the jocks?' Jennifer knew she was being unfair, but she had a number of things on her mind and Cassie had been making life difficult for both her sisters recently.

Cassie almost reacted, her desire to snap a retort almost too much to resist. However, there were bigger things at stake.

'Did you see Naomi? Did she say anything about ditching school today?'

Surprised at her twin's unexpected line of questioning, Jennifer was momentarily taken aback.

'What makes you think Naomi would ditch school? She's never missed a day of school in her life. You know she plans to be President one day, right?' She was making a joke, of course, the two girls often referring to their elder sister as 'Miss Perfect' and speculating on what her goals in life might be.

Cassie nodded her head back towards the direction of the street running outside the school.

'I saw her drive past. And I saw Bethany. I think Naomi was following her. Did she say anything about it before we left the house this morning?'

Jennifer's eyes widened, and her head turned to look at the direction of the street as if her elder sister might still be there.

'Naomi was following Bethany?' Jennifer questioned. 'What was she thinking?'

'She was probably thinking that she can prove me wrong,' Cassie replied uncharitably. 'She probably plans to follow her and find out where she lives. No doubt Naomi has some grand plan for revealing Bethany's real identity just so she can rub my face in it later.'

Jennifer shook her head, surprised at her twin.

'Naomi is not that petty, Cassie, and you know it. We've got no reason to trust Bethany. If Naomi is following her, it's probably so she can protect us.'

Cassie knew Jennifer was right and wasn't going to get drawn into an argument.

'Whatever,' she snapped. 'I'm going after her.'

Jennifer's eyebrows hiked up her forehead. 'You're ditching school too? You'd better hope mom doesn't find out. She'll ground you for the rest of the year.'

'You're not going to come?' It was clear from Cassie's tone that she expected her twin sister to be at her side.

'Ethan,' Jennifer replied somewhat cryptically. When Cassie's forehead wrinkled in confusion, she added, 'Didn't you hear the questions mom was asking Robbie this morning? It was obvious that she thinks

Ethan could be involved in the magical attacks. She was trying to establish an alibi for him. That's why she was quizzing Robbie about Saturday night.'

Cassie swung round to look back at the gaggle of boys gathered under the oak tree. The whole group was chatting, looking at their phones, and gathering around one because somebody had something cool to show everyone else. She had almost got to be part of that group, but now she was looking at Ethan and questioning whether it was he who attacked her and Jennifer at the woods yesterday.

She was still staring at them when Jennifer spoke again.

'I'm going to watch him. We're in the same class this morning anyway. If he is the one, he'll be bruised, and it won't take much for me to check that. All I've got to do is bump into him.'

Cassie's head was nodding, though she was doing very little to control it. Her thoughts were whirling, attempting to work out what she needed to do. A few moments ago, it had all been clear, now she felt she had conflicting priorities.

'If it is him, Jen, then he knows who we are.'

Jennifer corrected her sister, 'You mean he knows what we are.'

'This is dangerous, Jen, you should come with me to find Bethany or Naomi or both of them. What if Bethany is exactly what I hope she is? The three of us could learn so much together.'

'What if she isn't?' Jennifer replied, doing nothing to hide the worry in her voice. 'The three of us could be walking into a trap. Stay here and help me identify whether it is Ethan or not,' she begged. 'If we knew it was him, we could find a way to let mom know.'

Cassie glanced across at the street outside the school again. Cars, kids on bikes, and those who lived close enough to walk, were still streaming through the gates. If she didn't go soon, it would be too obvious that she was ditching school and she wouldn't get out. It was now or never.

With a shake of her head, she backed away a pace, saying, 'I'm going, Jen. Come with me.'

Jennifer countered instantly. 'Stay here and help me,' she repeated her previous request with added urgency.

Cassie felt torn, but ultimately, as she always did, she believed she was right. Another glance at the gates told her she had to get moving.

'Don't do anything until I get back. I won't be long.' With that, and with her twin hissing urgent demands that she return fading behind her, Cassie hurried toward the school gates.

.

Chapter 19

Just a little more than a block away from the school, Naomi ditched her car to go on foot. She'd caught a glimpse of Bethany between the trees outside the school. She was absolutely certain of it, but had lost sight of her just as quickly.

It was creepy enough that the old lady was hanging around outside the school, but made far worse that she took off just as Robbie's car with Jennifer and Cassie in it arrived. What was it that made her leave? Was it as simple as wanting to get one of them at a time, or all three of them together? She'd seen the twins, but Naomi was fairly certain Bethany hadn't seen her.

Confronting the old lady felt like a risky thing to do, and Naomi was only able to convince herself to do so because it was broad daylight. The old lady wouldn't risk doing anything with so many potential witnesses around, surely?

It proved to be a moot point, because five minutes of searching convinced Naomi that the old lady had given her the slip. Whether it was deliberate or not, she could not guess.

Back at her car, she paused to look around once more, then tutted when she remembered the option of using her second sight. A slow blink allowed her to engage it, and suddenly she could see the magical energy flowing through the city's ley lines beneath her feet.

To her left and right, in front and behind, Naomi checked for any sign of a person drawing on the earth's magical energy, but there was nothing for her to see.

Failing to catch up with Bethany did not change her plans for the morning. That she was ditching class felt like a radical move, but only because it was her. The lectures at college were not mandated, and nothing would come of her missing a few hours. She planned instead to use the time productively in the pursuit of some answers.

Had she looked in her rear-view mirror as she pulled away, she would have seen her younger sister running down the street towards her car. That she failed to do so, changed everything that was going to happen that day.

Naomi was heading for Sarah Kirke's house. She knew the young police officer was at home recovering from her injuries from overhearing her mother talk about it. Sarah used to babysit all three of the girls when they were young enough to need such a thing. Naomi could not claim that she knew Sarah well - she hadn't spoken to her in several years, but she believed it was her best place to start.

It took so long for Sarah to get to the door that Naomi was beginning to believe the injured police officer wasn't at home after all. She had been about to turn away when she saw a shadow pass through a beam of light inside the house, and moments later was able to make out the shuffling form of a person coming towards the door.

The inner door opened, a surprised face looking out through the screen to the young woman on the doorstep.

'Hi,' Naomi waved a cheery good morning.

Sarah's face wrinkled a little, and her lips moved before the dots in her head finally aligned.

'Naomi?' she sought to confirm that she recognised the person on her doorstep.

'How are you feeling?' Naomi asked, because she thought it was a good opener. She made her face take on a pained expression, as if wincing along at Sarah's obvious discomfort.

Now that she knew who she was talking to, Sarah relaxed. She'd been quite tense since the attack, though she was refusing to admit that to anyone and had thus far refused the counselling sessions that were offered to her.

With a smile, she commented, 'Like my car got flipped over by a supernatural.' She laughed a little at her own line and pushed the screen open. 'Come in out of the cold, Naomi,' she invited.

Once inside, Naomi had to force herself to steer away from the subject that brought her to Sarah's door. She wanted desperately to get down to business, leveraging the one relationship she thought she might be able to use to find out more about the mysterious old woman.

They made small talk for a minute or so, Naomi asking about Sarah's injuries, and what it had been like. Posing obvious questions that Sarah had already been asked dozens of times before about what she had seen and who it could have been. Were there any clues as to the individual's identity? Naomi made a joke about asking her mother and how the seasoned detective had refused to divulge any information.

Sarah had no idea why Naomi had come to her door, but was far too polite to question her directly. It was actually quite nice to have someone new to talk to. She hadn't seen the young woman since she was a girl, and at nineteen there wasn't actually that much age difference between them anymore. She figured her guest would get around to the real reason for her visit soon enough, and was only made to wait just a couple of minutes.

'Shall I make us coffee?' Naomi offered. 'You might have guessed already that there's another reason for my visiting you other than to make sure you're doing okay.'

'So what is it?' Sarah was glad Naomi hadn't felt the need to beat around the bush for too long. 'Oh, and yes please on the coffee, thank you. I hope instant is ok, my machine is on the fritz.'

Naomi got up, crossing the room to find her way to the kitchen, and checking over a shoulder to make sure that Sarah was staying where she was - the injured cop ought to be resting.

'I wanted to ask someone about how to find another person's identity. There's an old lady who's been watching us, kind of like a stalker.' Naomi found the jar of instant coffee, and some mugs in a cupboard above the kettle. 'I'm not suggesting she's dangerous,' Naomi added, 'But I'm not sure she's given us her real name. I've got a photograph of her, and I was hoping you might be able to tell me how to use it to find out who she is.'

This was not what Sarah had expected at all, but when her guest came back through carrying two steaming mugs of coffee, she was quite content to help. It would give her something to do other than watching daytime TV.

'That will probably depend on the quality of the picture,' Sarah remarked, gratefully accepting the mug of coffee, and placing it on a coaster on a side table to her left.

Naomi wasted no time in putting her own coffee down to pick up her phone. Moments later she had scrolled to the picture and was showing it.

'Is this any good?' she asked.

It wasn't like a mug shot, with the face filling the screen, but it was taken almost face on even though it was from a distance. Using two fingers, Sarah zoomed in a little.

'Yes,' she nodded her head, 'this ought to work. OK if I just send this to myself?'

Naomi was thrilled at the result. She hadn't been sure how her request for help might be received. It felt a little dishonest to come to Sarah's house, appearing out of the blue and after several years. It was true that she felt concern for the woman she knew – mom said she was badly injured, but Naomi couldn't hide that she arrived with ulterior motives guiding her.

If Sarah minded, she showed no sign and was fiddling with Naomi's phone again, picking up her own phone when it beeped, and handing Naomi's back. Naomi got to watch as the cop pressed a couple of buttons and then placed the phone to her ear.

'Yeah, hi, Dean. I just sent you a picture. Can you run it through facial rec and see if anything pings back, please?' As if something had just occurred to her, she added, 'Hold on a second.' Placing her right hand across the phone's mouthpiece to muffle her words, she aimed a question at Naomi, 'I don't suppose you have a name for this lady, do you?'

Naomi almost blurted that she'd already performed the name check using her mother's login and felt her pulse rate quicken as the guilt of doing so resurfaced.

Composing herself, she said, 'Bethany Cromwell, but I have no reason to believe that's a real name.'

Sarah relayed the name to Dean at the other end of the phone - one of her colleagues down at the station. For the next few seconds Naomi listened to the one-sided conversation as clearly the person at the other end was inquiring as to Sarah's well-being and health. He must have said something funny, because Sarah giggled at one point, before excusing herself and ending the call.

Unable to keep a lid on her excitement, Naomi asked, 'How long does it usually take to get a response?'

Sarah picked up her coffee and blew across the surface for a second before taking a sip. Her cop brain had kicked in and the next thing she was going to do was begin to carefully quiz her young guest on precisely what this was all about. Clearly there was something clandestine going on or, in Sarah's opinion, Naomi would have asked her mother.

Nevertheless, she replied, 'We'll probably have an answer before we finish our coffees.'

Chapter 20

Beneath the trees lining the avenue outside the school, Cassie spent ten minutes looking for any sign of Bethany or her sister, Naomi. There was no sign of Naomi's car - something Cassie believed would be far easier to spot than either of the individuals.

Had Naomi scared Bethany off? Was Bethany there looking for Cassie? More than anything Cassie wanted answers. The old lady seemed almost too good to be true. More than ever following the attack yesterday, Cassie wanted to learn what she was capable of and develop her own skills. Bethany Cromwell presented the best and simplest opportunity to achieve that, but not if she had questionable motives.

Cassie didn't want to agree with Naomi, but she couldn't deny her own concern that the old lady might be somehow linked to the hooded figure who attacked them. That the hooded figure was the same one responsible for the recent attacks was not in question so far as she could see.

Cassie planned to find the old lady. She had to live somewhere, right? If Bethany Cromwell was a fake name as Naomi suspected, then there was little hope of finding her. However, Cassie was willing to bet the old lady had given her real name, in which case it had to be listed somewhere.

Like a bolt of lightning striking her skull, Cassie yanked her phone from her pocket. There were still phone listings, right? It felt like a long shot, but she got a hit straight away. B Cromwell - there was only one of them in the phone book - Cassie smiled at the irony that she referred to it as a phone book even though it was entirely digital - and the name came with a phone number and an address.

Setting off towards what she believed to be the old lady's house, filled her with mixed feelings. Uneasiness was at the top of her list, but also a sense of purpose. There were altogether too many unanswered questions, and too many things to worry about for her to not find out whether the old lady was really on her side or not.

It was with that in mind that she crossed the road and quickened her pace.

A quarter of a mile away and paying little attention to the tutor at the front of the class, Jennifer was watching Ethan. He didn't appear to have a limp or to be favouring any part of his body because it was sore, but did that just mean he had taken some good painkillers this morning?

Periodically, Jennifer was engaging her second sight, curious to see whether she would notice Ethan drawing energy or not. What she was doing was making her feel uncomfortable - nervous and agitated.

Two rows behind her, she could hear Pandora Simmons whispering to Becky Munroe and could guess what it was about. She'd come up behind them on the way into class and overheard Pandora spewing awful trash about her sister. On any other day, she would slam Pandora, getting into her face to make it clear her trash talk wouldn't be tolerated. However, today the jealous inclinations of a spiteful girl were trivial. She wanted to determine whether Ethan was the one behind the recent murder and that took priority over everything.

However, after watching him for half an hour, not only had he shown no inclination to draw the slightest amount of elemental energy into his body, which he would need if he wanted to engage his own second sight, but he also hadn't once looked her way. Surely, if he were behind the attack on her and Cassie yesterday, then he would be unable to control the urge to glance. They had escaped him, so even if confident of his own abilities over hers, he must at some level be concerned that she knew who he was.

At least that's what Jennifer was telling herself, and Ethan's coolness was unnerving her. Her plan to bump into him as a ruse to check for bruising remained her plan, but she had intended to do that with Cassie around to back her up. Now alone, the confidence she required to carry out such a task was evading her.

When Mr Hargreaves at the front of the class made a show of clearing his throat, Jennifer twitched her eyes in his direction and was startled to find him looking her way.

'Is there something more interesting over this side of the room, Miss Stevens?' he demanded to know.

Her face reddening as the majority of the class turned to look her way, Jennifer mumbled an apology and fixed her attention on the interactive board to her front.

Figuring out whether Ethan was supernatural was going to have to wait.

Chapter 21

Cassie looked down at her phone, checking the address against the house she could see to her front. Now that she had found it, she was having second thoughts about what to do next.

There was a car parked on the drive - a BMW3 series. Is that the sort of car that the old lady would drive? Cassie knew she was asking silly questions of herself that she couldn't possibly answer as a stalling tactic. Standing on the opposite side of the street, in the shade of a large tree, she argued with herself about what to do.

If she wasn't going up to the house, her journey to find it seemed a little pointless. Of course, she had no idea if anyone was in. If she found nobody at home, it didn't mean that Bethany didn't live here. She could be at work. She could have gone shopping.

Then why was there a car on the drive? An annoying voice at the back of her head questioned.

Before she could argue any further, movement caught her eye. Someone was coming around the side of the house. Her heart skipped, her breath catching in her throat as she looked to see who it was.

Stepping out from the shadow cast by the house, Cassie saw that it was a woman, but it was not Bethany. The woman she could see had to be twenty years younger. At least.

Cassie's feet twitched as indecision ruled. Then with a growl of annoyance at allowing her fear to control her actions, she pushed off to cross the road, making a beeline for the lady as she approached her car.

'Hello,' Cassie called, raising her arm to attract the lady's attention. The woman had plipped her car open with the remote and would be getting in it if Cassie didn't stop her.

The lady's name was Veronica Cromwell. Of African descent, much like Bethany, she looked up with a curious expression at the girl hurrying towards her across the road. She paused, her hand gripping the door handle of her car and she waited to see what the girl wanted. Veronica thought the young black girl was about the same age as her eldest daughter, and thought for a moment that she might be one of her daughter's friends.

'Can I help you?' she inquired politely. She wasn't in a rush to get anywhere, and the girl clearly wasn't trying to sell her anything.

Now she was closer to the house, Cassie could see the word Cromwell on the mailbox. Hope bloomed in her head as she guessed that Bethany would be this woman's mother. The age gap was about right.

'Hi, sorry for stopping you like that. My name is Cassie Stevens, I'm looking for Bethany Cromwell. Is that your mother?'

The woman narrowed her eyes slightly, studying the young girl with an air of curiosity.

'No, my mother's name is Helena. Sorry, you seem to have the wrong address.'

Momentarily taken aback, Cassie recovered quickly.

'Actually, I was just guessing that she might be your mother. I think the age gap would be about right. Perhaps she's an aunt instead? It's quite important that I find her.'

Veronica Cromwell was about ready to dismiss the young girl. She might not be in a hurry, but that didn't mean she had time to waste either. However, remaining polite, she removed her hand from the car's door handle.

'I'm afraid I don't have any relatives called Bethany. Perhaps you have the name wrong?' she suggested.

It hadn't occurred to Cassie that Bethany might be short for something, an abridgement or nickname. She knew that people sometimes use their middle names out of preference. Was that the case this time?

Why hadn't she taken a photograph of Bethany when she had the chance? Naomi had one - she could have had her sister forward it to her. That would have solved this situation. There was of course the option of phoning Naomi now in a bid to get it, but that didn't appeal even slightly - She was still angry with her elder sister.

Veronica decided she had no further need to wait. She had been polite enough, and listened to the girl, but she clearly had the wrong address. Opening her car door, she put one foot inside and paused for a parting comment.

'The only Bethany Cromwell I've ever known was my great great grandmother. I only know about her because she vanished when my grandmother was a little girl.'

Cassie blinked, the lady's words sinking into her head too late to stop the woman from starting her engine and driving off. It left her at the edge of the drive watching the car vanish into the distance as an unbelievable thought swam to the surface.

At the same time, but in a different location, Naomi was in pursuit of the same information. Just when she was finishing the dregs of her coffee, Sarah's phone rang. Sarah frowned down at it where it lay face up on the sofa to her right.

'It's Dean,' she remarked.

Holding her coffee cup in both hands, so that she had something to do with them while she waited to hear whatever news the on-duty officer might have, Naomi tried not to hold her breath.

Sarah thumbed the green button to answer the call and held the phone to her left ear.

'Dean?'

Naomi could hear that it was a man's voice speaking, but could not make out anything that was being said. All she had to go on were Sarah's facial cues and monosyllabic replies. They were insufficient to tell her anything of use.

'Really?' Sarah questioned what she was being told, and cut her eyes across the room at Naomi.

Naomi couldn't read the expression, or perhaps didn't want to. Sarah's eyes seemed to say that she didn't believe what she was hearing and that perhaps it was due to Naomi.

An icy stab of fear shot through her chest as she remembered hitting the hooded figure with her car yesterday. Had it been reported as a hit and run? Until that very moment it had not once occurred to her that anything might come of it. Now she felt like blurting a confession, getting her defence in early because it really hadn't been her fault.

Then again, she hadn't reported the accident. That made her guilty, didn't it?

Sarah ended the call with words of thanks and a promise to see Dean soon. It appeared her plan involved meeting him for a beer one evening after work though Naomi couldn't work out whether that was a romantic liaison or simply cops meeting in a bar local to the station.

Naomi expected the hear what Dean had to say, but Sarah was shuffling around to get up off the couch instead. Making small grunting noises of discomfort as she wrestled against the aches and pains and bruising in her body, she used her left arm to push against the sofa and stood up.

'He's just sent me an email,' Sarah remarked as she began to hobble across the room. 'I could look at it on my phone, but this will be easier on my computer. I just need a moment to log in.'

Naomi could see where Sarah was going - across the room there was a small desk with a tower computer and a monitor – an older model PC.

It took a moment to boot up, clearly not getting a lot of use, and Sarah had to ask Naomi to take the mugs to the kitchen so she could enter her police department portal login without risk of being seen.

Naomi was astute enough to know privacy was the reason for Sarah's request to load her dishwasher and let her know by asking if it were safe to return yet before she re-entered the room.

Sarah allowed herself a small chuckle.

'I'm sure your mom is super secretive with her password,' she commented as Naomi came to stand on her right-hand side. 'Where did you say you saw this lady?'

Naomi frowned, curious as to why Sarah wasn't opening the file so obviously waiting for her.

'The first time was outside a coffee bar near my college. She was looking through the window at me and looked away the moment I saw her. I think maybe I'd seen her a few times before that, but never really noticed. You know what I mean? Like your brain has registered something, but you don't really know what it means at the time. I took the picture of her yesterday outside our house.'

Sarah had been studying Naomi's face the whole time, which was making Naomi feel a little unnerved. That sensation got worse when Sarah asked her a question.

'What is it that you're not telling me, Naomi?'

Naomi felt her stomach tighten a little. There was plenty she wasn't telling Sarah or anyone else for that matter. Her need to keep terrible secrets had become a major factor in her life over the last few weeks.

To provide an answer, even though it was a lie, Naomi stuttered, 'I'm not sure what you mean.'

Sarah turned back towards the computer screen, swivelling the chair so she faced the keyboard. Her right hand had never left the mouse, though she needed to adjust its position slightly before she clicked to open the awaiting file.

Naomi was expecting to find a criminal record or something that she had failed to locate when she searched for it last night. Instead, what the screen displayed required her to squint just to make out what it was.

Over a mile away at the city library, Cassie was gawping open mouthed at a news article. The library's research and archive section was a wonder of modern research technology. After concocting a white lie about looking into genealogy for a school project on family, she had gained access to one of the computers and an authorization code to look up personal information.

The librarian had commented on how there were websites for this sort of thing, but then followed it up herself by remarking that they were not free to access.

It hadn't taken Cassie long at all to find what she was looking for, not that she knew it even existed for her to find. The very first hit at the top of the page when she searched for Bethany Cromwell returned an article from sixty-four years ago. Cassie knew she needed to read the words, but her eyes were still glued to the picture. It sat beneath a headline that read 'Local Woman Vanishes'.

There was no mistaking that Cassie was looking at the same old lady who had been training her to perform elemental magic less than twenty-four hours ago. Her hair was styled slightly different now, but even in the grainy black and white photograph, there was no question she was looking at the same woman.

Tearing her eyes away from the picture, Cassie quickly scan-read the article. Bethany had been a mother of five and had twelve grandchildren when she vanished one night from her home. There were three witnesses to her disappearance, all claiming the same story about seeing a strangely dressed man in a suit accompanied by another man wearing a hooded robe. They were reported to have fired glowing orbs from their hands to dissuade Bethany's husband from coming after them and then they vanished into thin air. The police had apparently arrested Bethany's relatives on suspicion of murder, but when no body was found, they were all released. The husband claimed his wife was taken against her will and the report made it sound as if he only narrowly avoided consignment to an asylum for his fanciful tale.

Cassie had no idea what any of this meant other than the very obvious fact that the woman she met yesterday was well over a century old. Why had she chosen to leave at that time? How long had she been back in the area? Or had she never truly left? How was it that she hadn't aged? Who were the two men that her husband and the other witnesses saw her depart with? Was it truly against her will? Or was she in fear that her abilities would be discovered and chose to run before her witchiness was discovered?

Cassie checked her memory to line up dates, quickly deciding that the *Salem Witch Trials* and all of that had taken place centuries before Bethany had gone missing. Were they still hunting witches in the mid-20th century? Cassie didn't know the answer to that question, but whatever the case she suddenly had answers and she needed to share them with her sisters.

Her muscles twitched as she went to rise from the chair, but she caught herself before she moved. With the click of the mouse, she sent the article to the printer, then looked around the room listening for a machine to begin whirring.

When one did, she rushed across to it, waiting impatiently for it to spew all the pages. They got roughly folded and stuffed into her shoulder bag before she hurried towards the library doors and the exit.

Chapter 22

Tugging her jacket around her neck to keep the cool autumn air out, Cassie was still going down the steps outside the library when she scrolled to find Naomi's name in her list of recent calls. All thoughts of trying to prove her elder sister wrong or getting one up on her had faded in the revelation of Bethany's history.

However, as she scrolled through her contacts, Cassie's phone kicked into life with an incoming call from the very person she wanted to talk to. Thumbing the button to answer, she wasn't given a chance to reply before Naomi began talking.

'Cassie! Cassie, where are you? You're not going to believe what I've just found out!' Naomi blurted her words, scarcely able to get them out fast enough.

The excitement in her sister's voice was enough to give Cassie pause. She was poised to explain what she had discovered, but something in Naomi's tone told her she didn't need to.

'Bethany Cromwell is her real name and she's one hundred and thirty years old,' Cassie guessed what it was that Naomi so desperately wanted to tell her.

There was stunned silence from the other end of the phone. It lasted long enough that Cassie thought she was going to have to say 'Hello?' but Naomi spoke before she needed to.

'Oh, my God! She's with you, isn't she?' Naomi gabbled her words in a panicked fashion, her free hand clutching at her chest as she began to hyperventilate.

When Sarah showed her the file Dean sent over, it had been with a raised eyebrow because the young cop believed she was being punked. Sarah went so far as to ask Naomi which of her colleagues had set her up. It was her assumption the photograph Naomi showed her was an elaborate fake cleverly made to look like a woman in the file who had clearly been dead for a very long time.

Naomi knew different, of course. The facial recognition software hadn't worked because it had nothing to compare Bethany to anywhere in the system. The grainy photograph, the same one that Cassie had seen, was all Dean had been able to find along with the article that accompanied it. He only ran the name check as an afterthought just before calling Sarah to tell her he'd struck out.

Naomi had no way to explain to Sarah what was going on. It was hard enough explaining it to herself. The whole magic gig was new to her, and she had no idea what the limitations or lack thereof might be. Could magic prolong life span? Had Bethany simply gone missing because she had to? Had she been under suspicion of witchcraft or something?

These were answers to be found later and Naomi applied the same logic to the pressing demands from Sarah who wanted to know what was going on. Still at Sarah's house, as the revelation of Bethany's truth sank in, all Naomi could think of to do, was call her sisters. When Jennifer didn't answer on the first attempt, she called Cassie and hoped the younger sibling might prove to be in a reasonable mood for once.

Now she was waiting for Cassie to reveal that she was being held captive, though Naomi bore a trace of hope that Bethany was indeed on their side.

'No, Naomi,' Cassie replied. 'I don't know where Bethany is. I thought maybe you would. I watched you following her outside of school.'

'Wait, what? Where are you?' Naomi demanded to know, her big sister voice suddenly back in place.

Cassie tutted and blew out an exasperated breath. 'I'm just leaving the library, Naomi. Tell me where you are, or better yet, come and get me.'

In a horrified voice, Naomi gasped, 'You ditched school?'

Cassie could feel her determined calm slipping away. 'Big picture, Naomi!' she railed. 'Big picture. You ditched school too! I'm pretty sure you did that so you could look into the same things I've been looking into.'

Cassie's feet were heading back in the direction of her school, but it was going to take her at least twenty minutes of walking to get there.

About to prompt Naomi into agreeing they needed to focus on the issue at hand, she was cut off by Naomi speaking.

'Hold on, I've got Jen on the other line,' she reported.

Cassie's line went abruptly quiet as Naomi switched between calls to speak to her other sister.

'Jennifer, where are you? We need to get together right now,' Naomi insisted before she gave her younger sister the chance to speak. Then she had to strain her hearing to make out what Jennifer was saying. 'What was that? I can't hear you,' she complained.

Raising her voice just a fraction in volume, Jennifer repeated what she had just said.

'I said, there's someone here using magic. Where are you?'

Naomi's heart thudded in her chest. 'You're still at school?' she asked, her own voice barely a whisper in deference to Sarah who was listening in just a yard away. Terrified that their conversation might be over-heard - Jennifer had just used the M word - Naomi fumbled to grab her bag from where she had left it on the couch. Waving to her host apologetically, she said, 'Sorry, I have to go. It was nice to see you. I hope you feel better really soon.'

Sarah got to watch in bewilderment as the young woman dashed from her house, forgetting even to shut the front door as she ran for her car at the edge of the street.

'Are you still there?' Naomi asked.

'Yes, I'm still here,' Jennifer squeaked. 'What the heck is going on, Naomi? Where are you? Cassie said she saw you outside our school.'

Ignoring her sister's questions, Naomi pressed to get an answer, 'Who's doing magic? Are you still at the school?'

Jennifer, the least easily agitated of the three, was getting agitated.

Taking a deep breath, so that she would not snap, she said, 'Yes, Naomi, I am at the school. I don't know who is doing magic. All I can see is a track of energy coming up through the ground. I'm trying to find out who it is now.'

Naomi got her car open and the engine started, but paused before she chucked it into gear. 'I'm going to get Cassie and we're coming to you,' she announced. 'Wait, are you in any danger?' she asked, the terrifying thought suddenly occurring to her.

'No, I don't think so. Whoever it is, they are on the other side of the gym, over by the sports pitches. I'm just going to try to get a glimpse of who it might be.'

'Could it be Ethan?' Naomi questioned.

Jennifer shook her head, though of course Naomi couldn't see her gesture. Whispering into the phone once more, she said, 'No. Ethan was standing just a few feet away from me when I first saw it. I was pulling up my second sight to see what he was doing, or whether he might attempt to draw on a line when he thought I wasn't looking. We're in recess now and I followed him when he snuck off with Robbie and a few of the other guys. It's none of them. That's why I'm trying to find out who it is.'

Naomi was gripped with fear for her younger sister. 'Just hold tight, Jennifer. We'll be there in just a few minutes. Don't get any closer, just try to keep them in sight if you can. I've got to go, okay? Cassie's on the other line, but we're gonna be with you really soon. Stay on the line.'

Naomi punched the button to reconnect her to Cassie and floored her accelerator.

'It's about time, Naomi,' Cassie complained the instant she heard the line reconnect. She'd been going nuts wondering what it was that was keeping Naomi so long and beginning to believe her older sister was doing it on purpose just to wind her up.

'Where are you? Naomi asked. 'I'm on my way to you. Jennifer says there's someone doing magic at the high school. She says she can see them drawing on a line, but she doesn't know who it is yet.'

Cassie gasped, shocked at the news. Questions formed an unruly queue in her head, the foremost of which was all to do with who it was and whether Jennifer was all right. Remembering though that she needed to tell Naomi where she was, she dealt with that first.

Naomi was coming for her, and she wasn't hanging around if the roaring sound of her engine in the background was anything to go by.

They were unprepared, none of them having anything more than rudimentary skills, but Cassie knew they were going to rush into danger with barely a thought for their own safety. They had to just to make sure Jennifer was safe, but it was more than that. If they didn't identify who the killer in the town was, it was going to be people like their mother who had to tackle him instead.

Chapter 23

They didn't have to find Jennifer when they arrived at the school – she was still on the phone, and they knew roughly where she was. She assured them she was still fine which allowed them to refocus their attention on finding the person who was drawing magical energy from the earth.

Naomi and Cassie each brought up their second sight the moment their feet hit the tarmac, and just as promised a tendril of golden elemental energy was trickling up through the ground to a point beyond the buildings to their front.

'On the sports field,' Cassie murmured. 'Just as Jennifer said.'

They hurried forward. The school grounds were littered with students of all ages, the lunch recess spilling them out of the buildings despite the cool autumn air. Naomi and Cassie understood well enough the desire for the freedom the outdoors presented as opposed to the often oppressive feeling of being inside the class and all the demands it held.

It worked to their advantage, since they were moving freely through a crowd, rather than finding themselves exposed as isolated individuals crossing the school grounds by themselves.

They rounded the edge of the main school building, checking over their shoulders to see if anyone was watching them. Lifting her phone, Naomi whispered into it.

'Jennifer, where are you? We're just coming up on the sports field.' Naomi had her phone turned right down so that when her sister's voice echoed through the speaker it was quiet enough that no one more than a yard away would hear it.

'I can see you,' Jennifer replied. 'Keep coming.'

Two seconds later, their sister stepped into sight, emerging from behind the bleachers. The three girls went into a huddle, putting their heads together, though none of them would look away from the thread of ley line energy across the fields for very long.

'What do we do?' Jennifer asked. 'Whoever that is, they've been out there for fifteen minutes now.'

Cassie's face twitched as she grimaced menacingly.

'We're going to introduce ourselves,' she growled, clearly meaning to start a fight. As she took her first step forward, Naomi grabbed her coat.

'What are you proposing to do, Cassie?' the eldest of the three girls demanded to know. 'Yesterday, whoever that is threw lightning at you. Or had you forgotten that minor detail?'

Cassie ripped her arm from Naomi's grip, twisting to face her as she snarled, 'And what do you propose? Whoever that is over there attacked and killed one cop and then attacked two more – badly injuring them. Then they ambushed Jennifer and me yesterday. We have no idea who it is, but we know for certain that he knows about us. At the very least, I intend to find out who is behind the recent attacks. Don't you think that might be a good idea?'

'Cassie's right, Naomi,' Jennifer pointed out. 'I want to know who it is too. I only waited because I knew you two were coming and then the three of us could approach together. We don't know that he means us any harm. Maybe we can find out what this is all about.'

Exasperated, but knowing she had no better suggestion to offer, Naomi blew out a hard breath of acceptance.

'Okay, but we need to have spells ready. If he so much as tries to form a spell, the three of us are going to have to get away and we will probably need to knock him down or knock him about at the very least.'

In response to Naomi's suggestion, flame jumped into Cassie's hand.

Naomi's eyes went wide in shock and both of her hands clamped against Cassie's to force them closed.

'No fire, crazy pyromaniac! How on earth would we explain it to the police, or better yet, mom if we burned someone?'

Annoyed that she couldn't employ what she knew was the coolest spell in her arsenal, but knowing she never would have been able to use on a person anyway, Cassie lifted her hand again. This time when she opened her palm, a small spinning vortex of air circulated an inch above her hand like a tiny tornado. It would have been invisible to anyone not gifted with second sight, but the three sisters saw Cassie's movements and the spell itself as a cascade of golden sparkles.

'Better,' Naomi remarked.

All three girls turned towards the woods on the far side of the sports pitches. The tendril of golden, ethereal energy seeping through the ground and into whoever was hidden out there was still visible. When the girls started walking, they were silent, each keeping their thoughts to themselves as they speculated about what or who they might find.

The silence didn't last long, and it was Jennifer who broke it.

'Girls, is it getting darker?' she asked.

Her question prompted Cassie and Naomi to look up and about at the sky above them. Neither had noticed it until Jennifer pointed it out, but the sky was indeed growing darker. Clouds were moving in from every direction, becoming blacker and thicker with every passing second.

That it was magic behind the sudden change in weather was not in question. Instead, each sister was questioning how much power an individual needed to produce such a spell. Mist began to drift in at ground level, covering the grass of the sports field and giving the woods ahead an eerie appearance that was only accentuated by the ever-darkening sky.

'What do we do?' Jennifer asked, the very timbre of her voice dictating that her vote was to turn around.

Before Cassie could respond, and to her surprise, Naomi said, 'We keep going.'

Behind them, the mist was thickening to the extent that it was hard to make out the school building's rising three stories into the sky, and still the sky continued to darken. It was as if twilight had descended five hours early, and shortly it would be full dark.

At the edge of the woods, Jennifer's left hand found Cassie's right before stretching out on the other side to grip Naomi too. Linked as they were, they felt a little braver, but their ability to perform magic was greatly reduced.

The mist parted before them as they reached a clearing. The sky had grown no darker, so the effect was still as if it were early evening - they could see each other and they could see the trees. There was one other thing they could see, and it was the hooded figure from the previous evening.

'Who are you?' Naomi demanded, operating as spokesperson. 'What is it that you want?'

The hooded figure stood over six feet tall. It was hard to make out his body shape, but it looked to be narrow at the waist and broad at the shoulder. The hood performed a perfect job of hiding the person's features. His hands were at his sides, and his stance was relaxed.

Was it the same person as yesterday? They just couldn't tell. The person they could see was the same height and shape as they remembered, but under the hood it could be anyone.

The thin line of elemental energy coming up through the earth was still there, fuelling him for whatever spell he might plan to cast.

Cassie shook off Jennifer's hand and increased her pull on the nearby ley line. Forming an air spell in her mind, she raised both her hands, conjuring the spell in her right hand while controlling it using her left. She was going to knock this guy on his butt.

'Yesterday you said we were more powerful than you'd been led to believe,' Cassie shouted across the distance between them. 'I don't think you know the truth of it,' she threatened. 'Why don't you pull back that hood and show us who you are?'

The hooded figure didn't even twitch. He was five yards away and looking right at them though his eyes could be closed for all the girls knew.

Naomi had been about to repeat her question, the figure in front of them giving no response thus far or even indicating that he had heard her speak. She got no chance to do so, because Jennifer suddenly gripped her hand so tightly that it hurt.

Naomi didn't need to ask why, because she saw the reason for her younger sister's fright the very next moment.

All around them, hooded figures were stepping out from between the trees. That they were all together could not be questioned – their hoods and pants were all exactly the same. It was as if they were wearing a uniform.

Still holding her spell, Cassie twisted to look at the new threat. Jennifer and Naomi did likewise, turning their bodies to look all around at the advancing figures. As the hoods – all men, the girls felt certain – formed a circle around them, the sisters backed against each other, so they were in a sort of triangle facing outward at the threat.

There had to be twenty of them, not that the girls had time or the presence of mind to count how many they were now up against.

Enraged by the terror she felt, Cassie threw her air spell, randomly picking a target because it was right in front of her. With a scream, she loosed her conjuring, anger and fear giving it strength.

To her mind it was going to bowl the hood she aimed at over onto his back, but to her great horror all he did was flick his right arm around in a circle as if parrying a punch. Her air spell deflected harmlessly into the leaf litter on the ground three yards to his right.

Before she could ready another spell, or question what move she could employ next, somebody finally spoke.

'There is no need for alarm, ladies,' a deep voice assured them. 'We mean you no harm.'

'Ha!' Cassie cackled. 'Which one of you fried my ass with lightning yesterday then?'

It had taken Naomi a moment to pinpoint which of the figures sur-rounding them had spoken. They all looked alike, dressed in the same non-descript black warm-up trousers and black hooded top, their faces hidden inside the dark recess it provided. The only difference between any of them was height and girth.

When the figure spoke again, Naomi was looking right at him.

'Yesterday's incident was unfortunate,' he remarked. 'Our master has a proposition for you.'

Picking up on what he had said instantly, Naomi questioned, 'Which of you is the master?' She was still trying to solve a crime. Hoping that in some way by revealing who was behind the murder of Officer Spencer, she might somehow be able to show that their use or ability to use magic did not make them the same as the supernaturals everyone was so terrified of. Naomi wanted to find a way to explain what they were to her mother, and perhaps in identifying the killer lay a path to absolution.

The hooded figure did not answer her question when he next spoke.

'You are outnumbered and outmatched, ladies. Please drop your spells, all of you. I will not ask again. If we have to take you by force, then we will do so. But I assure you, we intend you no harm. The world is changing, and soon it will be ruled by people like us. People who can control the elements. The most powerful among us will lead when the time comes and anyone who has the ability to stand against us will be destroyed. So I ask you again, one last time, come with us now.'

Jennifer's heart was beating so rapidly she thought it might explode in her chest. How could they have gotten it all so wrong? It wasn't one person that the police were after, it wasn't just one supernatural in the town who was killing and causing havoc and hurting people. There was an entire gang of them! If their matching outfits indicated anything at all, it was that they were organised. How could the three of them possibly hope to win this fight?

His voice sounding impatient, the one man who had spoken, growled out another ultimatum.

'What's it to be, ladies?' His final comment acted as a prompt as all around them the circle of hoods raised their hands and drew on the nearest ley line. With their second sight engaged, the three girls saw a rush of elemental energy flowing like a torrent through the ground beneath their feet.

The sisters responded, fear driving each of them to act in a manner that was natural for them. Much to the hoods' surprise, all three went on the offensive.

With a scream of rage that showed her teeth, Cassie ripped into the soil around them. For the last minute, she'd been pushing her thoughts outwards and downwards into the ground, looking for rocks, looking for anything that she could bind a spell onto. It was only the second time in her life that she had attempted to perform such a spell, but she learned a little yesterday.

Mostly what she had learned was that it was possible.

As the gang of hoods hefted air spells to buffet, batter, and bowl over the three girls, Cassie unleashed a spell she'd wound into the earth. It spewed rocks, dirt, and detritus into the air in a wide circle all around th em.

The effect was to temporarily blind everyone including the three girls as the air became opaque with the soil and rocks hanging in it. It was serendipity rather than strategy that her spell was released half a heartbeat before Jennifer and Naomi thrust outward with a wave of air. There was no tactic that allowed them to achieve such an effect, but the circle of soil hanging in the air was immediately thrust outwards to coat and confuse their attackers.

Jennifer squealed, 'Run!' thrusting off with her right leg to drive into Naomi and force her to move. Between them they snagged Cassie, dragging her along so that all three girls ran like a spearhead for a single point of the circle encompassing them.

Believing it no longer mattered if she hurt someone, and quite certain she didn't care, Cassie produced flame between both her hands. As she passed between two dirt and rock covered hoods, she thrust them out to either side.

Two thin jets of flame shot from her hands, igniting the hooded black tops. Like a six-legged beast, the three girls ran through the gap they created, but the tiny advantage they had gained ended in the very next second.

The need to keep the sisters in one piece was a major disadvantage. The hoods could not use flame or lightning for fear it might cause terrible harm. Nor could they manipulate the water inside the girls' bodies to raise or lower their temperature. To do such a thing safely required great finesse which none of them possessed yet. They were as likely to kill them which is precisely what happened with Officer Spencer. However, there were plenty of other spells they could employ.

The fleeing girls heard shouting behind them just as Cassie threw her fire spell. An instant later the ground beneath their feet bucked.

They couldn't see it, but an impossible wave had followed them across the ground, rising to a height of eighteen inches as it swept beneath their feet.

To amplify the effect and capitalise on the girls' momentary loss of balance, three of the hooded figures had thrown gusts of air at their backs. The combined effect was as if they had been catapulted into the air and then shot out of a cannon. Tumbling out of control, they shrieked and screamed until they crashed to earth several yards later.

They came to rest in a tangle of limbs. Bumped and bruised and wondering which way was up, adrenaline demanded they get up and get moving or find a fresh way to fight their attackers. However, the spells that tipped and then threw them were just the start of the hoods' onslaught.

A fresh barrage hit before any of them could get their feet pointing in the right direction to get up. The earth beneath them heaved once more, this time mounting up between them like a volcano rising from the ground. It split them apart, causing the sisters to tumble in different directions as the mound continued to grow and gravity dragged them down the sloping sides.

Somewhere in the melee someone was screaming. Naomi could make out that she was hearing agony-induced cries of pain. It wasn't her sisters though, it was the two hoods Cassie set on fire. It was awful, but Cassie had inflicted damage on the enemy. Enemy. The word stung Naomi's brain. How was it that they were involved in a magical fight and had an enemy?

Crying out in fear, Jennifer swivelled her head to look back the way they had come. The circle of hoods had closed and were coming at them as a squad. They were not hurrying, but with her second sight engaged she could see the spells forming in their hands, golden light tracing circles like a child twirling a sparkler on a dark night.

Abruptly, and in a way that astonished her terrified eyes, an invisible force struck the hoods at ankle height. It swept them from their feet like a scythe reaping corn.

Jennifer squealed when a hand grabbed her shoulder, yanking her upwards and away from the leaf litter and dirt in which she lay.

'Jen, come on!' Naomi screamed in her ear. She had also seen what had happened to their attackers and planned to get away from them in the momentary respite from their attack. Rising to her full height, and dragging Jennifer upright with her, she saw Cassie to her left. Cassie wasn't running, Cassie was trying to cast a spell.

Naomi choked in her surprise. Her younger sister had floored the twenty or so hoods with a single spell! Naomi had no idea how to achieve such a thing.

The hooded figures might have been knocked down, but they were getting back up. Caught motionless as she gawped at Cassie, Naomi was the first to be struck by a flying piece of stone.

The hoods were employing another manipulation of an air spell, one which used a projectile. The stones were small but that didn't mean they weren't dangerous.

Cassie cried out in pain and flinched when a stone caught her cheek. Naomi could see a small rivulet of blood on her sister's face, shining darkly in the dim light. She had to duck away herself, bringing up her coat to shield her face and crouching to protect Jennifer with her body.

Naomi's back was to her attackers - Jennifer cupped under her as she crouched, but she was completely pinned. The stones struck her clothing at a rate of dozens per second. It was torture, but to get away she would have to expose more of her body.

They needed to run. They needed to find a way to defend themselves. But without warning the bombardment of tiny stones stopped. No, she corrected herself, it hadn't stopped, she could still hear the tiny whooshes of air and the crack of stones hitting something.

It hadn't stopped, they had switched targets.

Risking a glance, she lifted her head just a little and lowered the coat that covered her face. Now able to see what was going on, she was shocked to find the hooded men were all facing a different direction, the flash and fizz of their spells aimed toward ...

They were fighting someone else!

Cassie's voice penetrated Naomi's thoughts as she shouted loud enough to be heard.

'It's Bethany! Bethany is fighting them!' Cassie roared.

It was true, Naomi saw. Across from them, and attacking from a different flank, the old lady who had a lot of explaining to do, so far as Naomi was concerned, was indeed trading blows with the hooded figures. What's more, she was winning and with a flash of understanding, Naomi realised it wasn't Cassie who knocked all the hoods down a moment ago, it was the old lady!

As if frozen to the spot, Naomi couldn't convince her feet to move, she was so transfixed by the sight to her front. The old lady's hands were a blur of golden light as she formed spell after spell. A little voice in the back of Naomi's head informed her that Bethany must be going easy. She knew the spells such as fire and lightning were possible because she'd seen them herself. That the old lady wasn't employing them had to mean that she wanted to win but did not wish to maim.

A shove from Cassie brought Naomi back to the now.

'Cast a spell!' Cassie yelled in Naomi's face. 'We have to help her! Throw everything you've got at them!'

Cassie was forming a spell herself, shouting at her sister, but with her attention on the enemy to their front. The tide of the battle had turned suddenly with their ally arriving and as Naomi watched, Cassie unleashed a blast of air. It was weak compared with using fire, but it disrupted and confused the hoods who were all battling against an old lady who was proving to be a match for their combined efforts.

Nothing they were doing was having any effect on the old lady, and as Naomi watched, she saw lightning arc toward the lone figure, only to be deflected into the soil by a flick of Bethany's hand.

Next to Naomi, Jennifer raised her hands and began to cast a spell.

Upon seeing it Cassie turned her head to shout, 'That rock there!' She pointed to a small boulder the size of a lunch pail. 'We can shift it between us!' she shouted to her twin.

Understanding what her sister proposed, Naomi got in on the spell too. Focusing her attention on the rock and casting an air spell with her hands, she reached out with her senses to feel the rock itself. She had never done anything like this, but knew it ought to be well within her ability - it was just a manipulation of an air spell which she had been practising for weeks.

The girls could not see it when silver light linked and enveloped them, but through the woods the woman fighting the hoods did.

Bethany had only seen such a thing once before and was so startled by it her defensive spell failed. A strike of lightning got through, blasting her from her feet, she flew backwards. Tumbling out of control, pain reporting in from all over her body, she could still not take her eyes from the sight of the three sisters weaving a spell simultaneously.

A bead of sweat dripped from Naomi's brow, running down the side of her face. The effort of focusing on the spell was making her breathing ragged, but the stone was lifting from the ground, buoyed up on a cushion of air. Thinking to herself as she strained to control the spell, she thought, '*This is hard.*'

Jennifer's voice echoed back, '*It sure is.*'

The two girls looked inward at each other, confused for a moment, but a roar from Cassie stopped them from saying anything.

Cassie was shouting instructions, 'On three we throw it with every-thing we've got!' She counted down and the three sisters converted the spell, thrusting out with their right hands as a physical action to help them control the magic behind the conjuring.

But instead of flying through the air as they intended, hoping it would strike as many of their attackers as possible, the rock chose to explode instead.

From her position on the forest floor, reeling from the effects of the lightning strike, Bethany got to watch as the three novice sisters underestimated their own combined power and shattered the rock into thousands of shards.

For the hooded figures, the effect was devastating. Tiny slivers of stone came through the trees and shrubs like a claymore mine exploding. The spells they were conjuring, believing they were about to finish off the old lady now that she was down, were gone in an instant, snatched away amid cries of pain and terror.

The clap of thunder that accompanied the exploding rock faded away into the distance, reverberating off nearby buildings until it could no longer be heard and an eerie silence settled over the woods.

Cassie could barely believe her eyes. Had they truly done that? She intended to throw the rock, hoping the blunt projectile would disrupt and annoy. Instead, it had ended the fight in one shot.

Or so she thought.

Not all the hoods were out of the fight after all. As some of them clambered back to their feet, cries of pain and general cursing filled the air as multiple hoods took the Lord's name in vain.

'We've gotta go!' Jennifer insisted, tugging at Cassie's sleeve. 'Right now, Cassie!' she insisted.

'No!' Cassie argued. 'We've got to help Bethany.'

Naomi and Jennifer both knew their sister was right, but to get to the old lady they would need to run past their attackers, getting closer to them than they already were. The men in hoods who were getting back to their feet were already drawing fresh ley line energy.

If they didn't run now, the sisters each questioned whether they would get another chance at escape. Caught by momentary indecision – their need to help Bethany fighting against the urge to escape – another glance made the choice easy.

Bethany was no longer anywhere in sight.

Chapter 24

Detective Michelle Stevens was just one of a dozen cops to arrive at the high school with her lights on and her sirens wailing. The message from dispatch was to get there as fast as possible. When Michelle heard it was her daughters' high school her right foot got about as heavy as it could.

Details of what they were rushing into were vague. The school reported a freak weather anomaly and Michelle could see it through her windscreen as she sped in that direction, directly above the high school, and stretching out to cover an area of possibly a mile or more, a thick black cloud hovered. It was unaffected by wind, the clouds everywhere else continuing to move westward.

That something magical was happening at the school was not in question in Michelle's mind and it filled her with horror.

Police cars converged on the school gates, forced to slow so they could weave through the evacuating students and staff. The principal had not hesitated to order everyone to leave the school grounds, a loud speaker message to go home was all it took.

Abandoning her car directly in front of the school entrance, Michelle raced to join a growing squad of officers who were looking for direction. Just as she joined them, a shout came from behind and they twisted to see a uniformed lieutenant approaching.

The officers, all in uniform except Michelle, looked to the senior man for orders.

Children and faculty members were still racing from the school, spewing out of the entrance just a few yards away. The stream of people was dwindling mercifully, most having already escaped the school grounds.

Ushering the school secretary, a woman in her late sixties out of the door, with his arm around her to hurry her along, Principal Geoffrey Blair paused to speak to the cops.

'There's something happening over on the sports pitches!' he shouted. 'We can see lights flashing between the trees and there was an enormous bang just a few moments ago. After that it went silent. I can't tell you what it is, but if you're going over there then I pray God goes with you.'

Without a further word, he carried on his way, escorting Mrs Velvik to get her to safety.

With a determined grimace, the captain gave the order to draw weapons. They had no idea what they were walking into, but even though no one said it, they all believed there was a supernatural on the school grounds. It was their job to face whoever it was, and none of them would voice the fear they felt, but they knew what had happened to three of their colleagues already and it filled their thoughts as they advanced.

Fanning out and approaching in a line spread across the sports field, a dozen cops with their sidearms drawn walked steadily toward the woods.

Had any of them chosen to look to the far left, they might have seen three figures sneaking behind the bleachers.

The sky above them was beginning to lighten, as the cloud sitting over the school began to break up. Michelle noticed, but did not know what to make of it. Was this a good thing? Did it indicate that they had missed whatever was happening? She dearly wanted to phone her daughters and find out where they were, but she was walking into potential danger and the officers to her left and right needed her to be focused on the task at hand.

Chapter 25

The school grounds were an apocalyptic wasteland when Cassie, Naomi, and Jennifer arrived back among the buildings. Everyone had fled, that much was obvious. But what did they do now?

There was no sign of anyone, but they had heard the police sirens approaching. It had sounded like dozens of them, so surely now the school grounds were swarming with cops. That their mother might be among the officers responding had occurred to them.

Should they leave the school grounds? Or would leaving now when there was no one else around make them easy to spot? How would they explain where they had been? Their clothes were muddy, they had bits of leaves and twigs in their hair, and there was a cut to Cassie's face.

But then again, would it be worse if the police found them still lurking in the school grounds? Would that then make the cops suspicious? Would they instantly assume the girls were involved? The police had to know that the school had just been the site of a massive magical battle. How could they not?

'I told you Bethany was on our side,' Cassie chose their brief moment of quiet to rub her sisters' noses in it. 'She's not working with the hoods.'

'Yes, yes, well done, Cassie. You were right all along,' drawled Naomi.

Breaking them up before they could start fighting, Jennifer said, 'Hoods, girls. Not just one hooded figure like we thought. How many were there? Twenty?'

Refocused by Jennifer's words, Naomi and Cassie looked inwards at their sister.

'What is it that they want?' Cassie asked. It was the most pertinent question, and all three girls knew it. The spokesperson for the gang had made it very clear that their master, which the girls had yet to identify from the twenty figures who attacked them, wanted them to join their gang. He spoke of events to come, hinting that the October 12th global supernatural event was the start of something.

'He talked about supernaturals ruling,' Naomi reminded her sisters.

'He was talking about demons and angels,' Bethany remarked, coming around the corner to join the sisters where they huddled in the lee of a building on the northern edge of the school grounds.

The three girls were startled by the sudden appearance of another person, then reacted in a mixed manner upon seeing who it was.

Naomi was brimming with questions, but still felt wary of the old lady as she approached them. Had she come to their rescue, and if so, what was her motivation? Did she also want the girls to join her because there was some magical battle for control of the planet coming?

Cassie felt nothing but joy upon seeing Bethany once more. She wanted answers on how it was that the lady had gone missing all those years ago and was here now when she should be long dead. She rushed to her, pulling the old woman into a hug, and laying her head upon Bethany's shoulder as she wrapped her arms around her.

Jennifer's dominant emotion was fear. Bethany was clearly very powerful - she had held off the twenty hooded figures and all the spells they could throw at her with ease until one slipped through. She knew nothing about the old woman and she had always been cautious of the unknown.

Posing the first of many questions, Naomi asked, 'You said demons?'

Greeting the eldest of the three girls with a warm smile, Bethany held out a beckoning hand for Naomi and Jennifer to come closer. Cassie was still touching Bethany, her left arm around the older woman's shoulders as she swivelled to face her sisters.

'I will explain everything, girls,' Bethany promised. 'I do not, however, believe it is a good idea for us to remain here.'

She got no argument from the girls, but she did get a question.

'The place is crawling with cops,' Naomi pointed out. 'How is it that you propose to evade them all?'

Cassie took Bethany's hand and tugged her towards the school building nearest to them. 'We can just stay here,' she suggested. 'It will give us time to think of what to tell the cops if they do find us.'

Naomi didn't like it, but she certainly didn't have a better suggestion. With a small nod of acknowledgement, she followed Cassie and Bethany towards the school building. Jennifer was right on their heels. They passed into the building to find warm air inside and it was only then that the girls realised just how cool they'd become outside.

'Demons,' Naomi prompted once more. 'I know a few things about you, Mrs Cromwell.'

'Bethany, please,' Bethany insisted.

'What is it that you know?' Jennifer asked, frowning at her elder sister because she didn't know anything about Bethany at all.

Her eyes locked on the old lady's, Naomi refused to look away when she said, 'You're over a century old for a start. Except you're not, are you? I think it more likely that you've stolen a dead woman's identity.'

'That's quite rude, young lady,' Bethany replied coolly. 'If you must know, I'm one hundred and thirty-six and I was seventy-three years old when I was kidnapped by a demon called Daniel. I've been in the demon realm ever since, only returning just a couple of months ago when another wizard, a German man called Otto Schneider, set me free along with a few hundred of my peers. I am ageing again now, but was sustained in the demon realm by a curse that froze my age.'

Bethany delivered her answer and looked around, meeting the eyes of all three sisters before pressing on.

'I think we should try to find somewhere comfortable. I for one would like to sit down, I'm feeling a little wobbly as it happens. Then I shall attempt to tell you a number of things that you do not know.'

Naomi wanted to argue, her mouth opening as she almost demanded Bethany start spilling the beans straight away. Decorum stayed her tongue for no matter what else she believed, she could see that Bethany was no spring chicken. If the old lady claimed to need to rest her legs, Naomi could not bring herself to argue.

Cassie was acting as a guide, leading the way through the school with Bethany's right hand hooked into her left elbow. They didn't go far, turning into the first classroom they reached. The chairs were far from comfortable, that not being their intended purpose, but they would suffice for now and Bethany murmured her thanks as she lowered herself into one.

'I missed the part where those gentleman in the hoods were telling you about what was to come, can you explain what they said, please?' Bethany requested.

Cassie got in before either of her sisters could respond.

'Only one of them spoke, and he said that his master wants us. He made it sound like he wants to recruit us. Who is their master?' Cassie begged to know.

'Who are any of them?' Naomi demanded, throwing another question into the pot even though her one about the demons was yet to be answered. 'Seriously, we need to know. They killed a police officer and hurt two more.'

Bethany accepted what Cassie told her with a short nod of her head as if it was what she expected to hear.

'I'm afraid I do not know who they are,' she admitted. 'I have been attempting to ascertain that for some time. Someone is recruiting those who demonstrate any level of magical ability. I have been trying to get ahead of whoever it is, trying to find who they might go after next which is how I found you.'

'You've been watching us for weeks,' Naomi accused.

Bethany nodded, not bothering to deny it. 'Yes, I hoped you would be approached, and I might discover the identity of the wizard behind the gang you just fought. Alas, I could hold my nerve no longer. When you saw me yesterday, I had already resolved to reveal myself.'

The girls were silent, absorbing what Bethany had told them until Cassie asked another question.

'He said the supernaturals were going to rule soon. He made it sound as if there was a battle coming. Is that what was happening on the news with all those skirmishes around the world a few weeks ago?'

Bethany sniffed in a deep lungful of air. Her eyes were cast down at the floor, looking into the distance or perhaps the past as she considered how to answer and explain.

'What I have to tell you will be hard for you to accept. I ask you to keep in mind what you know about me already. You know that I vanished a long time ago and I am here now looking exactly as I did when I was taken. I have lived far in excess of my expected lifespan, and I stand here before you able to wield elemental magic just as you can. You want to know how any of this is possible,' she said it as a statement not as a question. 'Many thousands of years ago, the planet was ruled over by a different race of beings. They were able to wield magic, but not the same magic that you and I are able to conjure; theirs is vastly more powerful. Humans lived amongst them as their servants or slaves, depending on one's viewpoint. Among them was a ruler, what you might call a king. He was betrayed and murdered by one of his sons.'

The frown of disbelief on Naomi's face continued to grow, but she held her tongue. Jennifer and Cassie were yet to form any opinion, listening intently to the old lady's words as she continued to weave her tale.

'In the moment when he died, that king released a curse that ripped all of his kind from the Earth and trapped them in a parallel plane. They have survived there along with all other magical creatures for more than four thousand years, but the death curse is weakening, and they are beginning to find their way back into the realm of man. It started centuries ago, the first creatures remembered only as nightmares and folk legends. Very few were able to travel between the realms, but their appearance resulted in the Grimm tales and the story of Count Dracula.

Naomi made a scoffing noise that Bethany ignored.

Pressing on, she continued her story. 'The earliest creatures to make it back to the realm of man were called the shilt. They are an asexual species who feed on life energy. Basically, they suck out a person's soul and that's probably where the vampire legend came from. The demons followed and it was they who began snatching humans. They wanted anyone who possessed magical ability to act as their servants just like before. It was a status symbol to have a slave. They called us *familiars*.'

'And that's what you were?' asked Jennifer. 'You were someone's familiar?'

Bethany nodded. 'Yes, my dear girl. There is a certain element of evil irony that a black woman just a few generations after slavery was abolished, would be captured and enslaved by a new race of masters, don't you think?'

None of the girls responded to her question, rhetorical as it was. They each lived daily with the topic of slavery lurking in their family's past and none of them wanted to discuss it.

'What I want you to understand is that there *is* a battle coming. It is one of the reasons why I sought you out. When Otto rescued the familiars from the demon realm, we were supposed to all come through together, but something went wrong, and we were split apart. I arrived back exactly where the demon took me in the street outside my home right here in Chippewa Falls. I have been surviving on the streets ever since, uncertain to whom I could turn and trying to come to terms with how much the world has changed since I left it. The death curse is failing. Soon, and I use the word soon because nobody knows when it will finally come to an end, it will fail completely and at that point the entire horde of demons will arrive back amongst humanity. They intend to take over.'

Naomi forced the disbelief from her face as she asked her first question.

'How many demons are we talking about? Is it millions? Billions?'

Bethany shook her head slowly from side to side. 'No. Thousands. Perhaps more than ten thousand. I do not know the exact number, but I do know that it is more than enough, and they come with other creatures besides.'

'Creatures?' Jennifer echoed, her voice filled with the dread she felt.

This time Bethany nodded. 'Yes, child. Supernatural aberrations the likes of which can only be found in your worst nightmares.' She swung her eyes to look directly at Naomi, able to easily identify that it was the elder sister she needed to convince. 'You are assuming the planet's superpowers will come together and their armies and weapons will be sufficient to defeat such a small enemy force.'

Countering the old lady's argument with a sneer on her lips, Naomi said, 'And you are going to tell me that all that combined military power will be swept aside by magic.'

'Indeed, it will,' Bethany replied almost apologetically. 'The combined might of the demons could split the Earth's very crust if they so chose.

They will happily lay waste to entire populations. They consider humanity to be an infestation upon the earth and something they must rid the planet of, reducing it down to a fraction of its current size so that the planet itself can recover and become the home they remember.'

The colour had drained from Jennifer's face as she absorbed Bethany's words. Cassie too was beginning to feel nauseous at the scope of what she was hearing.

'What can we do?' Cassie asked, fervently hoping that Bethany had something good she could reveal to them now, some plan that she and others like her would enact to save humanity. She had said that Otto chap saved lots of familiars - were they going to stand against their former demon masters?

'In truth, I don't know that there's anything we can do,' Bethany replied sadly. 'The most powerful familiars are no match against a demon. One of the things that came with the curse was immortality. It is believed that immortality will cease when the death curse fails and that being the case, it may be possible to kill them. However, that is not to say that they will be easy to kill. Their magic is entirely different from ours and they use something called source energy. Where we can access the magical energy contained in the planet's ley lines, they are tapping into the very power of the Earth itself. They can do everything that we can do and have thousands of years of experience. However, source energy gives them the ability to form and throw hellfire, a deadly bolt of magical energy that kills anything it touches. No human can survive it.'

Jennifer's forehead wrinkled. 'Hold on,' she begged, reaching into a pocket for her phone. 'Does it look like this?' She accessed the clip of Anastasia Aaronson firing energy from her hand and turned the device around so that Bethany could see it.

Bethany's eyes widened in shock as she took in the sight of angels and demons fighting each other in an old, cobbled street filled with modern businesses.

'What is this?' she started, barely able to believe her eyes.

At her side, and watching the same video clip, Cassie replied to Bethany's question.

'It's all over the internet. That's a girl called Anastasia Aaronson. We don't know anything about her, but it was finding this when it went viral that made us admit what we were. Are those the demons you were talking about?'

Bethany lifted a trembling arm to point at the screen. 'That's Nathaniel. I recognise him. The ones at the other end of the street, the ones firing the blue balls of light, those are angels.'

'That's blasphemy!' Naomi spat.

Bethany nodded her head. 'Yes, you would say that. I'm afraid though that everything you believe is about to be proven untrue. The very foundation of every religion on earth is based upon a false memory. Humanity remembers the magical beings that once ruled over them as God and his host of angels. But they are nothing of the sort and no one is coming to save you when the demons come for us.'

The rage welling in Naomi's chest filled her with a rush of blood. She had listened to what the crazy old woman had to say, but enough was enough.

Her arm came up to thrust an accusing finger as she prepared to rip into the blasphemous old hag.

The door to the classroom burst open behind her before she could speak, and armed cops streamed through the door. They were shouting orders and pointing their weapons. Jennifer and Naomi were both facing into the classroom, but Cassie was looking directly at the door when her mother came through it.

Chapter 26

There were eight cops in front of Michelle and by the time she had realised who was in the room, they were already grabbing her daughters and throwing them to the floor.

The force of police officers had entered the woods just as the weather anomaly began to clear and the sky above them lightened. All around was the evidence of something, the cops all on high alert as they moved through the trees.

The undergrowth was trampled - the result of the many feet moving across it, but more than that the ground was ripped up in several places as if exploded from underneath like a land mine going off perhaps. Pieces of trees were broken, and the cops found stones embedded in trunks and holes through leaves where clearly some form of projectile had passed.

It was clear that whatever had transpired in the woods beyond the school's sports pitches was over and the protagonists involved had already fled the scene. Feeling a mix of relief and disappointment,

Lieutenant Garrett believed the chance to catch whoever was behind it had been missed. He wanted the cop killer caught as much as anyone, but he didn't want to go up against a supernatural.

A shout from his right drove a spike of panic through his heart until he heard the report that injured boys had been found.

There were two young men dressed in their school clothes and lying just a few yards from each other. They had suffered burns to their arms and upper torsos and were both in a state of shock.

The call for paramedics to come to their location was instant, as was the search for other injured persons. The first cops to reach the boys questioned them on what had happened and who had attacked them.

Swiftly identified as Alexander Gudeon and Baxter Hayes – two seniors at the high school – they were equally swift to identify their assailant.

'It was an old lady,' claimed Baxter, his whimpered answer echoed by Alexander a moment later. They went on to describe her, both stating that she had appeared on the school fields and beckoned for them to help her with something before attacking them the moment they stepped into the wood line. They made it clear that she was supernatural and had produced the fire with her bare hands. They even indicated what direction she had gone in.

None of the cops had expected to catch her loitering on the school grounds so it was with great surprise when they heard voices coming from inside one of the evacuated school buildings. Cautiously and with their Lieutenant coordinating their movements, they carefully got into position.

They could see three young women in the room along with the old lady who they knew from the injured boys' description was the one they wanted. They could take no risks with the girls - the suspect might be holding them captive, or they might be with her. Once subdued they could ascertain the truth – it was the only safe play.

Bursting through the door, the officers rushed the four women inside the room. The first cop, a burly young man in his first year of service, tackled Naomi just as he would an opposition player coming off the line of scrimmage. She went down beneath him as he wrestled her to the floor, his sidearm pressed hard against the back of her neck.

'Don't move!' he screamed at her. 'Hands behind your back!' A colleague grabbed her arms to wrestle them into position, the cuffs ratcheting home a second later.

Slammed into the floor, the air left Naomi's lungs with a painful whoosh while fear jacked her heart rate up. With her face pressed into the floor, she got to see Jennifer land just a few feet away as she too was piled into the tile.

Before either of them could say anything, tape was clamped over their mouths to keep them shut. The girls couldn't know it, but in their terror, the police were guessing how the magic was controlled. By binding their hands and disabling their ability to speak, the cops hoped they could remove the girls' ability to conjure spells.

Facing the door unlike her sisters, Cassie got to react the instant the cops burst into the classroom. In that half second between seeing the first cops running at her sisters and then catching a glimpse of her mother coming through the door, she had tapped a ley line and was readying a spell in her mind. Had she been given an extra half second her hands would have been up to project a blast of air outwards to push the cops back.

She could see that it was uniformed officers coming at her and she did not wish to harm them, but her defensive reaction was automatic.

Her mother's face and the horror and shock contained within it stalled the spell before Cassie could conjure it. Then Cassie lost sight of her mom as the cops reached her and she too was wrestled roughly to the ground by three uniformed officers.

Her head struck the corner of a desk and that was the last thing she remembered.

Chapter 27

When she awoke a short time later Cassie was outside in the autumn air, lying on a gurney with both hands cuffed to the sides. Confusion reigned until she was able to work out what was wrong with her mouth - it was covered in what felt like duct tape to the tip of her tongue as she squeezed it between her lips. She couldn't lift her hands to get to the tape and when she lifted her head to look down, she discovered the reason she couldn't open her hands was because they were duct taped closed.

Bound and gagged, Cassie's panic rose swiftly, and she began to yell, the muffled sound filling the air around her as she begged someone, anyone for help.

'Hey!' a gruff man's voice snapped at her. 'Settle down there. Struggling will do you no good. No one is letting you out until we can be sure it is safe to do so.

The voice was coming from behind her, so Cassie stretched and twisted in a bid to see who it was. She tilted her head right back until she caught a glimpse of the top of the man's head. She didn't know who it was - just another cop in uniform. Where was her mother?

Detective Michelle Stevens was twenty yards away arguing for her daughters' release and trying very hard not to blow her stack.

'Detective Stevens you will stand down,' Lieutenant Garrett ordered. 'Nothing terrible is happening to your daughters at this time. I understand your concern, but you have to understand this: They were found with the suspect, a suspect who may be responsible for the murder of one of your fellow officers and the terrible injuries inflicted upon two others. Until I am able to establish that your daughters are not involved, they are not getting out of their restraints.'

'They are teenage girls!' Michelle raged. 'They live in my house with me and my husband, the pastor. Do you think we would not know if our daughters were supernaturals?'

'I do not care what you think you know, Detective. Until I can prove otherwise, your daughters will be considered highly dangerous. Now you can calm down and help or you can consider yourself relieved of duty.' Lieutenant Garrett fixed Michelle with a questioning look that invited her to challenge him. He had all the authority he needed to remove her from the scene and that would cut her off completely from her three girls.

Michelle had no idea what they were doing with the old woman or who she might yet prove to be. That she attacked and injured two school students was not being questioned, but Michelle could not believe for one minute that her daughters had played any part.

If she wanted to argue any further, she was denied the chance by a disturbance erupting to her right. Facing her, Lieutenant Garrett twisted to his left so they were both facing in the same direction and could see what was happening. All around them police officers were backing away and drawing their sidearms once more.

When a gap parted, Michelle saw what everyone was getting so excited about. The old lady, who a moment ago was gagged and bound just like her daughters, was now standing on the asphalt in front of the school where they had all gathered. Her cuffs were gone, and she was peeling the duct tape away from her face.

'Don't move!' more than one cop shouted.

Other voices bellowed, 'Raise your hands!' or 'Get on the ground!'

The old lady did none of those things. Frightened cops were reacting, and things were happening too fast for anyone to regain control before the first shot was fired.

The bullet came from the gun of a young officer called Mark Weirsbaski. He hadn't meant to pull his trigger, but the safety was off and the shouting from all around him ended in the slight twitch of his right index finger.

It hit an invisible wall of energy right in front of the old lady's chest and ricocheted off into the sky.

The thunderclap of the shot, and the shock of it failing to meet its mark stilled everyone for an instant.

Bethany moved her right hand in an almost imperceptible motion. It meant nothing to the cops around her but when the first of them yelped in pain and dropped his weapon, the sisters knew what she was doing.

In quick succession, all the cops had to drop their weapons or put them down. Several were wearing gloves which were smouldering from the heat Bethany had pushed into the steel of their sidearms.

With terrified faces glaring in her direction, Bethany spoke in a soothing tone.

'I can assure you there is no reason for alarm. I will come quietly, if that is the correct term to employ. Please do not expend any further bullets. I can assure you none of them will reach their mark. I am not resisting arrest, but I am an old lady and I do not feel like wearing handcuffs today, thank you very much.'

All around her, stunned cops exchanged glances. What were they supposed to do now?

Acknowledging that she had the floor for the time being at least, Bethany said, 'You can let the three young ladies go too, if you wish. I was hoping to kidnap them, but you interrupted me before I could. I don't suppose I shall get a second chance.'

From her position on the gurney next to the aid car, Cassie raised her head. What on earth was Bethany saying?

Naomi and Jennifer were having similar thoughts, and similar reactions, neither of them able to speak either. They were positioned out of sight of Cassie and of each other where the cops felt they could best control them.

'No doubt you have some questions for me at the police station,' Bethany remarked. 'Shall we go? I'd really rather like to get out of the cold.'

Lieutenant Garrett, utterly bewildered by this latest turn of events, was trying to rally his brain cells to come up with what he was supposed to do next. His captain was en route to get to their location and would arrive at any moment. However, Captain Frazier would expect a report the moment he arrived and to hear that Garrett had it all under control already.

While the cops wrestled with the latest turn of events, down by the waterfront the hoods were listening to their master.

Chapter 28

'Three girls! I send all of you against three little girls and you come back empty handed!' the words echoed around the room, the speaker raising his voice to match the anger he felt.

'Master, they had help,' a voice protested from the sea of bowed heads surrounding a singular hooded figure.

With their heads down, none of them saw the flick of their master's hand as his anger boiled over. The owner of the lone voice was lifted from the floor and thrown like a ragdoll against the wall five yards behind him.

The victim cried out in pain and fell to the floor groaning. No one else in the room moved. They dared not. They knew their powers were developing fast, but they would never be a match for the one who had found and trained them. They had been sent to recruit the three girls, that was their masters desire, and they had returned empty handed.

No one spoke, they were all too afraid of the repercussions it would bring. Instead, they waited.

'Who? Who is it that helped them?' their master demanded to know.

From his kneeling position, Robbie Cameron raised his head.

'It was an old woman, Master. I did not recognise her, but she was powerful. She was able to deflect our conjurings, and she was fast, Master. She held us all off with ease.'

The boys' master had been about to scoff at their feeble attempt to lie to cover up their abject failure, but the words died in his mouth. He had not taught them about defensive spells. So how could they know if they had not seen one for themselves?

'Describe her to me,' he instructed.

With the master's eyes trained only on him, Robbie swallowed hard and attempted to clear his throat so he might speak.

'She is an old woman, Master. In her seventies or maybe eighties. Of African descent with greying hair.'

'Was she tall or short?' the master interrupted.

Robbie gulped and provided the answer, 'She was short, Master. Maybe five feet and three inches. She had a slight build, bordering on skinny even.'

One place to Robbie's left, Ethan pulled back his hood and spoke up, 'She was there to protect the girls, master.'

With a flick of his hand, the master sent Ethan flying across the room as well.

Without looking his way, the master said, 'I did not ask for your opinion.' He turned away, taking his eyes from the insignificant pups he was training. Their ability to wield elemental magic was puny, and he wasn't sure he had enough time to train any of them to a level where they would be of real use to him. They would make fine foot soldiers though. Now that he was back in the mortal realm, he would age once more. The demons would come, he knew that, but would they come before his natural lifespan expired?

That was the question on which he was basing all his strategy. When Daniel the demon came for him that night, he hadn't known what his powers were. His own mastery of the elements was nothing short of infantile at that point in time, but he had used what he could do to further his career as a criminal.

Jake Starr had been stealing since he could count his age with one hand. Snatched from the mortal realm to be a demon's slave in the late 1880s, when he returned to the mortal realm, he found it bewildering. Nevertheless, he soon realised that what he could do to manipulate and control the elements gave him ultimate power over all mortals. He could live like a king. He could be rich, taking what he wanted and killing anyone who tried to stop him.

Only two things could disrupt that. The death curse failing and the demons arriving to claim the planet as their own. Or the humans somehow organising themselves to capture him. He could minimise the impact of both eventualities by surrounding himself with loyal servants of his own. That required him to find young, impressionable supernaturals, but those he had found thus far, such as the young boys assembled in the room, had limits to their ability.

But then he had spotted the three girls. Sisters with such untapped depth to their powers that he knew he had to recruit them. He would take them against their will, and he would terrify them first, bending them into supplication so they could not imagine disobeying his will. It would take them years to reach their potential but with his training they would become seriously powerful.

If the demons came it wouldn't matter how strong his students became – they would perish in an instant against Beelzebub and his minions. However, until that happened, against humans ... mere mortals would cower in Jake's presence. With an army at his disposal, he would be untouchable, and it was going to start right here in Chippewa Falls.

Limiting his exposure was a guiding principle, but staying behind when he sent the boys to do his bidding resulted in their failure. Had he gone himself, the three sisters would be his now.

Or would they? If the story of the old lady was true, and he knew in his heart that it was, then he had a new problem.

If there was another familiar in town, he would have to deal with her first. It was that or move on to avoid her and he would never consider such a cowardly approach.

Leaving the boys on their knees, he left the room to consider what his new strategy might be.

Chapter 29

Lieutenant Garrett remained suspicious enough to refuse to release Michelle's daughters despite their mother's continuing protests and the old woman's claim they were innocents. The old lady remained in their custody, though the term could only be applied loosely now since it was clear she could come and go as she pleased and there was little they could do about it.

His boss arrived, Captain Frazier taking over about a second after he stepped out from his car. Michelle wasted no time in getting in his face to address her concerns.

'Sir, my daughters are victims here, not part of the problem.'

'We don't know that, Sir,' Lieutenant Garrett spoke over the top of Detective Stevens. 'They were found with the suspect, Sir. She claims to have been holding them captive, but there was no sign to indicate that that is true.'

'My daughters are not supernatural's, Sir.' Michelle was doing her best to remain calm when what she really wanted to do was punch Lieutenant Garrett in the face.

Captain Frazier pushed past both officers, making his way towards the gathered cops and the persons taken into custody.

Talking over his shoulder, he said, 'I hear your concerns Detective Stevens. I will address them in due course. Needless to say, if your daughters have played no part in this they will be released as swiftly as is safe to do so.'

'But...' Michelle attempted to argue once more only to be cut off immediately by the captain.

'Are your daughters in need of medical attention? Are they currently in a life-threatening situation, Detective?' he paused long enough to wait for Michelle to answer his rhetorical question, and when he could see that she wasn't going to argue any further he nodded his head. 'Very well then. I think we all have work to do. Let's get to it.'

Tracked by the eyes of almost all the cops assembled in front of the high school, Bethany strolled across to a police car and paused at the back door.

'Is it alright if I wait inside? I rather think it might be warmer in there.' Her face spread with a warm smile as she looked about for someone helpful to let her into the police cruiser.

Captain Frazier couldn't believe his eyes.

'That's our suspect?' he blurted. 'Why isn't she in custody, man?' he aimed the question at his immediate subordinate, Lieutenant Garrett.

Garrett shrugged apologetically and mumbled, 'She was, Sir. But she decided that she didn't like that, so she removed her cuffs and her gag. She is offering to come peacefully,' he pointed out and then briefly regaled his superior with the story of the bullet that ricocheted off an invisible shield.

Captain Frazier insisted on a complete search of the school grounds and the school buildings, drawing more officers in from the city to assist. His boss was on the way, and he wanted to be able to reassure the chief that everything tenable had already been done to secure the area.

While that was happening, he sent Lieutenant Garrett back to his precinct with Bethany in theoretical custody at least. The three teenage girls who were found with the old lady were also escorted to the station, Cassie being given the all-clear by the paramedics before she was loaded into the rear of another police cruiser.

Michelle rode with Cassie, fuming that her daughters were still being treated as suspects and being dangerously vocal about it. It might create backlash, but concern for her career and her standing amongst her peers were the last things on her mind.

At the station she fought against anyone who attempted to get near her daughters. When the car she was in with Cassie pulled up, there were officers in uniform taking Naomi out of the car in front. A rage-filled warning from the feisty detective was all it took to make them back off, their hands in the air to show compliance.

Gathering her daughters together, their hands still bound and the hastily applied tape gags still in place, she marched them into the station through the back doors reserved for suspects and detainees.

'It's going to be okay, girls,' she assured them repeatedly. 'I will force the chief to accept none of you are supernatural and we will all be home drinking hot chocolate in front of the fire before you know it.'

The sisters didn't know whether to believe their mother, or whether their mother even believed what she was saying. She planned to cut out everyone and appeal directly to the highest police authority in the city – it sounded like a sensible tactic, but would they be released? All it needed was for one of the men inside the hoods to claim they saw the girls performing magic. No one would question it.

Naomi, Jennifer, and Cassie exchanged nervous glances as their mother led them to a door marked 'Interview Room Two'.

Just before they got to it, a tall man stepped into their path to block it.

'You want something, Alan?' Michelle asked.

'You can't put them in there together,' he stated firmly. 'Word is that your daughters are all witches.'

Michelle lashed out with a foot that caught the man between his legs. He clearly hadn't expected Michelle to react violently, but the mumma bear was angry and no one was going to mess with her cubs.

While her daughters gasped inside their duct tape gags and stared with shocked eyes at the man now on his knees, Michelle twisted around to glare at the faces all looking her way.

'My girls are victims. Do you hear me? They were being held captive, but all y'all are so scared you want to treat them like they might kill you just because they were in the vicinity of a woman who can do magic. Anyone else want to try to stop me from making my little girls feel safe?'

No one spoke. No one moved. Except Detective Alan Grant who had been dumb enough to challenge her and was now groaning at her feet.

Turning back toward the interview room, she nudged her fellow detective to one side with a foot and marched past him with her daughters in tow.

Lakota appeared in the doorway a moment later.

'You need a hand with anything, Michelle?' he asked.

Detective Stevens snapped her head around, but relaxed when she saw who it was. Now in the interview room, the one place she could think of to put her girls that wasn't a cell – no way was she letting anyone lock her daughters up – she needed to leave them to find the chief, but also knew that she couldn't.

'Lakota,' she sagged with relief. 'Thank goodness for you. Can you stay with my girls?' she begged. 'I have to see the chief. Someone has to get their brain in gear or I'm going to do something drastic.' She was removing the duct tape from Cassie's mouth and planned to remove the gags and cuffs from all three of her daughters before she left the room.

Lakota joined in, removing Jennifer's cuffs, and then starting on the duct tape wound around her hands to keep them shut.

The door to the interview was shut, but it opened again, the very man Michelle wanted to see appearing in the doorway.

'Chief,' she stuttered, wanting to start arguing for her daughters to be released, but he held up a hand to silence her.

Chapter 30

SIA Headquarters, Washington DC

Word of the attack at a high school in Wisconsin reached the ears of Ayla Pendragon at the SIA building in Washington.

'You said a weather anomaly?' she questioned the man delivering her report, a human called Bret Landing.

'That's correct, Mrs Pendragon. I have no visuals at this time, but I expect them soon. The local police have made four arrests, an elderly lady by the name of Bethany Cromwell – she is almost certainly a former familiar,' he told her about the record he'd been able to find of a woman by that name going missing in the forties. He had the advantage over the police of knowing what to look for when it came to odd cases such as this one. 'There're also three sisters, all teenagers. Details are sketchy, but they are either working with Mrs Cromwell or Mrs Cromwell was trying to stop them from hurting people. There have been a few incidents in that town in the last couple of weeks.'

'No need to worry about the visuals,' she replied dismissively, her thoughts already elsewhere.

When she escaped the demon realm with Otto Schneider, hundreds of familiars had gone with them. Otto wanted to free as many as possible and had found a way to break the bond that held them to their demon masters. They had been caught in the act of escape by a demon called Daniel – a sort of slave trader who spent his time finding and capturing humans to train and then gift to his fellow demons in return for their favour.

Ayla felt her top lip curl as his face swam into her consciousness. He had invaded her home, terrified her children, and almost killed her husband. If Otto hadn't been with him – himself a slave to Daniel at the time - the demon might have killed her whole family just to get her. All because she could wield elemental magic.

They had escaped the demon realm, but it had all been so rushed that no one checked who was among the familiars Otto rescued. Only afterward, when she found the first few of those who arrived back in the mortal realm, was she able to begin piecing together a list of those she needed to find.

Otto was off doing his own thing, unreachable unless she was in desperate need – something to be kept in reserve until she truly was – so she was the one heading up the identification and collection of the escaped familiars.

In theory they were all highly dangerous individuals. Their mastery of the elements made them into gods among the vanilla humans all around them. If they chose to wield their power against their fellow man, it would take people like the SIA agents to stop them.

Ayla doubted that would be necessary for all but a very few of those who were rescued. Some of the familiars had already come forward, identifying themselves cautiously to the authorities because they had nowhere to live and were terrified by the modern technology they couldn't hope to understand. The SIA picked up two familiars after they returned home to find their former spouses living with someone else. One had gone berserk and killed his wife and her new husband. He had been in the demon realm for less than five years. Long enough for his wife to have moved on, but not in his opinion.

The greatest threat though, came from a small handful of familiars who were considered to be likely to wield their power for their own gain. With the help of the familiars already found and recruited to the SIA, she had a short list of ones to be most concerned about.

On that list was a man who had shown great dexterity when it came to controlling the weather. It was just a combination of air and water spells when all was said and done, but the scale of it proved to be too much for most wizards.

Linking the death of a cop, reports of other clearly magical incidents, and now a freak weather anomaly in a mid-west city, Ayla felt she had good reason to believe they had found Jake Starr.

Bret raised his eyebrows upon hearing Ayla's thoughts.

'We already have a pair of agents in the city,' he revealed.

'What?' Ayla questioned, surprise at the news making her response come out harsher than she intended.

'I only just found out,' Bret defended himself. 'It would appear they believed they had found a familiar at work and wanted to get there first. I guess they were hoping to be credited with the find.'

'Get in contact with them and tell them to stand down. They can have the credit. Heck, they can have an extra candy ration and a big, fat medal, just get them to back off. If that's Jake Starr they are up against, they'll be dead before they have a chance to get within a mile.'

Pushing back her chair, Ayla got to her feet and grabbed her phone. She wasn't going to make it home for dinner tonight and needed to let her husband know.

Chapter 31

'They are free to go,' the chief of police interrupted Detective Stevens to deliver the news he knew she wanted to hear. 'I've just spoken to the victims of the attack this afternoon and they both confirmed your daughters were nothing to do with what happened to them.'

Michelle felt her head spin and her vision fog as relief washed over her. She hadn't voiced her thoughts, but she had been genuinely concerned her daughters might possess supernatural powers. It had made her question everything in her life, all the decisions she had ever made, the one time she smoked a joint in college ... what would it mean if her daughters were witches?

Now she could believe it really had just been a terrible case of wrong place wrong time and that evil old lady taking them captive. She would get them home and into the safety of their house. Quizzing them about what happened at the school could come later.

'Oh, thank, God,' she sent up a silent prayer, her head dipped to combat the wooziness she felt.

'We're free to go?' Cassie sought to confirm, her hands still cuffed and bound by duct tape.

The chief offered them a kindly smile.

'I'll need statements from you first, ladies. But, otherwise, yes, you are free to go.' He switched his attention to look at their mother. 'Detective Stevens can I have a quick word?'

Lakota promised to stay with the girls and continued working on the duct tape while Michelle stepped outside.

'*Naomi?*' Jennifer's voice echoed inside Naomi's head just like it had in the trees when they were fighting. Shocked by it, Naomi shot her head around to look at her younger sister. '*You heard that, didn't you?*' Jennifer questioned.

'*I heard it too.*' This time it was Cassie's voice that echoed in Naomi's head and all three sisters were looking at each other, their eyes wide with amazement.

'Hold still, Jennifer,' Lakota begged, trying to work the edge of the duct tape from her hands.

'*What is this?*' Jennifer asked, thinking the question at her sisters. '*How are we doing it?*'

Cassie replied, '*Bethany would know.*' For once, neither sister argued.

Instead, Naomi said, '*She told the police she was holding us against our will.*'

'*Why would she do that?*' Cassie questioned, her voice, like that of her sisters' appearing in her siblings' heads without passing through their ears.

'*So that the police wouldn't detain us,*' Naomi guessed. '*You saw how easily she took off the cuffs.*'

'*Then she deflected that bullet,*' Jennifer reminded them.

Naomi thought perhaps she had the answer worked out. '*Maybe she plans to escape custody but didn't want to have to bust us out. This way, we'll be outside, and she can join us.*'

'*I guess that makes sense,*' Jennifer acknowledged silently.

'Right, that's you done,' commented Lakota as he freed Jennifer's hands. 'You know you girls are awfully quiet,' he remarked, looking at the three sisters in turn.

Cassie almost commented that they were being quite chatty, only catching herself just in time because of course they were communicating ... how was it that they were communicating? She pondered the question, finding the only word that fit was telepathy. Pushing the subject to one side, because finding a name for it really wasn't important, she held up her hands so Lakota could deal with her bindings next.

Naomi made an insistent mumbling squeaking noise, pointing out that she was the only one in the room still gagged.

'I think I better deal with Naomi first.' Lakota left Cassie as she was so he could free Naomi first.

Cassie stuck her tongue out rudely before restarting their silent conversation.

'What are we going to do now?' she asked her sisters. If Xander and Baxter accused Bethany, and they are being treated for burns, then they are the two that I set fire to. We've just identified two of the hoods. What do we do about it?'

Naomi replied, 'Aren't you missing something, Cassie?' she asked, as if attempting to prompt an answer. 'What links those two boys?'

'They both go to our high school, dummy,' Cassie replied snarkily.

Jennifer's voice invaded their thoughts, 'No, Cassie, that's not what she means. They're both on the football team.'

'Just like Robbie,' Naomi pointed out as if it needed to be made any clearer.

Cassie's response was interrupted by her mother re-entering the room. She glanced about quickly assessing what was left to be done and went to Cassie to finish removing the duct tape around her hands.

Michelle had been curious to hear what the chief wanted to speak to her in private about, but had been surprised when he asked her to be forgiving of her colleagues. She wasn't happy about it, but she had to accept that he made some valid points. Lieutenant Garrett, Captain Frazier, and several of her other colleagues including Detective Alan Grant for that matter, were all acting out of character. The chief put it down to the stress of uncertainty and the unknown future they all faced now that they were ordinary cops trying to investigate supernatural beings.

It was all quite terrifying, and almost too much for her to think about. The chief insisted she go home, pre-empting her request because she was going to go home with her daughters regardless of what anyone said.

Although she couldn't hear it, her daughters were arguing.

'We need to go to the hospital,' Naomi insisted. 'Maybe Robbie isn't involved, and maybe he is. Not knowing is our biggest threat. We need to know who it is we're up against. I want to know which one of them is the master. Don't you?'

Jennifer jumped in before Cassie could retort. 'Naomi is right, Cassie. Maybe Robbie isn't involved at all, but we just don't know.'

Cassie growled her response this time, 'You are treating Robbie as if he and I are engaged to be married. I agreed to go on one date with him. I want to find out who's behind this just as much as the pair of you. But, when we find out that he's not involved, you two are going to pay for the pair of us to go to dinner somewhere swanky, agreed?'

Cassie's bindings came free almost exactly at the same time as Naomi's and finally all three girls were free to move and speak.

Michelle pulled Cassie into a hug and kissed her head. Then she moved to Jennifer and finally to her eldest, Naomi, gesturing with her hands that all three girls should come close so she could wrap them all in one big hug.

'You have to give statements girls. Obviously, I can't take them.' Turning to Lakota, all she needed to do was raise her eyebrows.

'Of course,' he replied. It would be my pleasure. I guess we can use this room,' he commented, looking about. 'I just need to set things up. Who wants to go first?'

Chapter 32

Twenty minutes later, the three girls were leaving the police station, the task of recording what they had seen and heard complete. It ought to have been tricky for them to all provide the same story regarding their time in supposed captivity with Bethany, but using their newfound telepathy they gave the same testimony almost to the word.

Not only that, while they waited for Lakota to finish, they spent the time discussing and rehearsing the next part of their plan.

On cue, Jennifer broached the subject, 'Mom, you're taking us home, right?'

Michelle twitched her eyes to look at Jennifer in the rear-view mirror, a ripple of confusion furrowing her brow.

'Yes, I'm taking you home, honey,' she remarked as if any other destination would be utterly ridiculous to consider.

Jennifer reached across the car to take Cassie's hand in hers, a gesture of solidarity as she carefully pushed their mother to reconsider.

'It's just that ... we're quite concerned about the two boys who were injured. Xander and Baxter are in some of our classes, and we've known them for years now, mom. I'm not sure who else is going to visit them, apart from their parents. Can we swing past the hospital?'

All three girls held their breath as they waited to see if their emotional blackmail would hit the mark or not. In some ways their mother was easy to predict, but these were unpredictable times, and they were not sure which way she would go.

Inside her head, Michelle was having a private argument. She wanted desperately to take her three little girls home. She planned to lock the door, put on a movie, and pretend that the world outside could not get to them. She did not want to admit how scared she had felt when she saw them with the old woman today. She wanted desperately to talk to them about it and at the same time never wanting to raise the subject again so long as she lived.

Another side of the argument was the charitable and Christian love she could hear from her little girls. They were concerned more for the boys who had been hurt than they were for themselves, and how could she argue against their desire to check on them?

With some reluctance, she looked at where they were in relation to the hospital and changed lanes.

'Okay, girls, but I don't want to be there for long. It's going to be a quick in and out, I'm afraid. We need to get home to your father too. He will be worried sick and keen to see you all safely back in our house.'

The line about their father wasn't entirely true. Michelle was yet to phone and inform him, and was content that he hadn't heard about the attack at their school yet for he would have phoned her if he had. She was going to contact him soon, now that she had the girls safely in her care.

At the hospital, she used her police credentials to snag a space next to an ambulance bay. The last thing she wanted was to delay getting home any longer because she was looking for somewhere to park.

They were out of the car and walking towards the automatic doors of the hospital's front entrance when the screaming started.

Chapter 33

The automatic doors opened as expected just as they approached them, but the sight inside was enough to stop them in their tracks.

People were running at them, or rather they were running for the doors that Michelle and her daughters were standing in front of. The sense of fear and panic was palpable - one only needed to look at a few faces to see they were all etched with the same horror.

They had to jump to one side to get out of the way as a flood of people burst into the car park.

'What's happening?' demanded Michelle, reaching her right hand to grip the butt of her sidearm. She left it where it was, but she was ready to pull it if she needed. 'Hey! Why's everyone running?' she shouted as the crowd surged past.

Spotting a bewildered looking security guard, she snagged his arm, gripped his bicep hard and used it to pull him from the surge of people.

He twisted around to face her, his feet barely under control. Once he was looking her way, she showed her badge.

'Why are you running away?' she demanded to know.

The man, easily a hundred pounds heavier than Michelle and five inches taller, yanked his arm free of her grasp and started moving again.

Backing away, he blurted, 'There's one of those supernatural's in there! He's killing people!' Then he turned and ran, putting his head down as he fled as fast as his legs would carry him.

Michelle turned to yell at her daughters – she wanted them to head back to the car and take it home. Though it was the last thing she wanted to do, she was a cop, and this was her city. It was her duty to protect the people even if it might be a suicide mission.

However, twisting around to shout instructions to her girls, she gasped in horror when she saw that none of them were there.

Cassie, Naomi, and Jennifer were thirty yards away and running into the hospital through the Emergency Room entrance. They had guiltily abandoned their mother the moment they engaged their second sight and saw the fat bead of ley line energy being sucked up through the ground beneath the hospital.

They were not around to hear the security guard's comment and didn't need him to confirm what they already knew: someone inside was wielding magic. That people were running away in terror made it clear the supernatural inside wasn't performing party tricks to entertain the kids.

'Are we really doing this?' Jennifer asked.

'I want to see who it is,' Cassie replied.

The girls were using their voices now instead of communicating telepathically. However, they all had their second sight engaged, the wide line of magical energy snaking up through the hospital acting as a landmark to guide them as they hurried along increasingly empty corridors.

Naomi, feeling a need to take charge, as she so often did with her younger sisters, moved ahead of them so she could look at them when she said, 'We're not gonna get too close, okay? I don't know who we are going to find, but that's an even broader stream of magical energy than we saw Bethany drawing.'

No further explanation was required. The girls had all seen their own connection to the ley lines increase in size over the last few weeks as they had slowly learned to control their magic. The width of the stream of energy they were heading towards dictated that the person drawing it was significantly more powerful than they were and probably stronger than Bethany too.

Back at the hospital entrance, Michelle screamed for her girls. She could see her car – she had parked close enough – and they hadn't gone there. So where were they? Her heart racing as she fought her rising panic, she screamed their names again.

There was no sign of them, and nothing to indicate which direction they might have gone in. That she couldn't see them terrified her because the car park was a flat expanse of asphalt. If they were not hiding behind a car, which she didn't think they were, the only direction they could have gone was inside the hospital.

How it was that she hadn't seen them go, and what could possibly have motivated them to run towards the apparent danger, Michelle could only guess.

Jostled by more people running by as they exited the hospital, Michelle gritted her teeth and tussled with what to do. She didn't get to choose though.

Two shots rang out, punctuating the air. The already panicked herd of humanity screamed and ran faster, streaming past Michelle and stopping her from getting into the hospital. Two more shots echoed through the hospital, putting steel into Michelle's spine.

She knew a police issue sidearm being discharged when she heard one. There was a cop inside, probably assigned to the two boys who were burned in the woods, and he or she was in trouble.

Michelle did her best to still her breathing. There were no other cops here that she knew of. It was just her. Drawing her sidearm and slipping around the edge of the dwindling crowd of people running from the hospital, she reached for her phone to call in what was happening.

Over a hundred yards away and two floors above their mum, the three girls were nearing the source of magic when they also heard the shots.

Still a pace ahead of her sisters, Naomi put out both of her arms to slow them.

Jennifer cried, 'Someone's shooting!'

Cassie murmured, 'Fighting back.'

Naomi almost said they needed to go back, but the memory of Cassie's argument – the one about their mother being among those who would have to face the supernaturals if other supernaturals didn't, echoed in her head. Mom was here and she would have heard the shots too.

'We need to press on,' she stated as boldly as she could muster. 'Mom will be heading this way. We need to get there first.'

Stepping around Naomi to get to the front and boldly walking into the open, Cassie drew a spell into her hands, calling on air in the belief she could channel it inside the confines of the corridor where it would create a far greater affect.

Naomi grabbed Cassie and yanked her back. 'What do you think you're doing?' she hissed urgently, refusing to let her sister's arm go. 'We're not here to fight whoever that is. We just want to identify them.'

Cassie yanked her hand away, snarling into Naomi's face, 'And what do we do if we are spotted?' She hitched an eyebrow. 'Don't you think it would be a good idea to have some kind of spell ready to defend ourselves with?'

'Okay,' Naomi relented. 'But defence only. Our skills are no match for whoever that is.'

Cassie snapped, 'You're not in charge, Naomi. Being older doesn't make you our leader.'

Getting between them, Jennifer ventured, 'What if we joined ourselves together again? When we did that, it was more than just the three spells combined, it was like our magic had been mathematically cubed to produce something many times stronger than any of us could perform alone.'

Cassie agreed, forcing Naomi once again to be the voice of reason.

'And how did we do that, huh? I certainly don't think now is the time to start trying to produce something we've done once by accident. What if it fails, and the person we're fighting kills us in retaliation?'

The sound of smashing glass ended their conversation abruptly.

Cassie was the first to react, taking advantage of the momentary distraction to get away from her sisters. She darted around the corner and into a new corridor, but she could already see that the person they wanted to find was no longer there.

With a grunt of frustrated anger, she started running, heading for where she believed the person had just been. The shouts of her sisters followed, but she did not slow down. A cool breeze had appeared in the corridor, telling her that the shattering glass sound they heard was a window breaking.

Cassie's determination to see what happened stalled when she spotted the blood on the floor, her eyes widened in horror when in the next second she saw the first body.

It was a doctor, the green surgical scrubs identifying the man as a member of hospital staff. Just a few feet away was another, this time a woman. Cassie could not see her face and was glad for it. The woman was lying on her front with her head contorted at an unnatural angle.

The smell of gunfire was stronger here and there was something else too. Something that reminded her of cookouts in their back yard.

Cassie's feet had come to a stop, seemingly without her instructing them to do so. Jennifer and Naomi appeared at her shoulders, each recoiling at the horrific sight.

'Oh, my God, who did this?' Jennifer mumbled, her voice so quiet it was barely a breath.

Cassie gritted her teeth, the revulsion she felt welling up in the form of rage that fuelled her to get moving once more. Strutting forward, her steps determined though her legs were like jelly, she drew level with the door from which the cold breeze blew and stepped inside.

She had a spell readied by the time she got there, telling herself, even though she knew it was a lie, that she was brave enough to deal with whatever she found in the room.

Bile rose in her throat, the contorted forms on the bed almost too much for her to take in. When she heard Jennifer retching behind her, she closed her eyes and turned away from the terrible sight.

There were two beds in the room, both empty, the covers thrown roughly to the side as if the person in the bed had left in a hurry. The empty beds of course were not what was disturbing the girls. It was the sight of the uniformed police officer that would haunt their dreams.

He was the source of the BBQ smell. They could only guess, but it seemed probable the fire spell had been conjured and used against him. He was almost turned to charcoal in places, and much of his uniform was burnt away, his sidearm was lying on the floor a yard or so from his right hand.

'He came to get them,' Cassie stated. 'The master, whoever that is, came back to get the two boys I injured.'

Neither Naomi nor Jennifer argued with her - they believed the same thing. A quick check of the chart at the end of the first bed showed the name of one of their classmates. It was all they needed to confirm their guess.

Forcing herself to fight against the desire to run from the room and banishing the image of his body from her head, Cassie went around the fallen officer to the smashed window so she could look out.

The hospital was a box shape with a hollow in the middle where a peaceful garden and courtyard could be found. One end of the space was dominated by a coffee shop with tables and chairs if patients or visitors wanted to sit outside. It was all abandoned now, of course, chairs and tables upended as people had panicked and run.

It had to be at least fifty feet from the window down to the ground below.

'There's no sign of anyone,' Cassie informed her sisters.

Back on the ground floor, Michelle was ignoring the order to wait for reinforcements to arrive. There hadn't been any more shots fired, so either the officer had a suspect in custody and needed backup where he or she was, or they were hurt which made Michelle's need to find them even greater. There would be officers joining her soon, but if there was an officer down somewhere in this hospital, and he or she needed her help, Michelle was not going to hide or allow her fear to make her wait.

She was, however, advancing cautiously. The part of the hospital she was in now seemed to be completely abandoned, she hadn't seen another soul for more than a minute and there were no sounds to suggest there was anyone around.

Looking about and tracking her arms to make sure that her eyes were looking wherever her weapon was pointing, she caught movement out of the corner of her left eye. Her head snapped around just in time to see a hooded figure appear on the other side of a window.

He had two young men in hospital gowns with him.

Detective Stevens was inside the hospital, moving along one of the inner corridors, and right next to the garden and courtyard enveloped in the middle of the building.

Had she been looking the right way a few seconds earlier, she would have seen the hooded figure landing, daintily stepping down onto the grass having manipulated an air spell to control his descent. Regardless, Michelle believed she was looking at the person Chris and Sarah described as their attacker.

Her heart rate spiked instantly, adrenaline powering her muscles as she started running. She needed to find a door that led from the hospital into the courtyard. Spotting a sign hanging from the ceiling that advertised 'coffee garden', she sprinted. Gripping her sidearm tightly in her right hand, Michelle pumped her arms and legs to get outside before the suspect could evade her.

Constantly checking to her left as she passed each window, she could see him moving away from her. He did not appear to have any idea that she was coming for him, and she hoped that would give her some advantage. Scenarios played through her head in the few seconds she got to consider what she was going to do.

Could she just shoot him, aiming to wound rather than kill so that perhaps she could have him cuffed before he could perform any magic? How would that look on her report? It went against all of her training and every protocol in the police manual. She could see the man's hands - they were placed to the left and right against the back of the necks of the young men either side of him.

They had dressings on their hands and on their faces. Michelle noted them when she first spied the trio, but only now did she sense what she was seeing. The boys were facing away from her, but she didn't need to see their faces to know they were the two who got burned in the attack at the high school.

They had survived one magical attack, only to be taken now by whoever was inside the hood.

Michelle hit the door with her right foot leading, kicking it wide as she brought her sidearm up to control it with both hands.

'Freeze!' she screamed at the hooded figure ahead of her. The two boys to his left and right twisted around at the sound of her voice, their faces filled with shock. The man in the hood did not turn around, not immediately, but he did stop walking and dropped his arms away from the boys.

'Chippewa Falls PD!' Michelle shouted. 'Put your hands on the back of your head and get on your knees.

In the hospital room above, the three girls all heard the shouts from below and recognised their mother's voice. They ran to the window, looking out and down at the scene below them. Half a second was all they needed to assess what was happening and how much danger their mother was in.

Jennifer sucked in a deep breath ready to shout a warning only to find a hand clamped across her mouth.

The hand belonged to Naomi, who whispered insistently, 'If you do that, you'll get her killed. We're going to have to control this if we want to save her.'

Next to her, Cassie was sucking in as much ley line power as she could, feeling it filling her body as she prepared a spell.

Naomi spoke quietly, but with authority.

'We need to get mom out of the way, that's the only way we can save her. Cassie, I want you to direct whatever you've got at that man in the hood. We know Baxter and Xander are with him, so if they get hurt at the same time, I just don't care. Jennifer and I will attempt to push that coffee stand over. If we're lucky it will form a physical barrier.'

Cassie saw what her older sister had planned. The coffee stand was a mobile thing on wheels. It was designed to move forward or back where it would be stable. If they could make it move, they could use it to separate their mother from the supernatural.

Was this the master they were looking at now? There was no way to be sure, but Cassie suspected that was the case.

Jennifer drew in ley line energy of her own, whispering, 'We cannot let mom see us.'

Cassie bared her teeth as she conjured an air spell. She wanted to follow it up with something else, but had no idea how quickly she could move from one conjuring to the next.

Naomi whispered, 'On my count.'

But it was too late for that, because Cassie was already unleashing what she had in her arsenal. It took effort for Cassie to stay quiet when she released her spell, she wanted to scream as if that would give it extra power. The funnel of air shot across the open space of the courtyard. Her aim was true, but the spell lacked the power required.

Shocked into motion by Cassie jumping the gun, Naomi conjured her own air spell and directed it at the portable cabin set up to serve coffee and other treats. Jennifer was already throwing what she had at it.

Michelle was watching the creep in the hood, he was turning around slowly, his arms up and spread to each side as he rotated.

'I said on your knees!' Michelle screamed, her right index finger twitching against the trigger of her sidearm. Everything in her brain was telling her to shoot now. She had to shoot him, or she might never get another chance. She might not get to draw another breath, but as she watched, the man staggered backwards, something pushing against his body and rustling his clothing and that of the boys either side of him.

The man in the hood snapped his head around and up to see where the spell had come from. He had not thought to engage his second sight, so used to being the dominant force, he was not wary enough to consider that another witch or wizard might be near him.

He was looking in the right direction, but he did not get to see the three girls, because a flare of flame was shooting at him. Just like with the air spell, Cassie was not practised enough to be able to produce the power she required to do any damage, not at this range. The flame hid her from view, but did nothing to the man she was aiming at.

Frozen by indecision, Michelle was about to scream another order when the coffee cabin suddenly began moving. Not only was it moving, it was coming right for her. She was just a couple of yards inside the courtyard and had to look around for a safe escape route as the wheeled menace came at her, picking up speed now that it was moving.

Jennifer and Naomi squealed with joy when they saw the mobile coffee shop begin to move. It was the encouragement they needed to push a little harder. Their mother had nowhere to go, except back through the door she had run out of.

They were so engrossed in watching what they were doing that they did not see Cassie coming for them.

Cassie had watched with frustrated disappointment as her air spell had almost no effect other than to distract the hood. Worse yet, the flame she conjured in the fastest time she'd ever managed, got three quarters of the way across the distance between them before faltering and failing. She wondered if her best effort had even managed to warm the air around the man's face.

As her flame died away, her eyes flared in horror as she saw the hooded figure's hands lifting in her direction. There was a swirling of air like a shimmering between them and she knew that something hard was coming in their direction.

Cassie had enough time to throw her body weight at her sisters. She drove them to the floor of the hospital room before the wall they stood in front of exploded over their heads.

In the courtyard, Michelle stole a final look at the man in the hood as she ducked back through the door, then the mobile coffee place slammed into the door frame and cut off her view completely. She ran to the right, finding another window to look through. Her brain was telling her that the man hadn't thrown the coffee shop at her, but if that was true then who had? Even now, as she looked at him, his focus was not on where she had been, but on something way above her head on the other side of the courtyard.

She gasped a breath, forcing herself to get moving again. Whoever the man in the hood was, he was a supernatural and that alone dictated she had to do what she could to stop him. That he was dressed similarly to the description given by Sarah and Chris only reinforced her intention.

She was terrified and alone, but she was still armed and a cop in this city. Forcing herself to get moving, the sounds of sirens outside filtered through to her ears. There were lots of them - blessed relief filling her heart as she pressed onward with the knowledge that reinforcements were right behind her. She yelled to draw whoever could hear her in the direction she was running.

'In the courtyard! He's in the courtyard!' she bellowed to bring the cops to her. Then she ran on, looking for another door.

Two floors above her, the three sisters, stunned, deafened, and covered in bricks, chunks of mortar, and pieces of window frame, were crawling back towards the door. Their eyes and noses were filled with dust and their ears were ringing from the sound of the wall coming apart right next to their heads. The majority of the blast had gone over them as they hugged the floor, Cassie's knee-jerk reaction to tackle her sisters saving all three of them.

They were battered and bruised though, not to mention partially deaf, and it was time to withdraw. When Jennifer suggested it, neither Cassie nor Naomi argued.

They wanted to know who the man in the hood was, but the chance to find out was already gone. They had been lucky to survive the encounter unscathed and had saved their mother just as they intended. It was enough for now.

If any of them had looked back through the ruined wall, they might have seen Jake Starr taking the two boys from their high school and lifting into the air.

As the cops flooded the lower level of the hospital, shouting instructions to one another and looking for the target they could hear Michelle indicating, Jake Starr and his two young apprentices flew up through the courtyard. Jake switched his spell in mid-air to blast out the glass above them, and then flew through the hole he created.

Chapter 34

Stumbling and coughing from the dust they inhaled, the three sisters found the side exit from the hospital and made their way outside. Now in the open, they looked around for the cops they'd been able to hear inside. They had half expected to find a phalanx of armed officers training their guns on them the moment they stepped outside, but exiting into what appeared to be a staff car park, they were pleasantly surprised to find themselves alone.

'I'm calling mom,' Naomi announced, pulling her phone from her pocket. 'We can tell her we ran off expecting her to be behind us when everyone ran from the hospital.'

'She's never going to believe that,' Cassie remarked.

Naomi narrowed her eyes at her younger sister. 'She will if we all stick to the same story, Cassie. What we've got to say is that we ran, and we hid, and then we looked for her.' Nodding her head to the street they could see beyond the staff parking lot, she added, 'We are at the back of the hospital right now. We can leave the grounds over there and work our way around to come back in the front. It won't take long. Then, we can identify ourselves to whatever cops we find, and they can tell mom we were coming into the hospital from that direction.'

Not giving Cassie any time to argue, Naomi punched the button to phone her mother. It connected instantly.

'Naomi!' Michelle blurted. 'Where are you? Are Cassie and Jennifer with you?'

Pointing to the road and starting to walk, Naomi replied to her mother. Cassie bit her lip and followed her sisters as they left the parking lot and turned right onto the sidewalk outside.

'We're all fine mom. We lost sight of you. We thought you were running with us as everyone ran from the hospital. But when we turned around there was no sign of you. We heard shooting, was that you, mum?'

It almost had been, but Michelle had resisted the urge to fire her weapon against what the courts would identify as an unarmed man.

Michelle was inside the hospital still, joined now by more cops than she could count. Uniformed or otherwise, on duty or off, all the cops within range of the hospital had scrambled to get there. They were combing the lower floors of the hospital wards, and SWAT was apparently inbound to bolster their numbers.

Nevertheless, Michelle believed their efforts were in vain. She doubted the man she had seen was still here. By the time she had found a way back into the courtyard, there had been no sign of him, and the converging cops would have found him swiftly if they were going to find him at all in her opinion.

It was bad news all round. Her report was that the hooded figure they were all looking for had taken the two boys and Michelle doubted the city had seen the last of him. With Naomi on the line, she chose to abandon the search to find her daughters instead.

'I'm making my way back outside now. Where are you?' she asked.

Naomi realised her error at this point. They were only just on the road outside the staff parking lot, and therefore on completely the wrong side of the hospital to the one their mother would expect. In a panic, she lied and said they were outside the coffee shop just around the corner from the hospital. They had ducked in there to wait for her, Naomi claimed. Then with the call ended and her mother undoubtedly hurrying to get to that point, she revealed the news to her sisters.

With a groan, all three started running.

They got to the coffee shop just before their mother came around the corner.

Michelle had started running the moment she disconnected the call with Naomi and didn't stop until she got to her car. There was a police cordon set up at the front of the hospital. That was mostly to keep people out, but the exit road was further blocked by a mobile command unit arriving to deal with the aftermath of the scene - the second in just a few hours to befall the city.

Michelle had to wait until the exit was clear and the mobile command centre had parked up on one side. She then had to show her credentials to the young officer controlling traffic in and out before she could leave the hospital grounds. A gasp of relief escaped her lips upon turning the corner and finding her three girls exactly where they said they would be. Abandoning her car at the curb, Michelle ran around the hood to get to them, pulling all three into a hug.

She stayed like that for a moment, revelling in the touch and warmth of her daughters and clinging to them as if needing their embrace to convince herself that they were real and unharmed. Standing back, she got her first proper look at them, Eyebrows dancing as she tried to work out what she was seeing.

'What in the Lord's name happened to the three of you?' she asked, taking in the grey dust coating their clothes and the tiny bits of what looked like mortar stuck in their hair.

Presenting her mother with a lie they had quickly rehearsed, Naomi said, 'We hid in an alleyway around the corner but somebody above us was throwing things out of the window. We kind of got covered in whatever this grime is.'

The three girls knew their mother wasn't going to let it go at that, so Jennifer distracted her with a request.

'Can we go home now, mum?'

Chapter 35

J ake Starr arrived back at the warehouse he was calling home to find his throng of apprentices waiting for him.

Baxter and Xander were enduring their great discomfort in silence for they knew well enough their master's tolerance for weakness. Jake Starr thought all the boys were weak and reminded them regularly.

When he found them, some were not only willing to accept his gift of training, but were excited at the prospect of all that he promised. However, they soon discovered that they had very little choice. Any who refused to join him, or were foolish enough to attempt to walk away, suffered terribly. He had yet to kill any of his apprentices, but the threat was always there.

If they failed to achieve a level of mastery which he expected of them in a given time frame, Jake would inflict upon them such tortures that they would all work doubly hard to avoid even witnessing it again let alone being the one to endure his judgement.

Their skills had accelerated swiftly, but they knew their combined strength was still no match for their master. They had no choice but to comply with all that he demanded of them.

When Jake discovered the three sisters, he intended to recruit them in the same manner as the boys. However, he questioned if the same tactics would work on them. In the 1880's he would have just kidnapped them, but astute enough to understand why that would draw unnecessary heat in the 21st century, he attempted to employ a more subtle approach.

His boys were going to befriend them, slowly selling the sisters the concept of Jake's bold new world. When Jake delivered his plan, he was pleasantly surprised to learn some of his boys already knew the sisters.

Robbie volunteered to seduce one of the twins, convincing his master that the youngest girl, Cassie, would be easy to hook. It might have worked too had Ethan not stumbled across the twins at the edge of the woods yesterday.

Ethan's impetuousness, the same rash impatience and overconfidence that drove him to rob the pharmacy, ruined any chance of the subtle approach working. Jake might have killed the foolish boy had he not seen so much of himself in Ethan's actions.

Telling himself he was nothing if not adaptable, Jake went back to his original plan to kidnap the girls. The boys could do it. He had enough of them attending the same school as the twins. They could get the third sister later. The cops would go nuts, but that held little concern for the former demon's familiar – he could lay waste to the entire city with little effort if he so chose.

That was not his plan, of course. Chippewa Falls was to be his new kingdom. Jake knew there were those who could stop him, which was why he needed to recruit an army. He was going to live the rest of his life the way he wanted, and his foot soldiers were going to do the work to make sure that happened.

Handing off the two boys from the hospital with an instruction to get them ready, Jake reflected that his harsh methods were paying dividends. His apprentices might have failed to corner and catch the sisters at the school as he instructed them to, but the two injured boys had shown quick thinking in pointing the finger at the one person in town who might interrupt his plans.

He wanted the girls. Not because they were more powerful than any of the boys, but because they were young and raw, and he could mould them. Also, if there were supernaturals in the city, they needed to be under his control, not able to learn from someone like Bethany and one day be able to stand against him.

He would bring them into his fold and bend them to his will. Or he would kill them, which was precisely what he knew he would have to do to Bethany. He cursed himself silently for being too preoccupied to notice another familiar in the city. He was yet to confirm it was her, but he felt certain it was. She was no match for him, but that didn't mean she couldn't disrupt his plans.

There were others too, clearly. He didn't get to see who challenged him at the hospital, but they had to be new to their skills for their attempt at attacking him was feeble. Had they shown more skill he might have sought them out and killed them. As it was, with the police closing in, he chose to return to his hideout.

It was time to enact 'The Plan'.

Barely keeping his anger under control, he thought about all that needed to happen now in a short space of time. He was ready, he knew that, but bringing the timeline forward so abruptly was making him feel on edge.

Approaching their master and refusing to show the nervousness they felt in his unpredictable presence – he always punished timidity – Robbie and Ethan, two of the older apprentices, voiced questions everyone wanted answered.

'Master what are we to do now? The authorities will be looking for Baxter and Xander and that old woman in the woods, Master. Who is she?' Robbie asked.

'She overpowered us easily, Master,' added Ethan. 'Can you teach us how to overpower her?'

Talking over their heads and raising his voice so all his apprentices would hear, Jake said, 'Gather round. Today is a day on which we can rejoice. You have trained and learned and practiced your conjurings. With time, your skills will continue to improve, but events have accelerated my plan and we have no choice now but to reveal ourselves.'

Mutterings rippled around the warehouse, whispered comments of surprise and questions voiced too quietly for their master to hear as they voiced their fears.

'The world is changing, and we will step out of the shadows and into the light. No one can stand against us – you have seen that. Only if they possess an equal ability to manipulate the elements can they hope to challenge us, but they are disorganised, and we are a growing army. Today we will add the three witches to our number and grow more powerful still. The old woman you met today has mastery enough to interrupt my plans, but I will not allow that to happen. I intend to kill her this day and we will seize control of this city.'

This time there were excited gasps and whoops from his assembly of apprentices.

'The authorities are about to be brought to their knees. They know to fear us, but today they will learn just how powerful we are. I will create an impenetrable wall of tornadoes around this part of town, trapping the population inside. Once established, the storm will be controlled by you, my apprentices, just as I have shown you. It will take more than half your number to keep the storm in place, but you will not let it fail,' the threat behind his words was unmistakable. 'I have tasks for the rest of you too, because in a few short hours, anyone who dared to stand against us will have been destroyed and the world will acknowledge a new ruler in Chippewa Falls.'

'Won't they send the army, Master?' a voice echoed out from the gaggle of apprentices.

Jake nodded his head. 'They will, but the soldiers will be turned to dust. When this is done, and the storm is dropped, they can send whoever they want, we have the power to repel them. We will live like gods and the good people of Chippewa Falls will do our bidding. The government will have to accept a new reality. We are stronger than they are and there is nothing they can do about it.'

Chapter 36

Agents Bueller and Wallace were listening to the radio. They had taken a light aircraft to the Chippewa Valley Regional Airport and hired a car when they arrived. Now driving through the city, it had been Debs' suggestion to turn on the radio.

The channel was tuned to something local, but half expecting to find the station midway through a song, they got voices instead and it was immediately obvious something had happened recently in the town. The deejay was chattering in animated terms about a strange weather anomaly and something that had happened earlier today at a high school.

When the high school was named, Debs was instantly on her tablet to find the location for it.

'It's less than a mile from where that robbery happened two nights ago,' she reported. Agent Bueller, in the driver's seat, glanced across at her tablet and she tilted it his way.

The deejay shifted to speculating that the event at the high school had been supernatural in origin, suggesting the weather itself had been controlled by magic. Then there was an unexpected pause, the man stopping midway through a sentence as if unexpectedly cut off.

Debs stared at the radio, the deejay started to talk again just when she was about to start poking buttons.

'Folks, I've just heard, there's been another incident. You heard it here first, folks. I am being told about an unconfirmed supernatural attack at Saint Joseph's Hospital. That's right, folks, this is Mark Levine coming live on Channel 5 where we bring you all the latest news. I'll have more on this developing story after these words from our sponsors.'

Debs' fingers flew over the keyboard, finding the hospital a moment later.

'They're all in the same area. No more than a mile or so between any of these points,' she remarked.

Agent Bueller sucked in a deep breath. 'Then that's where we will find what we are looking for. If it's not one of Otto's lost familiars, I'll eat my hat.'

'How far is it?' Debs asked.

They were on the fifty-three, a long road that bisected the town from southwest to northeast. Getting across town would take them twenty minutes from where they were, but the question then was where to go when they arrived in the general vicinity of the recent incidents.

They had the option of waiting. Once tuned into the local police band, they could react swiftly when the next incident went down. Alternatively, they could go looking, but even employing their second sight, finding the person they wanted in a city the size of Chippewa Falls was more than hopeful.

The answer to their dilemma arrived in the form of a phone call before either one could voice a suggestion.

Punching the button on the radio to turn it off and fishing her phone from an inside jacket pocket, Debs held it in front of her face to see who was calling.

With surprise in her tone, she told agent Bueller, 'It's Ayla Pendragon.' Thumbing the button to connect the call, she said, 'Agent Wallace.'

There was a surprising amount of noise at the other end, forcing Debs to strain her hearing when a muffled voice shouted at her.

'Agent Wallace, this is Ayla Pendragon. Are you already in Chippewa Falls?' Ayla was having to shout and doing her best to hold her hair in place as the downwash from the helicopter did its best to whip it about and drown out her voice.

With a questioning glance at her partner, Debs Wallace replied, 'Yes, we touched down just less than an hour ago. We're crossing the city now. There's just been another incident here, possibly two.' she reported.

Ayla shouted in reply, 'Yes, I know. I'm mobilising as many agents as I can right now. I should be there myself in less than two hours. I believe the familiar at the centre of this might be Jake Starr.'

The name didn't mean anything to the two agents in the car. There were hundreds of missing familiars and one of the SIA's highest priority tasks was to track them down. Information regarding the individual familiars was sketchy. There were very few photographs, except in cases where the familiar in question had been taken in the last couple of decades.

'Jake Starr,' Debs repeated the name.

Ayla waved to Bret Landing who was shouting to let her know the pilot was burning fuel and ready to take off. It was time to go, but not before she delivered the news she had for Wallace and Bueller and a warning she knew they deserved.

'He's dangerous,' Ayla reported. 'If this is Jake Starr, do not attempt to take him yourselves. He is powerful and he was a criminal before he was taken to the demon realm. He is almost certainly behind the recent murder of a police officer there. One other thing,' she shouted to make sure she could be heard. 'The police arrested a woman earlier. They think she's behind the attack on the high school, and perhaps she is. I'm trying to find out more about her. All I know at this moment is her name - Bethany Cromwell, and that she is definitely one of the familiars Otto rescued. I've reached out to try and find out more about her, but I cannot yet say if she might be working with Jake Starr or not. Go to where they have her in custody and make sure you detain her. I repeat, do not attempt to take on Jake Starr by yourselves. There will be thirty SIA agents in Chippewa Falls in just a couple of hours.' She gave them the address for the police station where Bethany Cromwell was being held and said she had to get going.

Debs made it clear they understood their instructions and ended the call, allowing Ayla to get to her helicopter.

In the silence that followed, Debs bit her lip. They were the first ones to arrive in the city and the acknowledgement for finding the familiar was to be theirs. This was good, after all it was why they'd rushed to get out of Washington DC. However, this was not going to be the simple collection of a friendly supernatural they'd been hoping for.

Agent Bueller's focus was on the road ahead as one might expect. However, he wasn't really looking at the road at all. His attention was on the sky, which he would swear was beginning to darken.

Chapter 37

The girls were quiet in the car as their mother drove them home. Or so their mother thought. Communicating telepathically the sisters were having a full-blown conversation.

'*Whoever that was, we haven't met him before,*' Jennifer stated.

Naomi had been about to make the same point. '*No, his display of power was far greater than anything the hoods in the woods were able to throw at us earlier.*'

'*Then I guess we finally got to meet the master,*' Cassie remarked. '*Do you think Bethany is strong enough to stand up to him?*'

None of them knew the answer to that question and it terrified them. It also prompted Naomi to speak aloud.

'What's going to happen to that old lady, Mum, the one who was with us when the police burst into the school?'

Naomi was riding up front in the passenger seat, her twin sisters in the rear. Michelle twitched her head and eyes across to the right, wanting to see her eldest daughter's expression. It was a subject they were yet to cover. What had they been doing with that woman?

Flicking her eyes up to the rear mirror so she could make sure Cassie and Jennifer were listening, Michelle broached the subject that had been troubling her since she first found them hiding in the school.

'What happened at the high school today, girls?' Michelle showed her daughters hard eyes before adding, 'Don't any of you dare lie to me. Bethany Cromwell claimed that she was holding you captive, but that's not what I saw. It looked like you were having a nice friendly chat. '

The lie slipped easily from Jennifer's mouth before either of her sisters could ruin things. She had no idea what Naomi might say, but she knew Cassie was itching to reveal the truth about the three of them.

'Are you kidding, mom? Do you not see the state of our clothes?' She looked down at herself to accentuate the mud and debris that coated her clothing.

Michelle barely even heard what Jennifer said because she was glaring at Naomi.

'What were you even doing at the high school this morning?' she demanded to know. 'You ditched your college classes, clearly and since I don't recall you ever doing that in your life before, there's going to have to be a good reason.' Michelle heard Cassie suck in a sharp breath as she prepared to give an answer, and snapped her head around to pin her youngest daughter in place. 'I want to hear it from Naomi,' Michelle insisted, verbally forcing Cassie's mouth to close again.

Squirming slightly, Naomi glanced at her sisters on the rear seat.

'Don't look at them, Naomi,' Michelle growled. 'I'm your mother and I'm a detective in this town. I want to know how mixed up you are in all of this. Are you supernatural's?' she voiced the question she promised herself she would never ask.

'What! Goodness, no, mom!' Naomi squeaked. 'The old lady has been tailing us for more than a week. Don't you remember yesterday when you wanted to know why the three of us crossed the road? It was because we'd seen her again. She's been popping up outside my college and outside the twins' high school. And we've seen her other places too. That's why I went to the high school today, Mom. Cassie called me and said that she was there, I came to the school and the three of us followed her across to the woods. When we got there, she was attacking those boys. There was fire and flame, and it was terrible.'

Jennifer got in on the act. 'It was truly awful, mom. We were running, but she caught up to us. I don't know how, but she did.'

Cassie's voice appeared in her sisters' heads.

'What are you doing? This was our perfect opportunity to come clean. How long do you think we can keep our true nature hidden for? It's going to be so much worse when mom finds out we lied directly to her face. I'm going to tell her the truth.'

'*No!*' Naomi's voice roared in Cassie's head. '*Bethany took the fall to make sure that we were not incarcerated. She had to have a reason for that. We must trust her. We're going to have to tell mom eventually, but right now is not the time.*'

Jennifer interrupted their mental conversation and the next question their mother wished to ask by jabbing a finger between the seats to point out through the front screen of the car.

'*Is anyone else seeing the sky darkening?*' the tone she employed was filled with dread.

Ahead of them, and quite unmistakably, clouds were gathering just as they had above the high school. Only this time, the patch of dark clouds was ten times the size or possibly more. And it was beginning to rotate already. They were driving straight towards it and before anyone could speak, fat raindrops began hammering on the windshield.

Michelle flicked her wipers to on, the steady swish swish beating the raindrops away as they came in even harder.

'What is this?' Michelle begged to know, though she expected no answer in return.

The girls knew or at least they believed they did. Just as before, the storm was powered by magic. The internal workings of such a conjuring were far beyond their scope to conceive, but each of them understood that it was nothing more than yet another manipulation of the elements.

Michelle's right foot grew a little heavier, counterintuitively going faster despite the freak weather now bombarding their car and filling the road ahead with a surface layer of water. She was on a mission to get them home.

Michelle had asked the question about their involvement with the old lady and received an answer from her daughters. However, though she prided herself on always knowing when the three of them were lying, on this occasion she wasn't sure. Did she want to know the truth? The question echoed inside her head.

What would it mean if they were lying? If her daughters were supernaturals … no, she dismissed the concept as ridiculous. She would know if they were. They were her daughters and she had to extend them some trust, just as her husband remarked.

Wind began to buffet the car as they came fully beneath the surging black cloud. There was a term filling Michelle's mind, and it was super cell, the type of storm cloud that creates tornadoes. Above her head as she stared upwards, she could see the enormous cloud rotating.

Racing onwards through the rain, Michelle watched as the streets began to empty. Traffic was dwindling as people looked outside and chose not to make that journey to the supermarket or the office. Those who were outside were curtailing their journeys and heading home or finding safe refuge. There was a storm coming and it was going to be a monster.

No sooner had she thought that, than the wind began to decrease, the rain was still falling, but not with as much force as before.

From the passenger seat, Naomi asked, 'Did we just pass into the eye of a storm?'

Michelle shook her head. She was not a meteorologist, but she knew enough to give an answer.

'No, that's not what this is. This is something else.' Her summation was accurate, for though she couldn't see it, just a couple of blocks behind her tornadoes were beginning to touch down.

Right in the centre of the storm in his warehouse location, Jake had his eyes closed and was pouring all his effort into creating the largest storm he had ever attempted to conjure. This was to be his master stroke.

Once this area of the city was cut off, he would hand the spell over to his apprentices. They had strength enough to maintain the storm even if they were too weak to create it. Then the world would see him. Whether it was fate that delivered him back to the mortal realm or blind luck, he didn't care, and he wasn't going to question it.

He was back and this was going to be his time.

Chapter 38

Michelle hurried all the way home, braking hard as she turned into their driveway and parking as close to the house as she could get. All four ladies bailed out, running for the house through the rain that continued to fall.

Coming through the door, Michelle was already calling for her husband.

'Richard! Richard! Darling, are you home?' She heard the door slam behind her, the sound of the wind and rain dropping instantly once it was shut outside. Muttering to herself she said, 'That man and his phone. He never remembers to take it anywhere. And when he does remember, he 'accidentally' leaves it on silent.'

A quick sweep of the house confirmed the girls' father was not there, and that only left a few likely places that he would be. Snatching up the house phone, Michelle dialled the number for the church.

The phone was answered almost immediately by Miriam Blackwell, the church verger.

'Pastor Stevens' office, Miriam speaking. How may I help you?'

'Is my husband there?' Michelle barked, knowing that the woman would recognise her voice.

'Goodness, yes, Michelle. He arrived half an hour ago. People are flocking to the church. They're afraid. Some are saying this is the great rapture.' The terror in Miriam's voice was clear as day. Whether she believed that this was the end of days or not, she was clearly disturbed by what was happening around her. She would know about the recent events at the school and the hospital, Michelle had no doubt - they were all over the news. Now this inexplicable and impossible storm had descended upon them, no wonder people were panicking.

Michelle wanted to see her husband. In truth, she was scared too. And though she wanted to bring him to the phone so that she could speak to him, she knew that he was performing his duty to the community - administering to his terrified parishioners. No, if she wanted to see him, she would have to go to him, but what better place for them all to be in such times than the church?

Grabbing her purse from the kitchen counter, she ended the call with Miriam and turned around to face her three daughters.

Suspiciously, they were in a huddle, but they were not talking even though it looked as if they were deep in conversation. What Michelle couldn't see was the battle going on telepathically. They were still arguing about the best way forward. Cassie's vote was to head back to the station and get Bethany. The master was out there, and they knew they needed Bethany if he were to show his face again.

He had conjured this storm; they were certain of it. Not only that, it was he who had sent the hoods to get them. What he wanted with them didn't really matter, because whatever it was, they wanted no part in it.

Their mother's voice interrupted their argument.

'Girls, what are you doing?' she snapped at them, narrowing her eyes in suspicion.

All three turned towards her with innocent expressions.

Prompting the other two to stay quiet with a telepathic thought, Jennifer said, 'Nothing, mom. We were just waiting for you. Is dad in church?'

Michelle continued to eye her daughters. There was something about them. Something about the way they were acting was making all her cop senses tingle.

'When this is done, ladies, we're all gonna have a very serious talk. Right now, yes, your father is at the church. And that is where we're going. People in the community are scared, so we're going to reassure them.'

Chapter 39

gents Bueller and Wallace were running for cover. They had watched the super cell form above their heads, the enormous black cloud filling the sky with dark threat. Lightning arced within the black mass, but still they had headed directly towards it, dutifully obeying their instructions to get to the police station where they would find Bethany Cromwell.

However, the tornadoes had begun to touch down before they could get under the storm, and it was blind luck that Agent Bueller was able to steer through a gap just before it closed. Not that he got through unscathed.

The wind, powerful and deadly, picked up the tail end of their hire car to throw it across the street. It hit a parked truck, sideswiping it before bouncing off. Bueller regained control long enough to put some distance between him and the edge of the twister before the car's forward velocity slowed to a stop.

The car was wrecked, and undrivable. And when they abandoned it, they did so into what felt like the full force of the storm. Defying the laws of physics and nature, the tornado wasn't tracking across the ground, it was rotating in place as if it was a fixed point on the map.

Buffeted and getting soaked, they continued on foot, looking for cover until they found an abandoned car and commandeered it.

Wiping the rain from her face and slicking back her hair where it hung bedraggled in her eyes, Agent Debs Wallace caught her breath.

'I've never even heard of anything like this,' she remarked between heaving breaths. 'This must be Jake Starr's work and that's good for us. If he is conjuring this storm, he won't be able to do anything else. This much effort will leave him unable to defend himself. If we can find him. We can neutralise him.'

Agent Bueller cut his eyes across the car to his partner. 'Our orders were specific. We're here to get Bethany Cromwell, and under no circumstances are we to attempt to tackle Jake Starr or whoever it is that's behind this storm.'

Debs shook her head. 'They gave that order because they don't know what's going on. Look at that storm,' she pointed an arm through the windshield and tracked the line of tornadoes, 'It's all around us. He's shut off the town. I don't think anyone else is getting in. We need to adapt our plan to the situation, Ferris. Who else is going to stop the person behind this?' She gave it a moment for her words to sink in, then pressed him a little harder. 'Think about it. If he is controlling this storm, how is he going to fight us?'

In the driver's seat, Agent Bueller gripped the steering wheel. He didn't want to show how nervous he was feeling - it all got very real very suddenly. If Debs was right, they were now locked inside an impenetrable shield of tornadoes and heading for a showdown with a wizard of immeasurable power.

He had a counter proposal though. If no one else could get in, maybe they could get to Bethany Cromwell and if she was on their side, maybe she could help.

Chapter 40

On his signal, more than a dozen of Jake's apprentices moved in to take over the manipulated air spell. The storm, now that it was in motion, created its own inertia. Like getting a heavy object rolling, all the effort went into overcoming the initial resistance. Now that the storm was in full force, it required far less effort and skill to maintain it.

Jake watched, observing his students to ensure they were sufficient for the task. Then, when he felt he was safe to do so, he released his own control on the storm.

Ethan and Robbie darted in to catch him as their master sagged.

'Master! Are you all right?' Robbie gasped.

Jake had not realised how much the enormous conjuring had taken out of him until he released it. Now he felt spent, and exhausted. Angry that he had shown weakness in front of his students, he flapped his arms at the two boys, pushing them away.

'Enough of this nonsense. Such a conjuring demands a great deal. One day you will learn how complex and all-encompassing it is. I was momentarily disorientated when I released the spell, nothing more.' Stepping back, Ethan addressed the fully-fledged wizard, 'Is it time, Master?'

Jake heard the quiet excitement in the boy's voice. They had a task to perform, but more than that, they wanted to make up for their earlier failing in the woods. Jake knew that it was not their fault, Bethany would prove a challenge even for him if he were to meet her one to one. Mercifully, with his army of students, that would never come to p ass.

He nodded his head. 'It is time. You know what you must do?'

Robbie and Ethan bowed their heads solemnly.

'Yes, Master,' they replied in unison. Eight of them were going, Robbie and Ethan leading the team as they turned away from their teacher and headed out of the warehouse.

Where they were, there was almost no wind at all, and the rain wasn't falling. Such was Jake's mastery of the elements that he could leave the area where he worked untouched while all around him the storm wreaked havoc.

Chapter 41

'Mrs Pendragon,' Ayla heard her name in the headset that covered her ears. 'We're getting reports of a storm ahead,' the pilot informed her.

'So go around it,' she replied, then added a question, 'How much time will this add to our journey?' she wanted to get to Chippewa Falls as soon as possible.

'No, Ma'am, the storm is blocking our path.'

Ayla frowned, attempting to understand what the pilot was telling her before she tore a strip off him. They didn't have time for foolish nonsense. With a jolt, her eyes flared wide – she didn't like what her brain was telling her.

'It's magical?' she sought to confirm.

The pilot shrugged, though in the passenger compartment behind him, Ayla couldn't see his gesture.

'That I cannot say, Ma'am. Chippewa airport is redirecting all aircraft away from the area. What do you want me to do?'

Ayla strained against her seatbelt to look through the helicopter – there was a gap through to the cockpit, but they were too far out from Chippewa Falls to see what might be happening there.

'Proceed to our destination,' she replied. 'But keep me informed if the situation develops.' cutting off her conversation with the pilot she reached across to her right to tap the leg of her assistant. 'Did you hear that?'

'Yes, Ma'am,' Bret replied. 'Do you think it's Jake Starr again?'

Ayla nodded. 'Yes, I do. See what reports you can get from whoever's on the ground. I want to know if any of our people made it into the city already.'

Giving her only a curt nod as a reply, her assistant busied himself with the task of trying to get in contact with whoever there was to answer. Communications from the helicopter were never great, but he was quickly able to raise a pair of agents who had been within driving distance of Chippewa Falls when Ayla had mobilised them.

When his conversation finished, he got his boss's attention.

'Ma'am, agents Farrow and Wellington are outside the city. They are saying the whole northeast of the city is trapped inside a wall of tornadoes. they said they tried to penetrate it, but it is too strong. In their opinion, the only way to shut the storm off, is to get to the person controlling it.' He didn't need to say that the person controlling it was almost certainly inside the wall of tornadoes and thus out of their reach.

Ayla received the news with a tight grimace. Whether it was Jake Starr or not, there was no longer any question that something serious was happening in the city of Chippewa Falls. A magical storm even her agents could not penetrate ...

'What about Bueller and Wallace?' she asked hopefully, 'Anything from them?'

Chapter 42

At the church, Michelle intended to run straight inside. However, they were not the only ones arriving at the church at that time. There were cars in front and behind them as they pulled into the parking lot, and she could see people arriving on foot - battling the elements in their bid to seek sanctuary.

As she watched, the umbrella beneath which Mr and Mrs Bennett, a lovely couple in their early eighties, were hiding, caught the wind and folded inside out. Mr Bennett's frail hand, his grip weakened with age, wasn't able to hold it and the Stevens ladies got to watch as it barrelled down the street.

Seeing the couple huddling together and leaning into the wind while the rain whipped against their clothing, Michelle started running toward them. Jennifer went with her, leaving Cassie and Naomi to help other people out of their cars and into the church.

Many of those arriving were fit and strong, but others were less so and Mrs Dumont was there with all four of her young children. Her husband, a marine, was serving overseas. Working together, Cassie and Naomi struggled to the front doors with Mrs Dumont and her kids, where they found Bob Mercer and Doug Tremaine standing by to help them inside.

They saw why the two men were necessary once they were inside and had to help them get the doors closed again.

The pews of the church were full to overflowing, all heads turning to see who the latest arrivals were. Michelle and her daughters had arrived during a hymn though it was coming to an end as they looked around to find empty seats.

Mr and Mrs Bennett murmured their thanks, keeping their voices low so as not to disturb the pastor's ministrations as the congregation fell quiet and he took centre stage once more.

Bob Mercer, his own family tucked away safely inside the church, touched a hand to Michelle's arm.

'What's going on, Michelle?' he asked. 'Do the police know anything? Is anyone coming to help us?'

'Girls, go find seats,' she aimed the instruction at her daughters before turning her attention to Bob. 'I don't think anyone knows what is happening, Bob,' she replied. 'I guess that's why people are coming here.'

'It is the end of days,' Mrs Bennett interrupted, while crossing herself. 'The Lord is coming to take us all home. Praise be to God.'

Mr Bennet gripped his wife's hand tightly, but didn't argue with her as he led her away to find somewhere to sit. Seeing the old couple coming, Betty Faversham and her husband left their seats, moving to stand instead.

When the Bennetts were out of earshot, Bob whispered, 'I don't think it's the end of days. I don't think this has got anything to do with God at all. I heard about that storm at the high school. My boy is in eighth grade there and he came home terrified. He said there was some kind of magical battle in the woodland beyond the sports pitches. What do you know about it?' he all but accused Michelle. 'My boy said there were dozens of cops there.'

Letting her emotions get the better of her for a moment, Michelle offered Bob a hard expression.

'I was there,' she growled at him, 'and I can assure you the police are as in the dark as everyone else. There're supernaturals in Chippewa Falls, yes. I don't think anyone is questioning that, but I'm not going to second guess my faith. Are you?'

Bob Mercer had been holding something back, waiting to see what Detective Stevens would say, when he asked her the question. She hadn't mentioned what he believed to be a highly pertinent point, so he levelled her with a fresh accusation.

'What about your girls?' he wanted to know. 'I heard they were taken away in police cars and they were not only in cuffs, but they had their hands and mouths bound.'

The hymn had ended, and the pastor was yet to speak so the church was silent when Bob revealed what he knew. Standing just inside the main entrance, Michelle and Bob were at the back of the church, but everyone in the congregation turned their way now.

In front of the altar, Pastor Stevens had his arms raised and had been about to say something inspiring. He was going to welcome those who had just arrived and attempt to once again reassure the members of his community that God was with them.

Like everyone else though, he heard what Bob said. However, unlike the rest of his congregation, he was questioning why his wife would have kept such a thing from him. Almost everyone in the church was swinging their eyes to look at the three girls huddled together in one of the rearmost pews. Those nearest the sisters were trying to back away from them.

Michelle could see the situation going south fast and went into a full cop mode.

'My girls were taken into custody as a precaution, that's all,' she raised her voice to make sure it would be heard by everyone in the church. 'If they were under suspicion, do you think they would be with me now? My girls are no more supernatural than anyone else in this community.'

'Then why were they gagged?' Bob wasn't willing to let go of the subject just yet.

'Are they gagged now?' Michelle rounded on him, demanding an answer to her rhetorical question. 'Are they gagged now?' Michelle repeated her question but this time in an angry voice.

Standing in front of the altar, Pastor Stevens spoke up, 'Let there be no raised voices in the House of the Lord.'

Michelle did not look his way, but held up a single index finger, her unspoken instruction to her husband that she wasn't finished yet and she was not to be interrupted.

She refused to break eye contact with Bob until he mumbled an answer.

'Well, no,' he replied too quietly for anyone else to hear.

Michelle took it as the prompt she needed anyway.

'Exactly. My daughters were treated harshly after being targeted by a supernatural. That person is currently in custody. The police are doing everything they can at this time. I find it needless to say, but if there is a supernatural behind this storm, they will be found and they will be stopped. I want to hear no further talk about my daughters.'

Michelle looked about, making eye contact with as many members of the congregation as she was able. Finally settling on her husband, she realised that she was commanding the attention of his congregation and needed to hand it back to him.

'Go ahead, dear,' she encouraged. 'I'm sure everyone would love to hear what you have to say.'

Cassie, Naomi, and Jennifer were yet to say a word since the accusing eyes of their community had all swung in their direction. Jennifer had stopped breathing for almost half a minute under the malignant, accusatory stares.

The worst of it was that their mother was wrong. They meant no one any harm and would all much rather be without the magical ability they now possessed, but they were stuck with it, and sooner or later everyone was going to know.

Chapter 43

I n his office at the police station, Chief of Police Matt Ericsson was on the phone to the mayor.

'Yes, your honour, we have a person of interest in custody,' he used the word custody even though it wasn't strictly true in Bethany Cromwell's case. 'But I do not think she is the one behind the storm, sir.'

Mayor Seymore Sixbury had a large glass of Scotch in his left hand while he held the phone in his right. He didn't have any ice for his glass, and he hated Scotch without ice. However, it was better to drink it neat than to reveal to his aides that he was drinking in the day again. Sending someone for ice would be a sure giveaway.

He drained the glass and put it back inside the left-hand drawer of his desk where it could not be seen. When he straightened again, he caught sight of himself in the mirror by the door. He knew it was vain to have it installed when he took office, but then he also knew he was a vain man. Was it wrong to check his appearance before he went out in public?

He was handsome and athletic. Combined with a healthy tan, a great smile, and a few right words, those shallow attributes had seen him into office with almost no votes going to the opposition. That he was a veteran of both Gulf wars and had a law degree from Harvard hadn't hurt either.

Now though, he was feeling the stress of office because people expected him to have answers.

'What makes you so sure?' Seymore demanded to know.

Sure? The word echoed inside Chief Ericsson's head. The only thing he was sure of at this precise moment was that he wished he'd heeded his mother's advice and become an accountant instead.

To answer the mayor, he said, 'Sir, Mrs Cromwell is sitting quietly in an interview room. If she's behind this storm, then she's doing it all very calmly.'

'An interview room? Did I hear you say she's in an interview room?' Mayor Sixbury echoed Chief Ericsson's words in a disbelieving tone. 'Why on earth isn't she in a cell, man?'

Chief Ericsson almost laughed at the mayor.

'She said she didn't want to go in a cell, Sir. I would ask you to remember that she can perform magic. She can deflect bullets and I witnessed her make everyone's weapon too hot to touch earlier today.

She released herself from a set of cuffs and removed her own gag. That I have her at the station at all is entirely at her own volition, Sir. So if she is willing to sit in an interview room, I think that's probably the best I can achieve. My question to you, your honour, is who is coming from the outside to help us? Surely, you must be in contact with the governor? What is the president saying about our current problem?'

Chief Ericsson knew it was unfair to press the issue with the mayor, he genuinely liked Seymore Sixbury and had voted for him when he ran for office. Pushing the onus back his way was a method to deflect some of the attention and potential blame away from the police department.

Mayor Sixbury was not used to being placed on the spot and he did not like it.

'You watch your tone, Chief,' he snapped in the chief's ear. 'The entire country, no, the entire world is suffering the same problems that we see here. I'm not hearing anyone else whining about it.' His choice to rant at the chief of police was primarily to do with covering up his own inadequacy. He had done nothing about the supernatural problem in their city. Frozen by indecision, the only thing he had done was work his way through a third of a bottle of fine Scottish whisky.

He had been made aware some weeks ago about a new organisation known as the Supernatural Investigation Alliance. They were heading up the supernatural problem, linking up with units already established in most of the world's countries. Sixbury was given the impression that the world's governments already knew about the supernatural problem before it exploded onto everyone's TV screens in October and had been preparing for it.

A knock at his door, an insistent one, stopped the mayor before he could say anything else. He quickly checked to make sure he had in fact put his glass away and looked across the decanter to make sure the stopper was back in it.

Snatching up a breath mint from the packet on his desk, he opened his mouth to call to whoever was outside to come in, but never got the chance.

The door burst open, the deputy mayor, a firecracker of a Native American woman called Cheyenne Summerhill coming through it with two of the mayor's aides on her tail.

It was her expression as much as anything that stopped Mayor Sixbury mid-sentence. Her face was white, her cheeks drained of colour as she rushed across the room.

'There are men outside!' she all but squealed. 'They're demanding you come out to speak to them!'

The call to the cops had already gone in from the security at the door to the mayor's building. Chief Ericsson was going to find out about it through one of his own men in less than a minute, but he heard the deputy mayor's words clearly.

Sucking on his upper lip, something he always did when he was nervous, Mayor Sixbury asked, 'What do they want?'

'They want to talk to you,' Cheyenne replied. 'There's three of them,' she revealed. 'They said that they are the ones behind the storm, and that they will lay waste to the city if you do not come out to speak to them.'

Chief Ericsson's voice rumbled in the mayor's ear, 'I'm sending everything we've got right now, your honour. Do not go outside.' Across town at the precinct, the chief of police had yanked his door open, and with one hand over the mouthpiece of his phone, was shouting instructions to get people moving.

Back in the mayor's office, Deputy Mayor Summerhill was still speaking.

'He says you have five minutes, Seymour, or he's going to destroy this building with everyone inside it.'

Standing just behind her, one of the mayor's most trusted aides said, 'That was more than three minutes ago, Sir.'

The three faces were looking at him expectantly. He knew they were all going to argue against him going outside, but he believed they also wanted him to do so. There were more than fifty people in this building, and he could not remain inside hiding like a coward when he did not know if the men outside even intended him any harm.

He put down the phone, cutting Chief Ericsson off mid-sentence and a sigh escaped his lips as he opened the desk drawer to retrieve his glass. He saw no need for further pretence, and he was in a hurry now.

Over his shoulder, as he crossed to the decanter, he said, 'Please inform the gentlemen outside that I shall be down momentarily.'

'Seymour, you can't!' protested Cheyenne.

He pulled himself a two-finger measure, then added a little extra because he didn't think two fingers would be enough.

Raising the glass to chin level, he sniffed the liquid as he swirled it around his glass and looked up to meet his deputy's eyes.

'Can you suggest an alternative course of action? They wish to speak with me, and since the alternative appears to be the destruction of this building and the death of everyone within it, I rather think I ought to see what it is that they want. Wouldn't you agree?'

He downed the liquid in two fast gulps, feeling it burn as it made its way into his body. He gave a slight shudder, then with purposeful strides he crossed the room to check his tie was straight in the mirror by the door.

'But what if they mean to harm you?' Cheyenne whimpered her question.

Seymore dabbed at a drop of moisture on his chin, removing it before he left his office, heading for the stairs and the lobby below.

His voice drifted back, 'Don't worry, Cheyenne, these are my constituents. I'm going to shake their hands and win them over with the same smile that got me voted into office.'

Chapter 44

Across town at the police station, all hell was breaking loose. Every cop in the building who was not assigned to an essential task that would tie him or her to their desk, was strapping on body armour and heading for the armoury.

The officers already on the ground in the city could be easily divided into two groups: those inside the storm and those outside. Those outside could do nothing but watch. Most of those trapped inside had returned to the station or done what they could to assist people affected by the storm.

There was a lot of damage, and casualties, but after the events at the hospital, it was unclear where casualties would be taken. Emergency management was yet to kick in to provide them with a new destination where the doctors and paramedics could set up.

Chief Ericsson arrived downstairs shouting orders as he came. They were all about to haul ass, the full might of everything he had available was on its way to the mayor's building. He was fed up being on the back foot. One of his officers had been killed, two had been injured, and now it seemed that the person or persons responsible were making themselves known.

Several gasps and a high-pitched squeal of alarm from Officer Cody Banks, focused everyone's attention on a singular point in the open plan office.

Bethany Cromwell, the detainee who had sat patiently for the last two hours inside an interview room while the cops tried to work out what to do about her was making her way back into the main part of the station.

What disturbed the people witnessing her decision to leave the interview room most was that she wasn't bothering to walk. Instead, her feet were floating six inches off the floor. There were small sparks like static electricity fizzing in her hair, and her clothes were swaying gently as if caught in an invisible breeze.

She touched down lightly onto the floor as if coming off a step and looked around at the assembled officers until she spotted Chief Ericsson.

'I believe the person behind your recent spate of supernatural crimes has announced himself, is that correct?' she asked.

Heads all around the room swivelled to look at the chief of police, since that was where the old lady was looking.

Rooted to the spot, the chief grumbled his response.

'We have an incident on Bay Street that appears to involve a supernatural, yes. Would you care to tell me who it is?'

Bethany held his gaze when she replied, 'I cannot be certain, but I believe the man goes by the name of Jake Starr. I will not know for sure if it is him or not until I meet him. Are you proposing to sacrifice your officers by sending them up against him?'

There was an angry curl to his lip when the chief next spoke.

'We are the police in this town. When there is a crisis, we respond. When the people are in danger, it is our job to protect them.'

'I rather think that will be difficult to do when you are all dead. I hope you will not think it to be hyperbole when I assure you he will not hesitate to unleash everything he has if you stand against him.'

From across the room Captain Frazier shouted a question.

'So what is it that you're suggesting? We should just sit here like cowards and wait for him to tear the city apart? You seem to know a lot about him, why don't you tell us what it is that he wants?'

His question was echoed by a lot of the cops in the room agreeing with his thoughts on the matter.

'As I said,' Bethany replied calmly. 'I cannot be sure that it is him. But I can assure you that whoever it is, they possess a great deal of power and I doubt they intend to surrender. The storm I can hear raging outside is a statement of intent. He means to crush anyone who defies him.'

'How do we know that you're not with him?' Chief Ericsson demanded.

Distracted by the question which she thought to be highly foolish, Bethany failed to notice the small movement as one officer withdrew the tazer she was carrying and in a snap of motion deployed it.

The prongs of the weapon struck the small of Bethany's back. She wasn't aware that such a weapon even existed. Her senses were attuned to the steel in the weapons each cop carried. If any one of them had shown intent to draw one, she would have neutralised them. The tazer though, it was mostly plastic.

Cheers echoed around the station as the old woman the cops all knew to be a supernatural and therefore someone who could not be trusted, twitched and collapsed. The officer closest to her threw himself at her when she hit the floor. In seconds she was cuffed, her hands pulled behind her back and they were discussing whether they ought to hogtie her.

A reel of tape appeared in someone's hand so they could gag her mouth, and the cops blindly removed from the playing board the one person who would have given them any hope against Jake Starr.

As two cops carried the old lady to a cell, the rest of the officers got on with the task of preparing to face the uncertain future they knew awaited them.

Chapter 45

Things had settled slightly at the church. Pastor Stevens was speaking in the pulpit, addressing the congregation with words to reinforce their faith. With Michelle standing in line next to her three daughters, no one dared turn around to look at them.

However, nothing was going to stop the mumbling and whispers that passed between everyone in the church. Suspicion was high, driven by fear and the desire to be able to regain the smallest modicum of control over their situation.

The church was a tinderbox. Rather than being a place of sanctuary or refuge, it wasn't going to take much to make people act in an irrational and dangerous manner.

Bob Mercer was still standing by the doors to the church when they exploded inwards.

The deafening noise that accompanied the splintering of wood and the screams of those nearest the doors silenced the pastor. Everyone's attention fixed on the entrance to the church. Where the wooden doors had once been, now an ugly hole showed the world outside.

The wind howled like a banshee, and rain was still falling. It was so dark beneath the clouds that it was as if night had already fallen.

Through the wreckage of the doors strode hooded figures.

Panic gripped the crowd pressed inside the church. They were hiding from the threat outside, but it had come to them, invading the sanctity of the Lord's house.

Those nearest the doors were trying to get away as the hooded figures spread out in the entranceway.

Michelle ripped her sidearm from its holster. She had never brought her gun into the church before today and hadn't made a conscious decision to do it this time. It was nothing more than an omission - the need to get her daughters to safety causing her to forget that she was carrying it.

She had no intention of shouting a warning this time. She could have brought down the man at the hospital if she had been brave enough to pull the trigger when she knew she ought to. The same mistake would not be made twice.

As if watching in slow motion, the sisters were screaming thoughts at each other. The hoods each had a thread of golden, magical energy seeping into their bodies from a nearby ley line and most had spells readied in their hands. The twisting constant motion of the elemental energy was visible only to the three sisters who each engaged their second sight as a reflex reaction to the doors bursting inward.

'*The hoods have come for us!*' yelled Jennifer, her thought echoing inside Cassie and Naomi's heads.

Seeing what her mother was doing, Naomi screamed her response, '*Mom is going to start shooting!*'

Cassie pulled hard on the same ley line feeding the hoods and screamed out loud, 'It's go time!'

Michelle's right arm was coming upwards, her sidearm lifting towards the hoods as they fanned out inside the church entrance, her left hand was coming up to join the right, to give support and steady her aim. She was paying no attention to anything but the targets to her front, all the sights and sounds around her became background events until an unseen force threw her hands upwards. The first shot exploded from her handgun, the bullet sending down a sifting of dust and plaster debris as it buried itself in the ceiling of the church.

The sound of the shot shocked people as much as the exploding doors and the sight of the hooded figures invading their sanctuary. But as all eyes turned towards Michelle, it wasn't the off-duty detective they were looking at, but the three sisters as they clambered onto the wooden pew and leapt into the aisle.

All three were crackling with power, the energy they were drawing far more than they had ever attempted or been able to claim before. They were motivated now, the danger was right in front of them, and there were dozens of innocent people between the girls and the eight hooded men now blocking the church entrance.

All attempt at pretence was abandoned as the silent argument raging between their heads ended with agreement. Now they had no choice other than to reveal themselves. It might not be what they wanted, but trying to hide had brought the hooded figures into their church. Their community, the people they knew, and their parents were all being endangered, and it was going to stop right now.

Cassie called forth flame into her right hand, her eyes narrowed fiercely at the centre mass of the hoods. They had formed an arrowhead just inside the church. On her left and her right, Naomi and Jennifer were both holding air spells, and the three were talking to each other. They didn't want to fight inside the church, but if they had to, they would force the hoods back outside by using Cassie's fire driven hard by their air spells.

However, the figure at the tip of the arrowhead reached up with both hands to pull back his hood and reveal his face.

'Robbie!' The flame in Cassie's hand sputtered and died as her disbelieving eyes widened.

'*Don't drop your spell!*' Naomi's voice reverberated in Cassie's head. '*Also, I hate to point this out, but I told you so!*'

Cassie knew she was wrong to do so, but she just couldn't believe it. She didn't want to believe it. Even though it made absolute sense, it seemed so unfair that the one boy she liked was her enemy.

Robbie let his hood fall around his shoulders and reached out with his right hand.

'Come with us,' he beckoned, his tone pleading. 'No harm will come to you or anyone else. A new era is dawning for mankind. The old gods will fall, and new ones will rise. That's us Cassie,' Robbie appealed to her in soft, kind tones.

Michelle shoved her way between her daughters, her gun trained on Robbie's centre of mass.

'All of you on your knees right now!' she commanded. 'Any of you so much as twitches and they get a bullet for their trouble.'

Cassie turned to face her mother, lifting her right hand as she formed a new spell. As gently as she could, she pushed heat into the molecules of the metal in her mother's sidearm.

'This is not your fight, mom,' she remarked as gently as she could. 'I know nothing about what is to come, but I cannot let you kill anyone. This is a fight that we must wage.'

Michelle fought against the heat searing her fingers for a few seconds, but with an angry snarl she let it go. It clattered to the stone floor and lay there with a slight heat shimmer rising from it.

From his position on the carpet where he still cowered, bruised and bloody from the exploding doors, Bob shouted, 'I told you they were witches!'

Naomi flicked a look in his direction, making him hug the carpet as he cowered before her gaze.

'Yes, we are witches if that is what you wish to call us,' she replied, her voice loud enough for all to hear. 'However, since the God we all worship permits us into his house, I take that as an indication that He sees us differently. Being able to wield what you all call magic does not make us evil. Only what we do with it defines us.'

No one in the congregation agreed with her, and the mutterings were becoming rumblings and soon turning into outbursts as people shouted their disapproval from within the crowd of people looking on. They wanted to be elsewhere, but were trapped inside the church with the very abominations they sought to hide from.

'Everyone, please!' called the pastor. His arms were raised as he called for a calm that was never going to come. The only thing holding back the congregation was their shared fear of what the hoods and the three sisters might do to them. But they blocked the aisles, spilling from the pews as they looked for any avenue of escape. The pastor could see his family, but he could not get to them.

Even though the clamouring noise around them grew in volume, Robbie could be heard when he repeated his request, 'Come with us. All of you. The master only wishes to help and guide and train. We will be the leaders in the new world.'

Cassie had no idea if Robbie even believed what he was saying. So far as she knew, their master and his students, including the boys she could see in front of her, were guilty of murder, assault, destruction of property, and goodness knows how many other crimes that were yet to be discovered. The storm alone had to have taken casualties.

However, when it all came down to it, they couldn't stay where they were, and if they attempted to fight the hoods inside the church, more people were going to be hurt. They were outnumbered eight to three.

Discussing it swiftly yet silently between their heads, the sisters agreed. Watched by the hoods, all three girls dropped their spells, hoping the hoods would not see it as an opportunity to attack.

'Girls, what are you doing?' Michelle begged as her daughters began to walk towards the hooded figures.

Cassie was the first to reverse her direction, returning to her mother and moving in close to hug her. Jennifer and Naomi did likewise, all three girls enveloping their mother for a timeless moment.

'It's alright, mum,' Naomi whispered.

Cassie pulled back a pace letting her mother go as her sisters withdrew.

Before she turned to go, Cassie said, 'We have no choice, mum, but if we can stop what is happening then we will do so. I'm sorry that we lied to you.'

'We are all sorry, mum,' Jennifer remarked. 'We didn't know what to do, we didn't know how to tell you. We haven't changed, mum, we're still your girls, and we can't explain how it is that we can do this now.'

Naomi took Jennifer's hand and then Cassie's, the three girls spinning away from the mother to go with the hoods. Turning her head Naomi offered her mother a slim smile and a parting comment.

'If God is picking a side in this battle, I think he is with us.'

Ahead of them the hoods were already moving back outside, Robbie and one other waiting just inside the doors for the three girls to move between them.

Michelle remained rooted to the spot until her daughters vanished into the storm outside. Losing sight of them broke the spell, her legs carrying her to the ruined doors where she screamed their names.

They were already nowhere to be seen.

Chapter 46

Agents Wallace and Bueller were on foot again, abandoning the car they found because it was wrecked.

The storm was all around them, but it wasn't coming any closer and it was so dark that the streetlights had come on. They had been, after much argument heading for the police station, where they believed the familiar, Bethany Cromwell, was still being detained. Those were their orders, and they could have got there if the sounds of a battle hadn't reached their ears.

Before either could ask what the rending metal sound and dull whump of explosions were, flashes of bright light filled their vision and a cop car sailed through the air, coming out of a side road to land right in front of them.

There had been no time to stop, so Agent Bueller trashed a second car in less than ten minutes.

When Debs engaged her second sight, she saw a huge channel of ley line energy being drawn through the ground. The sounds of gunfire and explosions left little doubt that the humans, almost certainly the cops, were fighting magical supernatural's.

They didn't argue this time. They could press on toward the station and maybe the familiar there would prove to be on their side, but there were people dying just yards from their current location and they were duty bound to respond.

They needed back up. They at least needed to let someone know what was happening, but they hadn't been able to raise anyone on the radio since they passed through the curtain of tornadoes. They were cut off, and so far as they knew they were the only supernaturals now in a position to do anything about what was happening in Chippewa Falls.

Both of them drew in as much magical energy as they could, tapping into what proved to be a rich source running beneath the city.

The sounds of gunfire were diminishing, the sporadic pops and bangs suggesting that the battle was almost over and there was almost no one left to fight. It could be the case that the gunfire was dying away because the humans were winning and there were only a few or possibly no targets left to shoot at. Neither Bueller nor Wallace expressed their thoughts, but neither of them believed that would be the case.

Far more likely was that all the humans were already dead.

They reached a smoke-filled street and crept along it, going as quickly as they could while sticking to the shadows. The acrid smell of burning plastic and rubber was everywhere, the smoke stinging their eyes and irritating their throats and lungs.

They pressed on, readying spells. Though both carried sidearms, such a thing had little purpose in a battle against another supernatural and would be called upon only as a last resort.

Reaching the corner of a building, Agent Bueller sidled up to it and peered around. Burning vehicles were strewn across the street, the whole scene one of devastation. They had reached an open area approximately triple the width of the road they had just left. To their front was what looked like a government office or a municipal building of some kind.

As the smoke swirled, they saw bodies littering the ground. Whatever had happened, they had missed it. But perhaps in that, there was a slight advantage to be had.

Hissing at his partner, agent Bueller said, 'Drop your spell.' When Debs looked at him with a confused expression he repeated his words, 'Drop your spell,' adding, 'He'll be looking, and he will see us if we are tapping a line. Just the two of us can sneak in and surprise him. He probably thinks he's beaten everyone - look at the bodies.' He indicated the destruction and horror laid out before them. 'We get in close without using magic and then we throw our spells. We will have the element of surprise on our side.'

Debs blew out an exasperated breath. 'Hey, I didn't want to live forever anyway.'

They both dropped their hold on the line, the magical energy within them and the spells they held evaporating into nothingness. Keeping to the shadows, they made their way forward. Burning buildings and vehicles created unnatural shadows, light flickering here and there to confuse. It mingled with the smoke filling the street and gave them excellent cover as they stole forward.

Without magic they could not engage their second sight, so were approaching their target with the belief that he would still be where they had last seen him.

Hunkering down behind a destroyed police van, they peered out, trying to catch a glimpse of whoever was there.

'There!' Debs squeezed Bueller's arm, jabbing a finger in the direction she had just seen someone move.' It was a guy in a hood.'

The smoke shifted, the figure appearing once more, though only for an instant.

Whispering as quietly as he could, Agent Bueller replied, 'Let's get a little closer before we tap a line.' He didn't wait for an answer, choosing to come out from behind the police van in a crouch and run across the road to find cover against another building as quietly as he could.

They knew they were yet to be spotted because no one was trying to kill them. Whether it was Jake Starr as Ayla Pendragon believed, or someone else they were going up against didn't matter at this point. They had a target and could ask questions once they had beaten them.

Fifteen yards away, Jake Starr was inspecting his handiwork. He had the remaining five of his students with him. He wanted his greatness to be observed and recorded. Wasn't that how it used to happen in the olden times? Heroes would take a bard with them who would then sing of their glory for years to come, songs being passed down from generation to generation.

That was what he wanted, and he had lain waste to not only the might of the police department, but also the local regiment of National Guard who had foolishly armed themselves and joined the fight.

He was looking for signs of life, reaching out with his senses to detect heart beats, and that was when he found two healthy ones moving directly toward him.

'Now!' Ferris shouted.

Both SIA agents tapped the line beneath their feet and sucked in the power they needed to fuel their spells. They expected to find a single figure drawing energy from the ground and that would instantly give them their target.

They didn't find one target though, they found six. As they brought their second sight into play, they could see them all at the same time and it caught them completely off guard.

Agent Wallace swung to her left as she detected a supernatural just a few yards away. Agent Bueller focused on one directly to his front and detected another just beyond him.

Both agents let rip with fire spells, the deadliest in their arsenal. Under no other circumstances would they have dared to use such a spell without first identifying who the target was. But in the wasteland that was the streets around them, they felt fully justified in their actions.

Startled by the suddenness of the attack, Jake Starr flinched away. Bright light, sudden and unexpected in the unnatural darkness hurt his eyes but it wasn't aimed at him.

An inhuman scream lit the air, followed by another, and another as three of his students became human fireballs. Jake hadn't seen them coming, but he knew instantly he was being attacked by two supernaturals. He had no idea who they were, or how they had snuck up on him, but he was charged with power and righteous purpose. This was his time, and no one was going to stop him.

With those words echoing in his mind, he brought everything he had into his core. He didn't choose fire as his opponents had; he was better than that. Deadlier. In the demon realm, he had been thrown into combat with other familiars much like gladiators entertaining a baying crowd.

Few familiars ever died, though it did happen, but entertainment was only part of it. The demons wanted their familiars to be powerful – it was bragging rights, but they also believed that when the death curse fell, their familiars would help them in the war that would follow.

Jake had fought many wizards and he always fought dirty. He had killed before and felt no resistance to doing so again now.

He powered the spell in his mind and gripped the liquid inside the two supernaturals' hearts. They dared to challenge him and now they would pay the price.

Agents Wallace and Bueller took a faltering step, initially questioning what was happening to them. It started almost gently as a warm sensation in their chests, but within a second the searing sensation had become abject and indescribable pain.

Having lived their lives in the mortal realm, neither Wallace nor Bueller had ever heard of such an abhorrent manipulation of the elements.

Knowing the fight was already over, Jake Starr forced yet more heat into their hearts. He could have stopped at that point – they were already beyond the point where they would recover enough to be a threat anytime soon, but with a final grimace of satisfaction, he made their hearts explode.

Debs Wallace stared down at her chest, a trickle of blood running from the right corner of her mouth, she remained upright for a few seconds, fighting against her sagging knees before collapsing to the paving slabs beneath her feet. Agent Bueller was already dead, his partner joining him moments later.

Chapter 47

When they left the church, the girls hadn't actually vanished into the storm, and they hadn't been whisked into the air by Jake Starr's students either. Mastery of the elemental forces to the point that one could manipulate air in order to fly was something that did not come easily. Robbie, Ethan, and the other hoods were a long way from learning such skills.

Instead, they had a van.

Though they knew their master was planning to unseat the mayor and take over the city, they had no idea how much destruction he would bring. The surprise they felt could be seen in their faces as they drove towards the burning police vehicles.

Cassie, Naomi, and Jennifer were huddled together in the rear of the van on one of the bench seats that lined the two sides. On either side of the trio and sitting opposite, staring at them with hard eyes, were six of the hoods. Robbie and Ethan were in the front.

The girls had exhausted their repertoire of 'Why are you doing this?' and 'Do you truly believe your master has your best interests at heart?'. Even questioning why they would follow a person who had so willingly murdered a police officer got them no response.

Falling silent, the sisters took to conversing telepathically instead.

'*Can they hear us if we talk like this?*' Jennifer asked.

Neither Naomi nor Cassie knew the answer to that question, but Naomi took a wild stab.

'*I don't think so,*' she hazarded, watching all around her to see if anyone reacted. '*I think perhaps this is something that is unique to us.*' She watched again, looking all around at the hoods.

They could see their faces now, recognising several more of the boys as kids who went to their school. They were younger than the twins and thus in different year groups, and the ones they didn't recognise were probably from other schools – there were plenty in the area.

None of them reacted to the conversation in the girls' heads.

'*I'm going to try something,*' Cassie announced. '*On the count of three I'm going to fill the entire van with flame and burn all of them alive,*' she informed her sisters. Then, before they could react, she screamed, '*Three!*' in her head, and looked around.

Jennifer breathed a sigh of relief. She believed Cassie was genuinely going to start burning everyone in the van. That would be bad enough, but she had no idea how her sister planned to not burn her and Naomi as well. That it was just a ruse came as a welcome surprise.

Seeing both her sisters tense up and then relax, Cassie gave them a one eyebrowed look of question.

'*You didn't think I was actually going to set fire to everyone did you?*' she asked. '*How would I pull that off without torching us as well?*

Naomi kept her eyes pointing dead ahead. Staring at a space between the heads of two hoods sat opposite her, her face was emotionless when she said, '*Okay, I think we can assume that the telepathy thing is limited to the three of us. This is good, now what are we going to do with it? We managed to get them away from the church, but the three of us are now trapped and outnumbered.*'

'*I don't want to meet their master,*' Jennifer remarked. '*We had enough trouble against his students earlier.*' She had more to say, but was cut off by Cassie's thoughts entering her skull.

'*Jennifer is right,*' Cassie agreed. '*Our best chance is to take out these idiots right now. If we allow them to deliver us to their master and the rest of the hoods, we'll stand no chance at all.*'

From the front of the van, Ethan turned his head to look back into the load area.

'What are you three doing back there?' He leered at them with an evil grin. 'I can see you pulling energy. If you attempt to conjure a spell, if I suspect that you are thinking of attempting to conjure a spell, the eight of us will render you unconscious. Do you know how we're going to do that?' he asked.

All three girls turned their heads to look his way. None of them knew the answer.

'I shall take that silence as a 'no',' Ethan licked his lips with delight as he thought about what he was going to get to do. 'It's actually a relatively simple manipulation of air,' he began to explain, 'and master has taught us a great many things. Things that you would never be able to discover by yourselves, but I shall reveal this one small trick.'

The van rocked slightly as Robbie slowed to drive over the limbs of a figure lying face down in the street. He was having to swerve around burning and ruined vehicles as if he were in a chicane. Glass and debris littered the road, making him question whether he might incur a puncture.

With a smile changing the shape of his face, Ethan drew on a nearby line and conjured an air spell into his hand. Closing his eyes, he visualised what he wanted to do in the way that his master had taught him. They've been forced to practise on each other, rendering unconsciousness over and over again so that they could practise fighting against it and perform the spell faster themselves.

'What you have to do, girls, is feel for the air in your opponent's lungs. Then simply prevent it from moving.' He stopped speaking as he released the spell, watching with glee as all three girls began to gag.

It was the worst kind of horror to suddenly find that you were unable to draw breath. In the confines of the van, penned in on all sides by their captors, the sisters were watched by smiling faces as their eyes widened and each of them clawed at their throats.

'Let them go, Ethan,' Robbie warned his friend.

Ethan kept the spell on, enjoying the show as the three helpless, but distinctly attractive girls demonstrated that they were completely in his power to control.

'Now, Ethan,' Robbie dropped his voice so that it became a threatening growl.

With a giggle, Ethan released the spell, but didn't take his eyes off the girls as each of them sucked in grateful lungfuls of air, heaving to try to recover the deficit of oxygen running through their bodies.

'*Now?*' asked Jennifer.

'*Absolutely,*' replied Naomi.

What Ethan and the other seven hoods in the van could not know, was that while they were being asphyxiated, the three girls were focusing on the spell, and commenting on how effective it was. It sounded simple to learn, and tapping a line already so they could communicate, they reached out with their senses to detect the air in the lungs of all eight of their captors.

Now that they were released, Cassie sucked in another deep lungful of air and lifted her right hand, her thumb extended to give Ethan a thumbs up.

He hitched an eyebrow, when she looked his way, clearly trying to get enough oxygen in her lungs to say something.

Offering Ethan a smile, she gripped Jennifer's left hand with her right. Naomi was already holding Jennifer's other hand, the three sisters linking their bodies physically as they prepared to deliver a spell with their combined force.

With her grin firmly in place, Cassie said, 'Thanks for the tip, Dick Face.'

This was the first time they had attempted to link spells as a deliberate act. When their conjurings combined in the woods earlier, it was a complete accident. However, while they were asphyxiating, their hurried conversation argued back and forth about what they had done and how they would produce such an effect again.

Cassie insisted they had to try something, and argued that perhaps together they would be able to create enough juice to overwhelm the boys.

The biggest concern was that Ethan and probably the others would all fight back, rendering them unconscious faster or perhaps employing a different spell the girls didn't know. Nevertheless, they chose to try.

The moment Cassie stopped speaking, Naomi yelled, '*Now!*'

They released the spell they were holding, feeling the air in the lungs of all eight hoods in the van. Silver light enveloped the sisters, appearing to them like a filter over their eyes as their spells combined. The hoods got to see it in all its majesty, but not for very long.

The sisters got to see panic in the faces of the boys opposite them, and indeed Ethan who was still twisted around to look into the back of the van. Cassie guessed the expressions she could see must be how they had looked when they first felt the spell enter their bodies.

In her sisters' heads, Jennifer's excited squeal echoed. '*Get ready for it, girls! They're gonna hit us any second.*'

They were expecting the spell to come back at them as the boys fought. But they didn't. Instead, the hoods collapsed. Almost all of them at once and less than two seconds after the girls unleashed the spell.

Staring at Ethan with a determined grimace on her face, Cassie got to watch as his eyes rolled back in his head, and he slumped over the back of his seat.

It was only then, that the girls realised their error. Robbie was slumped on the steering wheel, completely unconscious, and the van was out of control. Worse yet, they were driving directly towards a burning building, and without someone to stop the van, they were going to drive straight up the sidewalk and through the front façade.

Chapter 48

Ayla's helicopter had made it all the way to Chippewa Valley Regional Airport unscathed. The powerful storm was visible from where they were and had been so for the last fifteen minutes of their approach.

The enormous super cell hung like a cage over one small portion of the city, cutting it off completely. If there was a way in, Ayla and her team were yet to come up with it.

Her assistant had coordinated the other agents as they arrived over land. They were massed, almost thirty of them, half a mile from the southern edge of the tornadoes on highway fifty-three. All traffic on that road had already dissipated. Nothing could go north, and there was certainly nothing coming south out of the storm.

Speaking on the phone to Agent Morris, one of the few returned familiars who had immediately wanted to join the SIA, Ayla asked, 'What can you tell me?'

Agent Morris pulled a face and continued to stare at the threatening wall of swirling wind filling his vision.

'Not a lot. I realise that's not particularly helpful. There's no doubt that this is magical, but how it's being controlled I'm afraid I'm at a loss to explain. Most of us can create some form of weather anomaly, and the strongest of us on a good day might be able to produce a tornado for a few minutes. But this has been going on for an hour ...' he checked his watch, 'over an hour,' he corrected himself. 'There's no way this is just one person. If you want my opinion there's an entire team inside. If we go in shorthanded - assuming we can find a way in, that is - then we might end up with a lot of casualties.'

It was the last thing Ayla wanted to hear.

'Okay,' she replied, gathering her thoughts and challenging her brain to come up with something sensible to do. 'We're going to have to start looking for a way in. We have to be able to create a gap in the storm that we can get through. Otherwise, whatever is going on inside will just continue happening.'

Her biggest concern was that whoever was behind it, whether that be Jake Starr, someone else, or a whole team of them as Agent Morris believed, they would be strengthening their hold on the city. They would be able to take many hostages - a fresh and horrific thought gripped her when she realised that the people behind the storm could take the entire area hostage.

How could she then move against them? She knew well enough conventional weapons wielded by humans would have little effect. The

SIA would be forced to decide whether to go with a full attack knowing such a move might cost the lives of all the humans held captive.

Who could hope to balance that equation?

A shout got her attention.

'Mrs Pendragon, we have transport waiting.'

She turned around to find a trio of Humvees pulling to a halt ten yards away.

Starting towards them, she offered Agent Morris a parting instruction. 'Look for a way through the storm. I want everyone working on it. We have to get inside.'

She ended the call and dumped the phone in her handbag. They were supposed to be pulling the supernaturals of the world together, finding the familiars Otto returned and bringing together anyone who possessed the ability to perform magic to create a coalition force. The demons were coming, they knew that for certain. Fighting against each other ... fighting other human supernaturals was nothing more than a pointless distraction that could cost the whole of humanity it's freedom.

When she caught the people behind this attack, she was going to be forced to make an example of them. A few months ago, she had been little more than a mom, caring for her kids. Her father was a powerful man, but she had never had any designs on office.

Now she was leading a team of agents, and because of her father's connections to the White House, was becoming a voice within the supernatural community. Her life had changed too fast, but there was no one to blame for it.

If she allowed herself to think about all the things that were happening to her, to the people she knew, and to the planet, she might curl into a weeping ball and refuse to leave her bedroom. Humanity had no time for that, so with a grim expression dominating her beautiful features, she slid into the back seat of an armed Humvee and focused her thoughts on what she needed to do next.

Chapter 49

Naomi, Jennifer, and Cassie all rose from the bench seat in the back of the van at the same time. They could see what was going to happen and were lunging to get to the front of the van. Someone needed to grab the steering wheel, or they were going to become a horrible burning fireball.

The van bumped as the left front wheel hit a piece of concrete – debris from one of the buildings where Jake had been throwing lightning around. It jolted the three girls, sending them sprawling one on top of the other. The unconscious hoods all fell from their seats, landing on the girls as a dead weight.

The sisters fought to get up, but were battling not only against the weight of the boys pinning them down, but also against each other, each inhibiting the others as they attempted to rise.

The van bumped again, this time as it rode up onto the sidewalk. They were seconds from crashing through the front facade of the burning building where the inferno inside would engulf them.

'*A spell to push us backwards!*' Naomi shrieked in her sisters' heads. She still had hold of the ley line and was attempting to conjure the spell as swiftly as she could when unexpectedly the motion of the van changed completely.

The girls asked questions of each other as the rocking, rumbling feel of the surface beneath the tires abruptly ceased.

Jennifer was the first to get her head high enough to see over the seats, whereupon her jaw fell open and she gasped in wonder.

The van was flying.

It gently coasted around in an arc, floating a yard or more above the road as it wove once more between the destruction. Any questions regarding what was happening were answered in the next instant as the van's nose swung around to face a lone hooded figure standing in the street.

Jake Starr had seen the van approaching and knew his students had been successful in their mission to collect the three sisters he so dearly wanted to recruit. However, his excitement at the prospect of finally meeting the girls was short-lived. One moment the driver was steering carefully between the obstacles that otherwise blocked the road, the next it was veering to one side and mounting the kerb.

Reacting quickly, Jake seized the air around the van and lifted it into the air before it crashed. Using his hands to aid him, he controlled the vehicle's trajectory, carrying it away from the building it had been about to hit. Once it was out of danger, he elected to maintain control of it, allowing it to glide on a cushion of air until it touched down just a few yards in front of him.

Only moments had passed since he exploded the hearts of agents Wallis and Bueller. He had no idea who they were, and the underground life he had lived since returning to the mortal realm had shielded him from learning that an organisation such as the Supernatural Investigation Alliance might even exist.

Of the five apprentices he brought with him to kill the mayor and face down the city's law enforcers, only two remained. The other three were burnt badly enough that Jake ended their lives as a mercy. The survivors were behind him now, stunned into silence by what had happened to their friends.

That they might suffer injury or worse had never occurred to them, and Jake Starr had chosen to never point it out. The hoods were foot soldiers to him, although he recognised a need to develop and strengthen them, rewarding them, and promoting those who showed the greatest potential. He was going to rule here and that required having his own strategic defence force ready to ensure their way of life could be maintained.

The deaths of three was insignificant, but Jake made a mental note to use it as a learning tool to push the boys to practice harder.

Setting the van down, he made his way toward it.

From their position inside, the girls could see him approaching.

'Oh, God,' whimpered Jennifer. 'That's him, isn't it? That's the master.'

'I know that you are in there, girls,' Jake Starr's voice startled the three sisters.

They had reached the end of the mystery. A day ago – was it really that recently? - they had wanted to be able to identify Officer Spencer's killer and now they were certain it was the man calling to them from outside. A fat lot of good it did them. They might have got to the information before their mother, but was that actually going to save anyone now?

'We're going to have to go out and face him,' Cassie murmured, for once not sounding like she was spoiling for a fight.

Jennifer slipped her hand into Naomi's, wanting to feel her sister's support.

'Come along, girls,' Jake Starr called to them. 'I mean you no harm. I must say, I am really quite impressed that you have overpowered my students. I suspected that your abilities might be among the most powerful in this city. You are raw … untrained, however, with me to guide and mould you, what you can do now will soon seem utterly insignificant. I will ask little of you, only that you allow me to teach you, and help you to fulfil your potential as we claim our rightful positions in the new world I am creating.'

There was no threat in his voice. If anything, he was speaking in a soothing tone and his words were inviting. He could not fool the girls though; they could see the death and destruction around them. They had spotted the bodies strewn in the street and could see several lying on the paving slabs behind the sinister hooded figure outside.

He was a murderer, and they could never join him. But they also knew they did not have the power to fight him.

Or did they?

Engaging telepathy, Cassie asked what they might do if they joined their spells once more.

'*I don't think we ought to dare risk it,*' Naomi replied. '*We don't know enough about him. He is vastly more powerful than the boys we have taken on so far. Perhaps we can overcome him, but we may need to study him first and pick the right time to launch an attack.*'

'Using her actual voice, Jennifer asked, 'Where is Bethany?'

Chapter 50

Bethany opened her eyes, blinking in the dim light as she attempted to work out where she was and how she had got there. Memories flooded back in the next few seconds, filling her head with the same confusing sensation she experienced just before she lost consciousness. That the police had somehow knocked her out angered her deeply.

Someone laughed, 'Hey, looks like grandma's awake.' The voice belonged to Matilda Swanson, currently being held on her third case of prostitution in four weeks.

Bethany twisted her head slightly, taking in her surroundings. She had never been in a cell before, but it was not difficult to work out that it was where she was now. There were bars on three sides and a cinder ash wall on the fourth. One corner was dominated by a toilet everyone was keeping their distance from, and opposite Bethany, viewing her with mildly bored disinterest were six ladies. Their ages ranged from a girl in her late teens arrested for shoplifting, all the way up to Matilda who was forty-three.

Bethany wasn't lying on a bed, rather there was a bench along one wall. The cops had placed her there, not caring particularly whether she rolled over in her sleep and fell off. They had bigger concerns.

There was a duty officer just down the hall, or at least there should have been. The battle in Bay Street had been broadcast over the airwaves, the screams of terror and panic-filled shouts getting the attention of every cop at the station. On hearing the cries of their colleagues, almost all the cops left behind abandoned their posts to join the fight.

Not that Bethany was going to call for the duty officer to let her out, she had no need for such a thing. Sitting up on the bench, she paused for a moment to assess how she felt. All the women in the cell were looking at her, displaying nothing more than a passing interest because there was nothing much else to do.

With a deep breath to settle herself, Bethany filled herself with magical energy, drawing it from the earth to fuel her next spell.

When her hair began to float slightly and tiny crackles of light passed along the tips, the ladies in her cell backed away. No one needed to explain to them that they were trapped inside with a supernatural.

'Hey!' Matilda yelled, her voice joining those of several others as they screamed to get the attention of whoever might hear her.

Bethany ignored them all, conjuring a spell as she pushed her senses into the ground beneath her feet. It was concrete, but an earth spell would have the same effect regardless of the substrate involved. Stepping back from the point on which she was focused, she created a surge of energy to wrench the steel bars from the floor. Six of them ripped upwards and outwards, fanning out and away like stage curtains being lifted as the steel tore outwards from the cell.

Concrete shards spattered against the wall, creating a spark here and there as they collided with one another. Bethany had to duck slightly to exit the cell, but standing up on the other side of the bars, she used her hands to remove the creases from her clothes, tutted when it didn't work, and proceeded on a direct path toward the exit from the station.

Matilda needed about three seconds to convince herself the old woman had no interest in hurting her, at which point she dived through the hole in the cell to escape too.

Chapter 51

Both Cassie and Naomi had been pondering the same thing; questioning where the one person who might be able to stand up to the hoods' master might be. Was she still at the station? Was she among the dead now littering the plaza in front of the mayor's office?

Jennifer's sisters were yet to voice their curiosity because they both worried the latter would be true. It was too awful and final to consider. If Bethany was gone, who would come to their rescue?

'I shall grow impatient, girls. I am not accustomed to being made to wait,' Jake's voice had taken on a hard edge.

'We're going to have to go out there,' Naomi voiced what was obvious already. 'I don't think we have any choice about what we do, at least not for the time being. Do you agree?'

Cassie was staring at the figure ahead of them, her eyes narrowed, and her jaw clenched against the impotent anger she felt.

'Do I agree that we shouldn't try to fight him?' she asked a question rather than answering her oldest sister's.

Jennifer's voice trembled when she spoke, 'Come on, Cassie, we can't fight him. Look at what he's done to the cops. For all we know, Bethany is out there too.'

Cassie's lips were pressed close together, but she wasn't arguing, she was just upset that her sisters were right.

'Okay, we accept defeat. For now.'

Jake Starr was thinking about flipping the van, wondering if a good shake might wake the girls up when the side door popped opened. The three girls emerged one after the other, each eyeing him warily.

'Did you kill my boys?' Jake asked in a conversational manner.

'We are not killers!' Naomi spat, her words coming out more harshly than she intended.

'They are all inside the van still,' Cassie supplied a more accurate answer. 'They're merely unconscious.'

Jake Starr hitched one eyebrow, surprised yet again by the girls, though pleased might be a more accurate description of his feelings. He turned his head to look at the three boys loitering behind him and twitched it toward the van.

'See to them. Bring them around. We might not be finished here yet.' Turning his attention back to the sisters as his hoods took a route around them to revive Robbie, Ethan, and the others, Jake said, 'It would seem I was right about you, girls. You have great potential. You have received instruction from Bethany Cromwell, yes?' He didn't bother to wait for them to answer, pressing on to ask the question he really wanted them to answer. 'Where is she?'

Having posed the question he looked around, turning his head left and right and looking up at the sky to make sure no threat was coming from it.

'He doesn't know where Bethany is. That means she's still alive,' Cassie's voice echoed in her sisters' heads. The thought filled her with hope and that imbued her with courage. Bethany could give this guy a run for his money even if they couldn't, but they would be there to support her when she did.

Naomi, however, was less excited by the news.

'Cassie, it also means that she hasn't turned up for the fight. We've no reason to believe she ever intends to. Maybe she wanted to train us so that she didn't have to face him.'

Without warning, all three girls were blasted from their feet. A shock-wave that felt like a bomb going off lifted them from their feet, catapulting them backwards five yards. They had barely even seen Jake move, the spell conjured and deployed so swiftly they had no time to prepare themselves.

Coming back to earth, it was only due to their athletic prowess that the three sisters were able to get their feet down and land the right way up. Even so, they were now crouching and panting as the shocking suddenness of his attack drove fresh fear through their veins.

His hands were spread to his left and right, a fresh spell woven between them very clearly though they could not tell what it was.

'I can boil your blood,' Jake sneered in their direction. 'I can explode your hearts with a thought. Your ability to wield elemental magic is insignificant when compared to mine. When I ask you a question you will give me an answer. If you do not answer this time, I rather think I might just kill one of you to motivate the other two.'

Jake Starr was bluffing; he had no intention of killing one of the three girls. At least not at this point. He needed to see how strong they were first. Also, they were quite attractive and would make worthy mates once he ruled. Despite that, he was quite certain the three girls would not be so foolish as to challenge him to make good on his threat.

Unable to stop herself, Jennifer blurted, 'We don't know where she is. She was arrested after the fight at our high school and was taken to the local precinct.'

Naomi spoke up too, 'She's telling you the truth,' she tried to reassure the man threatening them. 'There's no need to kill any of us.'

Jake considered their response for a second. In some ways he was glad they felt a willingness to resist him. Just like with the boys, it was important that they understood how powerful he was. Break them at the start and it would make them so much easier to control afterwards.

With a nod of acknowledgement, he said, 'I don't believe you.'

Jennifer gasped in horror. 'No! No, we're telling you the truth. We don't know where she is!'

Cassie's voice filled her sisters' heads again. *'Still think we shouldn't fight him?'*

The three girls were spread out, all facing the powerful wizard as he began to point his finger at each girl in turn.

'Is he eeny meenying us?' Naomi gawped at the man standing five yards away.

Jake was, in fact, doing exactly that. His bluff didn't appear to have worked so now he was going to hurt one of them. The other two would talk and beg for him to spare their sister and he would do so. If he had to kill one of them then so be it. He would be able to find more supernaturals yet, but he would avoid doing so if he could.

Behind them, the sound of Jake's students waking those they had left unconscious in the van added yet more pressure. They had a wizard to their front who they couldn't hope to defeat and were outnumbered four to one by his hoods. They would exit the van shortly and the girls knew they would be trapped between the two.

Cassie was pointing out these obvious facts to her sisters in the seconds Jake took to decide which of them he was going to torture.

'If doesn't matter if we cannot beat him,' she argued. *'He is about to kill one of us and I'm not going down without a fight.'*

Jennifer felt sick to her stomach, but though she wondered if she might actually vomit, she agreed.

'*Let's do what we can. All together?*' she confirmed timidly, her hands shaking when she raised them.

'I'm going to hit him with fire!' Cassie announced, her defiant scream filling her sisters' head.

Jennifer and Naomi could fuel it, adding their power to increase the effectiveness of the spell, but Naomi had a better idea. The benefit of telepathy was one person's thoughts appearing inside another's head – it was instantaneous, no time required to express and explain.

Naomi's instruction altered Cassie's intention in an instant, her choice of spell changing with it.

Maybe they couldn't beat Jake, but could they distract his aim for long enough to get away?

The girls each formed air spells. Jennifer and Naomi sent their conjurings into the debris littering the street, flinging rock and muck at their opponent.

Cassie, meanwhile, spun around to face the hoods just exiting the van. She hit the van itself with a blast of air on its front right quarter. It spun the vehicle, scattering the hoods who were not able to produce a counterspell fast enough to stop her.

Jake laughed, entertained by their juvenile attempts to stop him. As each projectile came within a yard or so, he parried it harmlessly away.

It took minimal effort on his part, a simple air spell obeying his commands.

However, as the hoods turned to fight, Cassie pushed fire into the van's fuel tank. It exploded a second later, the resulting blast felling the hoods still too close to it.

Shocked at how coordinated their attack seemed, Jake nodded his head to acknowledge their skill, but he wasn't paying enough attention.

The explosion was cover for Jennifer who used air to shift a car which collided with a lamppost. It crashed to the street right behind Jake.

The sound of it so close behind him made Jake take his eyes off the girls and that meant he missed the road sign Naomi threw at him.

It almost struck him, getting close enough that he needed to flinch and act fast to avoid being injured. The amusement left his face, his hard features turning to stone as he genuinely considered killing one of them to prove a point.

They weren't there though.

The road sign hit a building on the opposite side of the road and crashed to the sidewalk with a clatter. When the sound died away, Jake looked around for the girls.

'Master!' called Robbie. He'd seen his teacher forced to duck. 'What can we do to help?'

The bright flare of burning fuel from the van had forced the hoods back. Eleven of them were reduced to nine as the blast threw two of them into stationary objects with enough force to knock them out again. Those left on their feet were ready to fight, too terrified of Jake to consider running away.

They had also lost sight of the sisters who had capitalised on the momentary distraction to drop their hold on the ley line and duck behind an abandoned police truck.

Angered by the question, Jake shouted, 'I have no need to employ your help, boy. Let this serve as a demonstration. This is how you fight supernaturals.'

Invisible, if only for a moment, the Stevens' girls could hear Jake's words and tried to strategize.

'*He'll see us the moment we draw on the line,*' Naomi pointed out. '*So we have to hit him instantly.*'

'*Do we combine spells?*' Jennifer asked.

'No,' Cassie argued. '*We should spread out. It will make it harder to take out all three of us at once.*'

'*We are not trying to beat him, Cassie!*' Cassie's desire to fight always shocked Naomi. '*The aim here is to get away. Why don't you blow some more stuff up?*' she asked rhetorically. '*You're good at that.*'

Cassie gave her elder sister a completely fake smile.

'*All right, I will.*'

Before either Jennifer or Naomi could respond, Cassie was drawing on the line again, her hands moving in a blur at they filled with golden light.

Jake had been about to push his senses out to feel their heartbeats – it was easy enough to find living beings – when he felt the sudden pull on the ley line. He was tapped into it, ready to deliver a spell of his own – one the girls would not enjoy.

Seeing Cassie flit out from behind a truck to his right, Jake used his second sight to find the other two girls and sent magic into all three.

Running to split Jake's attention, and hoping her sisters were doing the same thing, Cassie was shocked at the sudden pain she felt in her chest. Groping at her left breast, she could not prevent the cry of pain that left her lips.

Like a fire had been lit beneath her skin, her heart was beating at three times its normal speed and threatening to burst into flame. What had he said? Jake's words rang in Cassie's ears, "I can explode your hearts!"

Gripped by terror, Cassie fell to her knees, the pain she felt too great to resist. She could not see it, but Jennifer and Naomi were doing the exact same thing, clawing at themselves, and crying out in pain.

All Jake needed to do was push a little more energy into the spell and he could kill all three. Or just one – that would be more sensible, he acknowledged to himself. Which one though?

Cassie's left hand was on the ground supporting her weight as her right hand held her chest. Bethany had said there was so much for her to learn about how the elements could be manipulated by different spells. She had lain awake imagining what that might mean in practical terms, but her thoughts had been about making tea without the need for a kettle and keeping her ice cream cold on a warm day.

Using magic to inflict pain had never entered her head.

'Cassie!' Jennifer's plaintive wail filled Cassie's head. 'Cassie, he's killing us!'

Until that moment, Cassie had assumed it was just her and that he had finally chosen which of them to kill. Learning that her sisters were suffering the same torment ignited a spark in her soul.

Screaming against the pain, Cassie pushed off the ground until she was kneeling back on her haunches. There was a police car just behind Jake. It looked parked, but she knew the occupants had to be dead. Whatever the case, she felt convinced there was no one alive inside it when she created fire and blew out the fuel tank.

The shockwave kicked out in every direction, lifting the car a foot from the ground and launching Jake across the road.

His hold on the spell tormenting the girls dropped instantly, freeing them.

Cassie pushed off her knees. She could barely breathe such was the pounding in her chest, but that didn't stop her from ripping a fresh spell into life. More fire, this time aimed directly at her opponent and at a far shorter range than she tried at the hospital, shot from her right hand.

Jennifer and Naomi were in her head, the three girls hearing each other's thoughts as they all came together to fight Jake.

Jennifer conjured an air spell, the gust of wind she created picking up glass from the street. It peppered Jake just as Cassie's flames reached him.

He avoided both, shooting back five yards at an impossibly fast pace. His feet played no part in the motion, manipulated air allowing him to fly. The spells missed him, but Naomi was coming at him from yet another angle.

Her spell hit home.

That their elder sister produced flame shocked the twins, but there was no time to quiz her on the subject. If they had just gained an advantage, they needed to press it home.

Jake's cloak was on fire, but this was far from his first magical battle. With the flick of a spell, he rose into the air to avoid the fresh lance of flame. He had to change his spell to douse the flames, dropping from the sky again to catch himself before he hit the ground. He was going to hit them with a barrage of lightning that would leave them begging him to stop. Then he would torture all three and make them pick one who would die.

He knew the eldest sister would volunteer which was why he had already chosen to kill the meek one.

Seeing him evade their best attempts to overpower him – he just knew so much more than they did – the sisters knew they had just one throw of the dice left.

They needed to combine spells.

Unfortunately, they were yards apart and had perhaps half a second before Jake was going to attack.

'*Where did you learn fire?*' Cassie wanted to know, her thoughts reaching Naomi's mind even as she readied a new spell.

'*It was in your head,*' Naomi replied, her thoughts calm even though she felt anything but. '*I was listening when you conjured it and … well, I guess I could feel the spell and that allowed me to understand it.*'

'*How about earth?*' Cassie asked, thinking about how to do it inside her own head.

At the speed of a firing neuron, the same information arrived in the heads of Jennifer and Naomi. Jake was just reaching the apex of his upward thrust, his current spell focused on putting out the flames licking up the right side of his cloak.

'*On three?*' asked Jennifer.

Jake began descending, the flames out and a powerful spell filling the air above his head. Particles of water in the air began to rub against each other, agitated by magic to form static electricity he would unleash with devasting effect.

Below him, the sisters' minds united into one. Naomi spewed a jet of white-hot flame into his path while Cassie ripped rocks from the ground to send them skyward. Jennifer was supposed to be creating a downward thrust of air, the hope being that he would not expect it, but at the last moment, she chose instead to reach out with her consciousness.

The girls were spread across almost ten yards with Jennifer in the centre when the silver light sprang from her body to encapsulate all three girls.

Jake saw it from the air, trying to balance the need to control his descent with blocking the spells being thrown at him. The one constant for elemental magic is that only one spell can be created at a time. A talented practitioner can switch between spells at a surprising speed, but the limitation of one at a time remains.

Now falling to earth and beginning to wish he'd killed the girls at the start, he got to witness something he knew couldn't happen.

The three sisters were operating as one.

It was as if they were a single witch, casting multiple spells simultaneously and somehow generating more power for each of them as they did so. They were perfectly attuned, the potential inherent in their ability startling.

Unable to do three things at once, Jake applied an air spell to slow his fall, then parried the flame away, but in so doing he not only had to drop the lightning manipulation he wanted to deploy, but left the door open for Cassie's rocks to hit him.

Winded, he fell to the ground, landing hard though he tried to counter his fall at the last moment.

The girls questioned how they had just done what they had just done when they were dealt a harsh reminder that they and Jake were not the only players on the field.

Robbie and the hoods had waited impatiently as their master demanded, but seeing him fall and clearly now on the backfoot, they struck.

Lightning, the same spell Jake had intended to deploy, lanced across the field of battle from the hands of more than half the hoods. The younger ones among them were yet to master the technique with enough finesse to know they wouldn't strike themselves or their team members.

Half the hoods creating lightning proved to be more than enough.

In their moment of victory, just when Cassie, Naomi, and Jennifer intended to swoop on Jake and overpower him, they were hit with blast after blast of artificially created fork lightning. It was powerful enough to tear them from the ground, slamming the air from their lungs and blinding them as they each fought to stay conscious.

Rising from the ground, Jake lashed out with a shockwave of air. Aimed at ankle height, it swept the legs of all his students, sending them tumbling painfully to the street.

'I told you I didn't need your help,' he spat, rage descending behind his eyes like a river of blood. He had shown weakness before his students – letting three novice girls get the better of him. His plan to kill one had to be abandoned now – he needed to know how they combined their spells.

It was an ability he'd never heard of once in his century and a half of life. Had Bethany taught it to them? Where had she learned it?

He would find out soon enough. The girls were down, smoke rising from their clothing as they gasped for breath and attempted to get back on their feet.

Their brains were scrambled, the ability to communicate telepathically momentarily shut off by the barrage of electrical shocks that racked their bodies.

'That was impressive,' Jake acknowledged, standing over the three girls. 'But you should have kept your ability to combine your spells a secret until you were strong enough to stand a chance against me. You could have learned from me and with training developed the power and skill you would need to win. I will enjoy breaking you.'

Everyone but Cassie was facing the wrong direction to see the new player arrive.

Chapter 52

Bethany walked out from between two burning buildings, smoke billowing in her wake.

'Not so fast, Jake Starr.'

Jake whipped around, twisting his body to face the new threat.

To his left, he caught a glimpse of the hoods as they were sent sprawling yet again, this time not by his hand, but by Bethany's.

'I'm sorry, boys,' she called to them. 'I mean you no harm, I genuinely don't. Your so-called master has led you down the wrong path. He is not going to be a king in the new world. He isn't going to be anything other than a slave like everyone else when the demons come.'

Jake whipped out a lightning spell, a ferocious fork of light arcing through the sky toward the old lady as she ambled across the sidewalk doing her best to avoid the debris littering it.

Almost nonchalantly, she conjured a spell of her own, casting a stream of water into the air between them. The lightning hit it with explosive power, fusing with the water molecules as the charge dissipated and the water became steam to float into the dark sky.

Bethany kept coming, walking slowly and eyeing her opponent warily.

'Did he even tell you about the demons?' she asked.

Naomi had her hands back under her body. Pain was reporting in from every part of her. Her head was ringing, just like Jennifer claimed hers did when she got hit … was that really only twenty-four hours ago? Her hip felt sticky, and her hand came away with blood on it when she touched it to her jeans.

The road where she had fallen was covered in glass – it was a wonder she wasn't hurt worse. To her left, Jennifer was on her knees, getting up but doing so slowly and clearly feeling just as much pain. Beyond her, Cassie was on her feet, but carrying her left arm as if it were broken.

Muttering from the hoods resulted in a shouted question.

'What demons?' Ethan wanted to know.

Jake replied, 'She's trying to trick you, boys. This old woman would have you scurry about like well-behaved mice, sticking to the shadows and telling you your power is to be hidden, not celebrated.'

'Your master is making up for lost time,' Bethany calmly remarked. 'For over a hundred years, he has been the familiar – that's slave or plaything to you and me – to a magical being far, far more powerful than either he or I.' She used her words to disguise the air spell she launched at him, gripping the oxygen in Jake's lungs as a feign to make him react before pulling the ground out from beneath his feet.

He fell into the hole as it opened beneath him, but only descended a few inches before he was able to drive air beneath his body to thrust himself back into the sky. He landed with a flourish two yards from where he had been, closing the distance between himself and Bethany as he threw his next conjuring in her direction.

Going for her heart, he focused on the water inside it, sending heat to make it burst.

Calmly, Bethany focused her own spell on the same organ, cooling her heart before Jake's spell could have any effect.

'You do not have to die with him, boys,' Bethany assured the hoods. 'But you do have to pick which side you fight on. Do you really think Jake represents what is best for you? How many people has he killed now?'

'We take what we desire because we have the might to do so,' Jake sneered. 'You could too, Bethany. The demons will come, but we have no idea when. Perhaps by the time the death curse fails we will have lived our natural lives.'

'Perhaps,' Bethany agreed. 'But do you really think you can fight all of humanity, Jake?' Working on a complex spell for the last few seconds, she forced water to coalesce into balls the size of musket shots up high above her head, then allowed gravity to take them as she switched spells to send them flying down toward her opponent.

Jake sensed them coming at the last moment, forming a wall of flame above his head to disarm the danger they represented.

Dropping his spell, he spread his arms and looked around. 'The police and army came against me and look what I did to them with a few simple spells. Imagine what I can achieve with an army of wizards at my side. They will flock to me, Bethany. You should join me now while my offer is still good. No one is getting through that storm until I let them.'

'The storm,' Jennifer's voice made its way into her sisters' heads. It sounded far away but they were recovering – enough so that they could once again speak telepathically. *'How is he controlling the storm?'*

Naomi supplied the answer. *'The rest of the hoods. They must be doing it for him.'*

'Is that possible?' asked Cassie, gritting her teeth against the pain in her left arm.

None of them had thought to question how he was able to fight them, or Bethany now, and keep the storm in place. That only about half of his hoods were present should have tipped them off, but now that they thought to look for them, the concentration of ley line energy being sucked through the earth into a singular spot was easy to see.

It was two blocks away, maybe more, but it had to be where they were located.

'We have to stay here and help Bethany fight him,' Cassie insisted.

Naomi's argument came back instantly.

'She is his match, Cassie. We can help her most, and the people of this city, by taking down that storm.'

'You don't know that!' snapped Cassie, trying to form a spell. Her brain felt half fried by the lightning attack, and she could feel shock from her injuries making her want to lie down. *'If we all fight him together, we will win!'*

'If we fight, then he will call upon his hoods to fight. If we go, we can draw them away. We have to trust Bethany to hold her own against him,' Naomi refused to back down. *'I am going.'*

'I'm going too, Cass,' admitted Jennifer, her meek voice sounding apologetic.

Cassie swore, something the three girls almost never did. She was about to call them both cowards when Bethany interrupted her.

Grunting between breaths, the old lady shouted across the divide, 'Girls, I need you to find the source of this storm and shut it off.'

Jake ripped another spell at her, rage driving him to score the first point as he found a way around her defensive spells when he launched his next spell into the building behind her.

Dozens of windows exploded outwards, showering the area with a downpour of tiny glass shards. Bethany wasn't swift enough to deflect them all, but feeling the sting of pain as hundreds of them punctured her skin, she repeated her instruction.

'Go! Find the source of the storm. I will hold him here!'

Naomi and Jennifer ran at Cassie, wasting no time in their bid to get away from the battle.

Jake twisted his body to launch a spell at their backs and might have landed it had Bethany not been so determined to ignore her wounds. She could feel blood trickling down from her skull, the wounds were painful, but not life threatening.

Her biggest concern was for how long she could fight him. She was an old lady, and returning to the mortal realm had hammered that home in the most serious way. Given a choice, she wouldn't be fighting Jake at all. Or anyone for that matter. It was a strange kind of cruelty to find herself back in the city in which she grew up. She had so many memories, but everyone she knew then was long dead now.

There had been several nights since returning when she considered taking her own life. There was nothing for her to live for, and the demons would come soon enough, bringing fresh horror and destruction with them. It was only when she spotted someone else drawing from the ley lines that she wondered if she might find a new purpose.

Now that purpose was the three sisters. They possessed a surprising power and she found herself questioning how many more like them there might be. Could humanity make a stand against the demons? Was it possible to fight back when the death curse failed? Wisdom told her nothing could stop the super race of magical beings set to invade the Earth. However, seeing the three girls weave two spells while the third linked their energies to multiply the effectiveness exponentially, she had to question what else they could learn to do.

Thanks to Bethany's efforts Jake's spell missed its mark and the girls ducked around a corner and out of sight. Forced to deal with the threat to his front, he screamed curses at the old lady and shouted orders at his students.

'Stop them! If they bring down that storm, anyone who didn't die trying to prevent their success will wish they had!'

Jennifer and Naomi had scooped Cassie and were running, all three ducking behind a police van to get out of sight. They didn't stop, the trio running hard toward the source of the spell and throwing spells to clear their route as they went.

Jennifer had proven they did not require physical contact to link their spells and power – experimentation to figure out what they could do could follow if they survived – but since they were all touching, the air blasts Naomi produced were strong enough to flip cars.

They did not see Robbie and the other hoods, but they heard Jake's command to stop them at all costs. The hoods would be hot on their heels, but the girls had a head start and that made it a straight race. The sisters had to get to the source of the spell controlling the storm and the hoods had to get to them before they did.

Only one of those two things could happen.

Chapter 53

Turning hard left when they reached West Central Street, the girls cut through behind the library. There was a fence ahead of them, cutting the library car park off from the auto and tire place next door. Naomi threw a car through it, making an opening they could use before they even had to slow their pace.

The sound of metal being tortured rang out behind them – the battle between Bethany and Jake was yet to be decided. An explosion boomed, the concussion from it shifting the air more than a block away in such a manner that it hurt the girls' ears.

'Are the hoods behind us?' Cassie grunted, biting down against the pain in her arm.

Jennifer twisted her body, checking behind but unable to see where Robbie and the others had got to.

'I don't see them,' she reported.

'Well, we didn't lose them,' Naomi made her thoughts clear. 'They will have gone another way and they know where we are heading. If we don't get there first, we will be running into a trap.'

'We might be running into a trap anyway,' Jennifer pointed out. 'They have phones, you know.'

The cheery thought filling their heads, the sisters stopped talking to focus on running. Emerging from the forecourt of the tire place, they hit West Spring Street and went straight across it. The channel of energy was right in front of them now, an orangey gold beam filtering upward like magma attempting to reach the surface. The river was ahead, and the moment Jennifer made that remark telepathically, all three girls knew they were heading for one of the warehouse units that bordered it.

There was a road that bordered the river – West River Street, so the warehouse had to be this side of it. They were almost there, but they still needed to find their way in.

And they needed to be wary.

Two blocks behind them, Jake's rage was reaching a level beyond apoplectic. It was impossible to find an opening because the old woman wasn't trying to fight him. Every move she made was defensive. It was as if she didn't want to win. There was no attempt to land a worthwhile counterstrike now that the girls were out of his sight, all she wanted to do was …

With a shriek of rage, he understood Bethany's tactic. She wanted to delay him, to slow him down and keep him focused on her. He couldn't go after the girls because to do so would expose him to an attack from the old woman.

Paradoxically he couldn't stay where he was to fight her because she could continue to parry his spells. Eventually, he would break her down – she looked to be breathing heavily as the effort of the fight exhausted her, but he couldn't wait that long. She was conserving energy, doing the minimum she needed to frustrate his efforts.

He couldn't let all he dreamed of be snatched away. Not now when he was so close. If Bethany hadn't shown up, he would have control of the city by now. With a fat percentage of the police lying dead in the streets, the rest would be in disarray. They could send fresh forces from outside when he decided it was time to drop the storm, but he would kill them just as easily. Soon they would stop sending men to die and accept they needed to negotiate with him.

Bethany was ruining it all. He could see her strategy, and now he knew how to beat her.

Chapter 54

Lightning stabbed the ground five yards in front of them, the magically produced element arcing across the concrete and into cars to their left and right as the sisters skidded to a halt.

Another blast struck, this one closer, but before another could touch down, the girls reproduced the trick they saw Bethany perform.

It was Jennifer's idea, telling her sisters to produce water spells as swiftly as they could. Exactly as they saw Bethany tackle the lightning sent by Jake, they pulled moisture from all around them to create a shield of water like a sheet hanging in the air.

The next strike could not get past it, diffusing harmlessly to earth as the girls watched with breathless satisfaction.

Jennifer held out her arms, staying in the middle of her sisters as if the role had been assigned to her. Silver light glowed all around them, both Naomi and Cassie holding flame in their hands even though Cassie was struggling to hide the tremors shaking her body as shock continued to grip her.

'We have the high ground,' shouted Robbie, his voice echoing down from above them.

The girls tilted their heads, looking around until they could spot the hoods on the second story of the industrial unit they faced.

'Do you really think you can beat us?' Naomi asked, sounding a lot calmer than she felt. 'You remember what happened in the van, right.'

'You remember what happened at the edge of the woods?' Ethan shouted back.

'That was you, was it?' asked Jennifer, a steely edge to her voice. She wasn't sure where it had come from, but she liked it and the attitude she could feel behind it. 'You did a good job of covering up your bruising.'

'It wasn't that bad,' Ethan laughed back. 'Your bitch sister is a terrible driver. She only caught me a glancing blow. A few painkillers was all I needed to throw you off the scent.'

'Was it you who flipped the police car outside Collins' Pharmacy?' asked Naomi.

Again, Ethan's chuckle echoed through the darkness. 'It sure was. You should have seen their faces when I hit them. I could have killed them just as easily, turned their car into dust with them inside it, but I spared them their lives.'

'So generous,' Jennifer remarked.

Gritting her teeth, Cassie bit down on her discomfort to voice a question.

'Were you ever interested in me, Robbie?'

'Sure he was,' Ethan laughed. 'The moment our master told him to get close to you, he got really interested.'

The sound of the two boys squabbling filtered through the air before Robbie replied for himself.

'I have always been interested, Cassie. Truthfully, I didn't think you were bothered about me, and I only found the courage to ask you out because I was told to. We can still have that date, Cassie – the world is going to change, and we can be the ones changing it. You've seen the news.'

'Do you seriously believe that?' Naomi snorted with derision. Jennifer shushed her into silence so Cassie could speak.

'I'm not going to join you, Robbie. Your master is a homicidal maniac. He kills people and that makes you a killer too.'

'No! No, I've never hurt anyone,' Robbie protested.

'Yes, you have, Robbie,' Cassie raged, her voice almost a screech. 'By failing to stop Ethan you allowed two cops to get hurt. By failing to identify Tammy-Jo Spencer's killer, you allowed your master to kill dozens of people here today. You gave Ethan an alibi, you threatened a church full of people. It shames me that you would believe for one minute I could ever be okay with that. Now step aside or get ready to die because we are about to destroy that building and we will do it with you on it if we have to.'

'Ha!' Ethan laughed at Cassie's threat. 'You don't have anywhere near the juice required to bring down a building.'

'We almost beat your master a few minutes ago,' Jennifer raised her voice to be heard.

'Look at them, man,' Ethan egged Robbie on, whispering in his ear to scare away any doubts he might be having. 'Cassie is injured for sure. We can take them.'

'You got lucky, that's all,' Robbie shouted across the divide. 'There are too many of us for you to fight.'

'No,' Naomi assured him, 'there isn't. Last warning, boys. Thou shalt not kill just got put on hold. For the good of this city and the people within it, we will do what is necessary.'

She didn't mean it though. The girls were communicating telepathically the whole time they were talking verbally. They didn't know if they could bring down the building – they had no idea what they could or could not do together, but they had a different idea anyway.

One that didn't even require them to move.

However, Naomi's threat tipped Ethan over the edge, his immediate response was a fresh barrage of lightning. Like a ripple spreading outwards from him, the other hoods joined in, multiple sources of lightning illuminated the darkness as the boys sought to end the fight.

Chapter 55

It took Jake more time than he wanted but he gradually forced Bethany to rotate clockwise. He needed to get past her and knew that if he tried to fly to get there, she would knock him from the sky the moment he left the ground.

To achieve that which he wanted, he was going to have to switch places with her, making it so she was out of position. She had him pinned in by the buildings around him. If he tried to hide behind a van or truck, she would launch it at him. If he tried to take off to get away, she would pull lightning from the sky or employ an air spell to throw him into a building. With his own efforts focused on flying, he would be a sitting duck to her next attack.

She blocked the way he wanted to go, but he had slowly moved to his right, hitting her again and again on her left side with earth spells to create holes she had to step away from.

It was turning the table on her. By targeting the ground by her feet and not her directly, it was far harder for her to deflect the spells. She could use a quick burst of flight to move herself before returning to a defensive posture – there was too little time in between for him to get a spell in – but she couldn't shift her efforts to the earth to fill the hole in again.

He was driving her back and circling around, he was almost where he wanted to be. He took another step, glanced over his shoulder like a pitcher checking the bases, and took a step backward.

Bethany realised with a cry of horror what her opponent had been doing. His shift in tactics had confused her. For the last few minutes, he had been making it easy for her to defend against his spells. It was as if he wasn't even trying to hit her. All she wanted to do was keep him where he was, keep his efforts on her, and that had been working just fine. When the girls crashed the spell that was holding the storm in place, then she could consider what came next, but now Jake was going to escape her, and she was abruptly left with no choice but to attack.

If she didn't, he was going to get away from her.

Chapter 56

'*Can you hold it by yourself?*' Jennifer asked, the effort of her own spell beginning to feel like the hardest workout she had ever performed.

Grunting with the strain of keeping the lightning at bay, Naomi replied. '*We need to find out.*'

So far, the hoods on the warehouse had flung lightning bolt after lightning bolt at them, but failed to employ any other spells. An earth spell from the hoods might have disrupted the conjuring the girls were working to manipulate, but either the boys didn't know how to perform one, or it just hadn't occurred to them.

They had tried to freeze the water spell Naomi was using to keep the lightning at bay, but she simply renewed it every second or so, thwarting their efforts.

Jennifer had to trust that Naomi could keep them safe from harm because Cassie needed her to help with the spell she was focussed on. Her twin was whimpering from the terrible demand of the conjuring.

What they were attempting to do was far beyond anything they had ever tried before. They knew that in essence it was just a water manipulation, but it certainly didn't feel like it.

Water was easy to manipulate, even easier than air in some ways, but that also depended on what you wanted to do with it. To make it rotate inside a glass – easy. To lift a one-hundred-foot high waterspout from the river – hard.

The hoods had no idea what the girls were doing. Their focus was on keeping them out of the warehouse. If they couldn't get inside, the sisters couldn't hope to stop the spell powering the storm. None of the hoods believed the girls could bring the building down – if they could, they would have done it already.

The waterspout was taking an age to build. The sisters believed they would get one shot at flooding the warehouse. Push enough water through it and those inside would be swept along with the tide, unable to maintain their grip on the spells they conjured.

When Jennifer lent her strength to the spell Cassie held, Cassie almost collapsed from the relief she felt.

Nodding her thanks, she stuttered through gritted teeth, '*We just need to get it a little higher. We will lose half of the volume when we tip it.*'

'*Or we could just pick the whole thing up,*' Jennifer suggested.

Cassie knew she didn't have the strength for that, but before she could remark, the effort required to lift the water reduced by more than half.

With her sister weaving the same spell it was the effort cubed again, not just doubled.

They didn't need to see the water on the far side of the warehouse to know it was there, they could feel the enormous ball of liquid rise from the surface of the river.

Chapter 57

Now able to back away from Bethany, Jake knew he could take off and fly if he wanted. The buildings were not so tall now that he was away from Bay Street. The storm was still in place too, the flashes of lightning bouncing off the clouds above his head enough to convince him his boys were holding their own.

He wasn't going to take any chances by leaving them too long – the girls' power was shocking, but he also wasn't going to rush and risk giving the old lady an opening.

She was flagging, it was obvious for anyone to see. Worn down by age and the injuries she had sustained in this fight, Bethany was gasping for breath and finding it increasingly difficult to keep her arms up.

Sagging from the continued effort, she gave Jake the opening he had been so patiently waiting for. On the offensive as she tried to stop him escaping, he felt it when her spells began to lose their punch. Her next conjuring missed its mark completely and he threw a truck at her.

She had been attempting to hit him from his blind side with a manhole cover, but when he deflected it easily because it lacked zip, it gave him the opening he needed to launch a new offensive. The truck proved to be all he needed.

Like braking a car in an emergency when your brain knows a collision is unavoidable, Bethany could do nothing but focus all her effort and energy on stopping the truck from killing her.

Altering its trajectory or opting to fly out of its path were just two options she could select. The flying thing though exposed her to the same danger that had kept Jake grounded for so long. If she took off, the likelihood that he would hit her in the air was too high.

So she deflected the truck instead, conjuring an air spell to stop the heavy vehicle safely before stepping around it to throw a fresh spell at Jake.

In that instant, she knew she had made the wrong choice. If she had flown, Jake wouldn't have knocked her from the sky because he was no longer anywhere in sight.

Chapter 58

T he water reached a height Cassie was content with in a matter of seconds once she had Jennifer helping her.

'How much longer?' Naomi begged to know. *'I'm not sure how long I can hold them.'*

She didn't realise how accurate her statement was. Goaded by Ethan, Robbie was leading the hoods to a new strategy. The sisters hadn't tried to advance in the two minutes since they arrived, and the hoods hadn't been able to drive them back. Staying where they were and doing the same thing again was going to get them nowhere.

However, as they descended the fire escapes, two at a time so the rest could continue to fling spells at the girls, Robbie saw a fast-moving object appear out of the corner of his eye.

He flinched, reacting by pulling more line energy to form a new spell, but the form changed direction, heading for the concrete where it landed thirty yards behind the girls.

'Enough,' roared Jake. He wanted to salvage what he could from the situation. In an ideal world, he would be able to keep all three sisters and train them, but the opportunity for that particular future had passed.

Picking Naomi because she was closest, he focused on her heart.

The shout from behind them shocked Jennifer and Cassie, the twins jerking spasmodically as they jumped in fright. Unintentionally, they released their hold on the spell they shared. It was only for a moment, but that was altogether too long for them to regain control over it.

The enormous wobbling ball of water hung in the air for just a split second before gravity claimed it. None of the hoods, not even Jake saw it coming. Only the girls, screaming warnings to each other knew what was about to happen.

But here is something the girls didn't know. One cubic metre of water weighs one metric ton. You might be thinking that it's just water and it will flow around and over stuff. Well, yes, but not that much, not when it comes that fast, and not when you drop it from a great height.

The warehouse didn't exactly explode, but the water hit it like a bomb, crushing the roof like a house of cards and flowing through the lower levels like someone flushed a toilet and the hoods inside were the undesirable contents of the bowl.

Robbie, Ethan, and the other hoods on the first story of the building were ejected from it without the option of using the stairs. The hoods who had made it to the ground floor already fared little better, a torrent of water hitting them like an oversized water cannon.

Cassie, Jennifer, and Naomi knew it was coming, their telepathic communication allowing them to all be on the same wavelength. Despite that, they were not prepared for the amount of water coming their way and were picked up by the resulting wave as it spilt from the ruined building and hit them like a Buick to the face.

The spell Jake had just sent at Naomi - intended to kill her in just a couple of seconds - dropped when he saw the water bomb dropping from the sky. He got enough time to question what he could possibly do to avoid the deluge heading his way before he too was engulfed.

Bodies were spun, looped, rolled, and discarded as the torrent spent itself and flowed away.

Naomi floundered for a second, fighting to get herself the right way up when the water receded, and she found herself beneath a blue sky.

Jennifer too, on her back as the water carried across the asphalt, saw the sun suddenly reappear.

'No!' The scream of denial from Jake was nectar to Cassie's ears as she rolled to a stop, clutching her wounded arm and wincing.

The storm had dropped and that meant ... what? What was to stop him raising a new storm?

Cassie rolled to her right, protecting her damaged left arm as she got her knees back underneath her body.

'*The fight's not over,*' she sent the thought to her sisters. '*We still have to stop him doing it again.*'

Jake was getting to his feet. There was blood coming from a terrible wound on his head, but he was up, and he was looking for someone to kill.

When he spotted Jennifer, it was obvious where his eyes were focussed.

The scream of fury that left his lips would stay with the girls forever, but the spell he cast didn't reach its mark because Bethany dove into its path.

Putting herself between Jake and Jennifer, Bethany absorbed the explosive shockwave of air and her ruined body fell to the ground far beyond saving.

It stunned Jake, though only for a second. His storm was gone, the sky above clearing from the centre outwards and even though he knew he could reform it, he couldn't do that and repel an attack. His students were all down, none of them coming to assist him as they ought.

He was going to kill the girls, women yet again proving they are more trouble than they are worth – especially the pretty ones, but as he rose to his full height, he found the three sisters all staring at him.

They had spells in their hands, and they were wrapped yet again in that unearthly silver light.

'You believe you can best me?' he spat at them.

Jennifer shrugged. 'I think we'll let electricity do that.'

Jake heard the sparks above his head as the sisters manipulated the air around a pylon and ripped it from its mounts.

They were all still standing in an inch of water, but as the pylon fell, trailing electrical cables and a deadly charge with it, Jennifer closed her eyes and pushed all the water away from her and her sisters.

Jake watched the sparking thing fall, wondering what it was until it touched the puddle he was standing in. Then he didn't think anything at all.

Jennifer had to hold the water spell on for longer than she wanted to, tears running down both cheeks as she kept her sisters safe.

They had killed a man. It wasn't an accident, and they couldn't tell themselves they hadn't made a conscious choice to end his life because they had. They discussed it at length telepathically in the final seconds. Though they accepted he had given them little choice, they regretted it nevertheless and knew it would always haunt them.

The pylon's electrical cables fizzed and popped in the water, sending current to the earth before shorting out and dying. Only when she was certain they were safe did Jennifer risk dropping the spell keeping them from being shocked.

Then, like a pin to a bubble, they all ran to Bethany. Jennifer's water spell had kept her safe from the electrical charge too, but there was nothing they could do to save her.

'Help is coming,' cried Jennifer, prompting Naomi to get her phone out. It seemed like such a mundane thing now, using a phone to call for help. Was there even anyone out there?

Naomi sobbed when she got a dead tone and checked her screen to find no bars showing.

'I think the storm knocked out the towers,' she cried.

'Stop worrying, girls,' Bethany begged, her voice little more than a whisper on the breeze as she laid cradled in Jennifer's arms. 'An old lady is swapping her life for three young ones. Trust me, that is not only a good deal, but it's one I would make again and again.'

'But we don't want you to go,' wailed Cassie, overcome with emotion.

'Maybe not, dear, but you don't have a say in the matter. I'm tired, girls. I could tell you that I am eighty-nine years old, but in truth we all know I have lived far longer than that,' Bethany croaked. 'It's time for me to go and you shouldn't mourn me. Remember me maybe, but don't be sad at my passing. Know this, girls, you are strong, and you are unique. I have been alive, and I have been around, but I have never seen anything like the three of you.'

'Stay with us,' Cassie begged. 'Teach us how to use what we have.'

Bethany offered her a smile. 'There will be others to teach you, child. Others who know better than me how to get the best from you.' She coughed and spasmed, pain tearing through her broken body until she lay still again.

'Bethany?' Cassie tried to get a response. 'Bethany,' she repeated the old woman's name with more urgency.

'She's gone,' sobbed Jennifer, able to feel the stillness of Bethany's body through her skin.

The sisters, the witches of Chippewa Falls sat on the soaking wet ground and cried until the SIA arrived.

SIA Headquarters Washington D.C. Three Weeks After the Events in Chippewa Falls

'Are you sure you are ready for this?'

Otto Schneider took a pace back to look at the three girls and to let them consider his question. His thick German accent notwithstanding, they could understand what he was saying well enough and ought to be giving him an answer.

A twitch of annoyance ruffled Otto's upper lip.

'You're doing that telepathy thing again, aren't you?' he asked though he wasn't really asking. He had been alerted to the three sisters' unique abilities by Ayla Pendragon while the mopping up operation in Chippewa Falls was still counting bodies. He and Ayla had enough history that she believed he was the right man to coax their skills to the best they could be.

He doubted that was true and planned to replace himself the moment a better mentor, in the form of another familiar, could be found.

Nevertheless, the girls were about to be tested and it was against a set of opponents they were not expecting.

Ayla and the other supernaturals massed beyond the storm that cut off the north-eastern part of Chippewa Falls had rushed in the moment the tornadoes fell. They had tried to find a way to break through them and were still trying – though with far less hope – when the storm abruptly died.

Streaking toward the drifting ley line energy being unconsciously pulled by the sisters as they used it to communicate telepathically, they arrived at the terrible scene of destruction on Bay Street.

There were two dead SIA agents: Wallace and Bueller, and nearby to them three young men who had very obviously been burned to death by magic. There were eighty-three dead cops and almost a hundred dead national guard. There were dead civilians too, including the mayor.

It took the SIA a little bit longer to locate the sisters, who by then had dropped their connection to the ley line beneath the city. There, Ayla's people found two more dead supernaturals, both identified as returned familiars – a terrible loss in humanity's preparation to fight against the demons.

They also found twenty-one live supernaturals not including the three sisters. The electrical charge from the downed pylon hadn't carried far enough through the water to be able to hurt the hoods over by the partially destroyed warehouse.

Robbie, Ethan and nineteen others were taken away by the SIA as 'persons of interest' and given a simple option – play nice or get neutered. It wasn't often that Otto agreed with anything the SIA said, but this time he was on board.

Actually, since Ayla took up a senior role, he found himself more and more willing to listen – she clearly had the ear of influential people and was bending them carefully to her will.

So, Jennifer, sporting a black line painted vertically across each cheek below her eyes, Cassie, her left arm still in a cast, and big sister Naomi, were about to demonstrate what they could do against a force of superior numbers.

Otto had deliberately chosen the former hoods and put them back in the clothes they were wearing when the SIA took them just to see how the sisters reacted. Their emotional stability and maturity would indicate how big a part they could play in the war that was to come.

With a nod of his head, a button was pressed in the control room above and the girls were given access to a controlled battle space.

Cassie saw Robbie and two sets of eyes went wide as they both gasped in surprise.

The End

Author's Notes

H ello, Dear Readers,

The Realm of False Gods remains an enigma to me. This series has my best review rating, yet it consistently sells fewer books than any other series I write.

Why continue?

The answer is fairly simple but has two parts. Firstly, I really enjoy the books and my style of writing is such that I don't know what is going to happen when I sit down to write. Thus, I find myself keen to write the stories just to see how it all ends. Secondly, I feel a responsibility to my readers. While I sell fewer books in this series, I still have a stack of loyal fans who want more. Like me, they want to know who will win and what part Anastasia, Otto, and the other characters will play.

If I were a business focussed solely on profit, I would never write another book in this series. Thankfully, I left all that profit nonsense behind me, and I live for the art of the story. The way I see it, if you get the story right, readers will find you. It might take a while, years even, but have the respect to write the story the way it should be told.

Stan Lee never had any idea his crazy superhero comics would propel him to superstardom. Not that I put myself in the same league as Stan Lee (who would be a Sir Stan Lee Knight of the Realm as bestowed by the Queen if he were British), or expect to experience one percent of his success.

My point is, you cannot guess what is around the corner and should be able to smile about where you are long before the next corner is revealed. Otherwise, a person might spend their lives hoping the thing to smile about is right around the next corner and never actually get there.

I can tell it is late and I am tired because I have fallen into my rarely seen or heard philosophical mode.

I finished this book with a final flurry of almost fifteen thousand words in one long go. Writing stories is like that – hard to get into sometimes, but then gathering pace until you hit a massive crescendo at the end. I consciously try to write that way, though only you, the reader, can determine how often I manage to pull it off.

It is coming up fast on 0200hrs here in my corner of England. It's the first of November and Christmas feels about ready to deliver an unexpected uppercut even though we all know it is coming.

My children are still of an age - six and eighteen months - when the fairy lights and elves are all really quite magical. The great joy of my chosen profession, selected after I cast off the awful corporate hell, kill-each-other-for-a-percentage job, is that I can pick and choose my hours. I might be tired because I stayed up late to get a book finished, but in December I will quit work at 1530hrs every day to join my family for Christmas movies and hot chocolate on the sofa.

It is a trade off I can get behind.

I am set up to write the next book in this series and even have the cover which you will find on the next page. It will be a few weeks before I get to it though, my schedule demanding I attend to the start of a new series first.

The witches will be back – the three girls having a pivotal part to play in the conclusion of this series though they are likely to feature again before we get to the final books. Next up is the long overdue second tale featuring Zachary, the immortal werewolf who just wants to be left alone. If only his righteous need for equality and justice didn't demand he act all the time.

Take care.

Steve Higgs

<u>**More Books By Steve Higgs**</u>

Blue Moon Investigations
Paranormal Nonsense
The Phantom of Barker Mill
Amanda Harper Paranormal Detective
The Klowns of Kent
Dead Pirates of Cawsand
In the Doodoo With Voodoo
The Witches of East Malling
Crop Circles, Cows and Crazy Aliens
Whispers in the Rigging
Bloodlust Blonde – a short story
Paws of the Yeti
Under a Blue Moon – A Paranormal
Detective Origin Story
Night Work
Lord Hale's Monster
The Herne Bay Howlers
Undead Incorporated
The Ghoul of Christmas Past
The Sandman
Jailhouse Golem
Shadow in the Mine
Ghost Writer

Felicity Philips Investigates
To Love and to Perish
Tying the Noose
Aisle Kill Him
A Dress to Die For
Wedding Ceremony Woes

Patricia Fisher Cruise Mysteries
The Missing Sapphire of Zangrabar
The Kidnapped Bride
The Director's Cut
The Couple in Cabin 2124
Doctor Death
Murder on the Dancefloor
Mission for the Maharaja
A Sleuth and her Dachshund in Athens
The Maltese Parrot
No Place Like Home

Patricia Fisher Mystery Adventures
What Sam Knew
Solstice Goat
Recipe for Murder
A Banshee and a Bookshop
Diamonds, Dinner Jackets, and Death
Frozen Vengeance
Mug Shot
The Godmother
Murder is an Artform
Wonderful Weddings and Deadly
Divorces
Dangerous Creatures

Patricia Fisher: Ship's Detective Series
The Ship's Detective
Fitness Can Kill
Death by Pirates
First Dig Two Graves

Albert Smith Culinary Capers
Pork Pie Pandemonium
Bakewell Tart Bludgeoning
Stilton Slaughter
Bedfordshire Clanger Calamity
Death of a Yorkshire Pudding
Cumberland Sausage Shocker
Arbroath Smokie Slaying
Dundee Cake Dispatch
Lancashire Hotpot Peril
Blackpool Rock Bloodshed
Kent Coast Oyster Obliteration
Eton Mess Massacre
Cornish Pasty Conspiracy

Realm of False Gods
Untethered magic
Unleashed Magic
Early Shift
Damaged but Powerful
Demon Bound
Familiar Territory
The Armour of God
Live and Die by Magic
Terrible Secrets

About the Author

At school, the author was mostly disinterested in every subject except creative writing, for which, at age ten, he won his first award. However, calling it his first award suggests that there have been more, which there have not. Accolades may come but, in the meantime, he is having a ball writing mystery stories and crime thrillers and claims to have more than a hundred books forming an unruly queue in his head as they clamour to get out. He lives in the south-east corner of England with a duo of lazy sausage dogs. Surrounded by rolling hills, brooding castles, and vineyards, he doubts he will ever leave, the beer is just too good.

If you are a social media fan, you should copy the link below into your browser to join my very active Facebook group. You'll find a host of friends waiting there, some of whom have been with me from the very start.

My Facebook group get first notification when I publish anything new, plus cover reveals and free short stories, but more than that, they all interact with each other, sharing inside jokes, and answering question.

f facebook.com/stevehiggsauthor

You can also keep updated with my books via my website:

g https://stevehiggsbooks.com/

www.ingramcontent.com/pod-product-compliance
Lightning Source LLC
Chambersburg PA
CBHW070418170726
48291CB00002B/256